Julianne's he
pounded wild

Ian's fathomless ~~regarding her so~~ intently that Julianne found it impossible to swallow. Carefully setting her fine china plate aside, she took a tiny mouthful of wine.

"I seem to be unable to eat," she said. "Perhaps I wasn't hungry, after all."

Ian moved quickly, closing the distance between them in a single step. Cupping her chin in one hand, he tipped her head up until her eyes met his.

Julianne's skin seemed to burn where his skin met hers. For seconds she could only stare. Ian's eyes were suddenly no longer unreadable. In the inky depths passion burned with an almost frightening intensity.

"Maybe," he said, stroking her face, "food isn't what you're hungry for."

ABOUT THE AUTHOR

Like her heroine, Julianne, Kit Bakker originally hails from Mississippi and comes from good Cajun stock. The tragic story of her ancestors' exile from Acadia is movingly retold in Kit's first Superromance, Book One of our Cajun Melodies series. Blessed with a close-knit family and a devoted husband, Kit makes her home in Arkansas. She is the proud mother of two teenage daughters.

Julianne's Song

KIT BAKKER

Harlequin Books

TORONTO • NEW YORK • LONDON
AMSTERDAM • PARIS • SYDNEY • HAMBURG
STOCKHOLM • ATHENS • TOKYO • MILAN

Published January 1990

First printing November 1989

ISBN 0-373-70387-2

PROLOGUE

HE WAS DYING. Soon his eyes would close and he would drift away into sleep, a sleep from which he would never awaken. The thought did not fill him with the despair it once had, only a bittersweet yearning for time he didn't have, for memories he would never know.

February winds raged through the cracks between the timbers, mocking his earlier attempts to fill every opening with thick mud. *So be it,* he thought. Someone else would repair those cracks after he was gone. Maybe someday his son would come back to farm the lands his father held so dear.

Drawing the woolen shawl closer, his thoughts returned to the parchment that he clasped in his thin fingers. The letters, written with such love, were blurred. He wondered if she would be able to read the words that had cost him so much effort.

If she ever received his letter. There were many leagues separating this isolated farmhouse in windswept Acadia from the home he'd never seen in the faraway Louisiana Territory, separating him from the young wife who'd cried so at their parting, from the son he would not see grow to manhood. Paul Gaston. A good name for a fine baby boy. He coughed. Of course, he'd forgotten. The little boy was a baby no longer.

For a while his thoughts wandered. How many years had gone by since the tragic winter of 1755? Paul Gaston would be four...no, five years old now. Had it been so long? Would Paul Gaston resemble his mother Anne, with blue eyes inherited from some ancient Breton ancestor? Or would he look like his half-Gallic, half-British father, dark and slim, with hair the color of raven feathers?

The man trembled; another spasm of coughing forced rational thought from his brain. It would not be long now, and still one task remained.

Ignoring the pain that shot through his body, he raised himself to an upright position, then forced himself to walk the few steps to his destination. He held on to the walls of the cottage, paying scant attention to slivers of wood from the rough boards. It no longer mattered.

He took the small pouch from its resting place close to his heart. Besides the land and the farmhouse it was all he had left. There was only one treasure he could leave his Anne.

As his fingers searched for the place he knew she would find on her return, a sudden thought struck him. Although the effort cost him dearly, he shuffled back to the wooden chest where he had laid his last letter to Anne. His fingers shook almost uncontrollably as he folded the stiff parchment, then stuffed it inside the bag. Someday she would read his words. He was sure of it.

His mission finally accomplished, the man, his breathing labored now, could no longer stay upright. He crawled back to his pallet, drawing the feather comforter about him as best he could. Then he closed his eyes and thought of Anne.

"THIS COLD seeps into a man's bones and into his heart, my friend," the priest exclaimed as he entered the farmhouse. He clapped his hands to rid his heavy gloves of their accumulation of snow. "I came as soon as I received your message."

There was no answer from the pallet near the stone fireplace. Only silence greeted him.

He walked to the pallet for a last look at the man he'd known so well. Then he stopped, amazed by what he saw. On Gaston's disease-ravaged face was an expression of such joy that the priest was momentarily stunned. He stood still for a moment, thinking about all the times they'd shared.

An occasional drink of wine, the wedding to Anne, filled with such happiness, the birth of little Paul Gaston, and then, of course, the sad parting that neither man had forgotten. The priest would remember forever the fierce faces of red-coated soldiers, would always hear the cries of families as they were forcibly separated. *Ah,* he thought, *always the sad memories mingled with the happier ones.*

Looking down at his comrade's face, the priest knew that someday Gaston would find his beloved wife. Then they would be separated no more. He placed a hand on Gaston's cool forehead and began to intone the ancient words he'd said so often of late. A great peace came over him as he thought of the new home his friend had found at last.

CHAPTER ONE

"I WONDER if this place is haunted."

Julianne Blanchet stared at the ramshackle farmhouse as she picked her way along the stone pathway.

Patches of green crept along rotted timbers that barely qualified as walls. The house sat in an almost accusing silence, as if staring back at the two who had dared to intrude upon its long isolation.

Despite the warmth generated by the June sun, Julianne shivered. People had lived here once, perhaps her own ancestors, if the conclusions she'd recently reached were accurate.

What had their lives been like? she wondered; her eyes roamed what was left of the roof. What tragedies had these walls witnessed, what celebrations of life? Had this been a house of happiness, strengthened by the laughter of children, the love of men and women? She closed her eyes for a moment, recalling the family stories she knew so well.

"No sane ghost would take up residence here. The place is a ruin."

Startled by the interruption, she turned toward her father. He was complaining again, as he had so often throughout this seemingly endless day.

Maybe coming to the farmhouse first had been a mistake, she told herself again. Maybe they should have gone straight to their inn, so he could rest. Today's journey had been tiring, it was true. They had stopped both in Boston and in Montreal on their long flight from South Mississippi to Nova Scotia. Later there had been the ride from Halifax to Wolfville in the car they'd leased for the summer.

She searched his face for signs of strain. But her father seemed calm, with no telltale whitening about the eyes.

"Maybe with some renovation the place could be made livable. I like it." That was true, she realized. The house and the acres of farmland surrounding it drew her with an almost irresistible pull.

"You would. I can imagine the stories already going around in that head of yours."

His displeasure momentarily forgotten, Dale grinned at his daughter. "The Cajun Story Lady finds yet another source for the tales she tells so well." His words mocked gently, but his pride in her was evident.

Julianne was a weaver of words, a teller of tales. She reached back for the legends, for the misty stories half-forgotten by people reared in an electronic age. Celtic and Indian tales, Norse sagas and Greek myths mingled with the happy stories of her Cajun forebears to make up her repertoire. She brought her myths and fables to children in elementary schools, to libraries and local radio and television programs.

Her pride and joy was a cultural center for Cajun children, a place where they could learn about their Acadian ancestors, the Expulsion from New France, and the preservation of their heritage in a new land. They learned legends, sang melodies, and studied exhibits that told the history of the Cajuns.

Julianne had founded the center, which was located in South Mississippi. She was also its director.

She smiled back at him. "I'll never get rid of that nickname, will I?"

"It suits you. There aren't too many people who tell stories for a living."

He turned his attention back to the house. "I suppose you want to look at everything?" he asked, although he already knew the answer.

She tucked her arm through his, hoping his good mood would last. "Of course."

They walked around the outside, both cautious as they avoided fallen timbers and dislodged rocks. Afternoon sunshine danced off the roof, gilding the stone chimney that seemed to be the only solid part of the entire structure.

"It's such a contrast to the land itself," Julianne said as she looked out across the rolling farmlands thick with apple trees and grasses. There were still blooms on the wild rhododendrons, although she knew the peak growing season had already passed. Other wildflowers scattered soft colors throughout the meadows.

Like the house, the lands had long been abandoned. No crops had been planted here for many a year, but there was little evidence of decay, only a lush fertility as far as she could see. She could feel why her ancestors had loved this land so fiercely.

"I don't see much use for this place, do you?" Dale grumbled as they came back to the front of the farmhouse. "It's too far-gone for renovation."

She suppressed a sigh. His mood had been too good to last, but then, he was tired. The summer might be difficult for both of them, she thought.

Julianne had moved out of her parents' home when she went to college and was used to an independent life-style.

Now she would be spending two months living with her father in a small inn, while she attended classes at the university. Two stubborn adults with their own ideas about everything, in very close proximity.

Patience, Julianne, she told herself. *It will take patience.*

"You've been testy ever since we left Ocean Springs." Julianne's tone was stern, although the look she gave her father was affectionate. "Try to be a little more positive, please."

"That's easy for you to say. Coming up here was all your idea, anyway. I was perfectly content at home."

He ran one hand through his dark hair, still untouched by gray, even though he was fifty-six years old. "Let's go to the inn. I'd like to see more of Nova Scotia than this old place."

"This isn't any 'old place,' Dad. According to Thérèse Blanchet, this is the same farm once owned by Gaston Blanchet, your great-grandfather many times removed. Our ancestors lived here. It makes me feel all tingly inside just to think about it."

"The only feeling I get is a sneeze coming on from all the dust. From the way the place looks, I'm sure there's dust everywhere."

Julianne ignored his complaints. "Let's go inside."

Something gray and furry scuttled into the dark interior as Julianne took one step closer. She stopped short on the threshold.

"Be careful," her father warned as he made his way over the ruined pathway. "That may have been a rat. They like to hang around abandoned buildings."

"That wasn't a rat. No self-respecting rat would turn out on such a glorious day, not even to this derelict of a house. I think it was a rabbit. We probably scared it."

Without stopping to see if Dale followed, Julianne pushed open the door that hung askew on its hinges. It tottered for a moment, then fell with a loud crash. Dust and the debris of many years swirled through the opening. Inside she could hear scampering sounds and creatures scurried into the afternoon sunshine.

Julianne jumped back. "I certainly didn't expect that." She turned to make sure her father had escaped any harm.

"Are you okay?" He surveyed her slender form, hunting for cuts or bruises.

She nodded. "Of course. The door didn't touch me at all. It only scared me a little, not like those poor animals that ran out."

"Poor little animals, my foot. Rodents and pests, probably."

He frowned. "Let's go check into the inn. We can come back and explore some other time."

Long strands of black hair framed her face as Julianne shook her head. "Come on, Dad. Just a few minutes more. Then we'll go check in. I promise."

Dale shook his own head, but followed his daughter into the house. "You always did know how to handle me to get your own way," he muttered. "Just like your mother."

Her mother. Julianne felt the familiar tug, the sense of loss she always felt when she thought of her mother. Had it really been a year since Lillian's death?

For a moment the memories overwhelmed her. It seemed such a short time ago that she was a child, running to her mother for hugs in exchange for scraped knees or bad dreams. Lillian had always held her close, then told her a story, turning any bad experience into a magical fantasy, where hearts never broke and knees were never scraped.

Julianne and her mother had become close friends as well as parent and child. She still missed her so much.

Julianne glanced back at her father, who was now absorbed in the task of putting the door back onto its stubborn hinges. Stray sunshine illuminated his face, highlighting the lines of care and strain that had appeared from nowhere during the previous year.

He missed Lillian terribly, she knew, although he seldom spoke of her. Still devoted to each other, they would have celebrated their thirtieth anniversary this year.

This trip was good for him, she told herself again, even if she was the only person who thought so. He'd griped and grumbled about leaving his large home for two months during the summer. "I've got too many things to do," he told her over and over.

She knew her father well. Left to his own devices, he would mope away this summer as he had the last, rambling around his empty house, losing himself in memories of Lillian. Oh, he dropped in at his office occasionally, "to check things over," but his supervision wasn't needed.

The company he had founded, nurtured through the lean years, and then turned into one of the largest commercial net manufacturers in the world, ran quite well without him. Everyone there was always polite; they listened to him attentively. Too attentively. "Like I'm the guest of honor," he'd said recently, after one of his increasingly infrequent visits. "Nobody asks me any questions or wants any advice."

No, she thought, he'd needed to get away, even if it had taken all of her powers of persuasion to convince her hardheaded Cajun father to come. Julianne gasped as she realized what he was doing.

"Dad! You shouldn't be picking up that door by yourself! That's heavy. It looks like oak."

She grabbed one end of the door, sneezing as a dust cloud settled around her head. "It certainly is heavy enough to be oak."

"Quit fussing! I'm perfectly capable of picking up this door. You hover around me like an old mother hen. How do you think I get along when you're not around?"

Julianne bit her lip. "You know you shouldn't overexert yourself. Your heart . . ."

"Is fine," he snapped. "The doctor told me at my last checkup I should get regular exercise, that I shouldn't be afraid of normal activities. The one thing I don't need is a daughter worrying herself sick about me."

Then his face softened. "I'm okay, really. I guess I'm not used to having a grown daughter to worry about me. I still think of you as a little girl. It's difficult to remember sometimes that you are an adult with your own home and a very responsible position."

She turned away. It was an old argument. Maybe she did "fuss" a little too much, but she had already lost one parent. She didn't want to lose her father, too. Trying to keep her self-control intact, she walked into the room to study the stone fireplace.

The door resisted going back onto its hinges, so it was several minutes before Dale completed his task. Then he put an arm around Julianne's shoulders. "I'm sorry I snapped. Maybe you're right, after all, chère. Perhaps I do need time away from home."

Chère. It sounded so good in his lilting, partly Cajun, partly South Mississippi drawl. He'd always called her mother *"Chère."*

"Maybe we both need time away, Dad."

She knew the words were true even as she said them. Since her mother's death she had immersed herself in the cultural center, working long hours. She'd told herself it was to ensure the success of the center, but she realized now it had also been a means to cope with the loss of Lillian.

They stood silently for a few moments, both lost in memories. Then Dale gave her shoulders a squeeze. "Are you ready to go yet? It's been a long day. We've got unpacking to do, and if I know my own daughter as well as I think, you're anxious to get started on your treasure hunt."

His words startled her. "Treasure hunt? I'd almost forgotten about it. Besides, Dad, there's only the slightest chance of finding Gaston's legacy to Anne after all these years. The only treasures I'm likely to find in Nova Scotia are legends and stories I can use in my work."

"Maybe," Dale answered. "But wouldn't finding something precious from one of our ancestors make a good legend?"

"You're right," she admitted. "I guess I don't want to get my hopes up. Chances of finding anything at all are so slim."

What was the "earthly treasure" Gaston had mentioned several times in his letters? she wondered. Gold? Silver? Precious gems?

Unlikely, she thought. Gaston was a farmer, a prosperous one by Acadian standards, but he measured his wealth in land and livestock. Unlikely, but not impossible.

"Now you've got me imagining things again. Old chests filled with diamonds and rubies, ropes of pearls, emeralds and gold coins." With mock ferocity she kicked at an old board. "They're probably buried under this old place."

"If you find a chest like that, save me some of those gold coins. You can have all the jewels."

She matched her father's impish grin. "Thanks a bunch. I notice you didn't offer to help dig."

"I'm retired, remember?"

Still smiling, she wandered about the house. Perhaps there would be time for a little treasure hunting. It would be a good break from studying. But there was time enough to think about that.

At the fireplace, Julianne reached out to touch the uneven stones. "It's strange, but this house has the oddest effect on me," she said. "I feel almost as if I've come home."

It was silly, she knew. Home was Ocean Springs, with its miles of white sand beach and the Gulf of Mexico beyond, the gray live oaks draped with Spanish moss, and humidity so thick that it sometimes took her breath away. Home was her own condominium facing the beach, her collection of handmade wooden furniture and simple baskets made by Cajun craftspeople. Home was the children who came to the cultural center, as often as not accompanied by their curious parents.

This was Nova Scotia, in a foreign land many hundreds of miles away. She'd never been here before, although she had heard the stories passed down through her family. How could it feel like home?

Coming up beside her, Dale said nothing for a moment. Then he stroked a lichen-covered stone. "The house has a presence about it, an almost tangible presence. It's like the house is listening to us, judging us. Maybe the house knows that our ancestor built it. Maybe it senses something different about us."

She nodded. "The fireplace is the heart of the house. It feels like a place for dreaming, for telling stories on endless winter evenings."

Her father laughed. The sound echoed eerily in the empty house. "Okay, Miss Storyteller. I think we've imagined enough for one afternoon in a strange country. It's time we headed up to the inn. I'm starting to get hungry." He gave her arm a gentle tug.

He was right. It was time to go. There was unpacking to do, and she wanted to call Thérèse Blanchet to let her know they had arrived. Julianne followed him out, but paused for one last look around before closing the door.

"I'll be back," she whispered. The house gave no answer.

"You need to lighten up. Think about it, Ian. Your last three books. Were they lighthearted and happy books for little kiddos to rejoice over? Hell, no."

The huge man paced about the book-lined room. "You covered divorce in the last one, dying in the one before that, and..."

"Cancer," his companion supplied. "How to live with someone who has terminal cancer."

"Precisely." Jock Palmer eased his bulk onto one of the sofas and picked up the teacup from the table in front of him. Holding the cup with nervous fingers, he balanced it on one knee. "Your last three books were nonfiction, which is okay, I suppose. But you do fiction so well. You know, if you don't want to write something upbeat, at least give horror or adventure a try."

"Are you telling me my sales are slipping?"

Setting his own cup on his desk, Ian Ross turned away from his agent. Taking two long steps, he walked over to one of the windows that framed his office. "I thought the books did quite well when I saw the royalties."

Outside the late-spring hillside beckoned, green and fresh. He could see his prize Guernsey cattle grazing placidly, soaking up the sunshine. He wanted to be out there, hiking through woodlands or maybe up the Cape Split Trail to where he could see and hear the magic tides ebb and flow. *Anywhere,* he thought. *I want to be anywhere but in here, listening to my agent tell me how and what to write.*

He fought back a grin. Jock had left New York, which he almost never did, and ventured into the wilds of Nova Scotia to talk with his favorite and most profitable client. Literary agents seldom made house calls, especially to foreign countries. Unless agent and client were good friends, he thought, realizing he'd known the red-haired giant for a long time. No, Jock was worried or he wouldn't have come. The least he could do was listen.

"Of course your sales aren't down," Jock was saying. "You're one of the best children's writers today. You know that. You've won every major prize for children's literature at least once. One of them four times. Even adults read your books. It would be easy for you to cross over to adult literature."

"No horror." Ian's baritone voice filled the small room. "Let someone else do it."

Hearing the firmness in his client's voice, Jock sighed. Were all these Acadians as thickheaded and obstinate as this one? He'd known Ian for years, but sometimes, and this was one of them, he felt as though he didn't know the man at all.

Ian grinned. "Yes, we are all stubborn. It's in the genes."

Jock stared, his mouth working like that of a beached fish. Although the room was cooled by breezes coming in through the open windows, perspiration beaded his forehead. "How do you do that? How do you know what I'm thinking, sometimes even before I do?"

The dark-haired man shrugged. "I told you. It's in the genes. I've heard that all true Acadians are somewhat fey."

"That's something else," Jock declared. "I've always wondered how you can be Acadian with a name like Ian Ross. Aren't those Scots names?"

"Yes. Marriage was common between eighteenth-century Acadians and the Scots who lived here in Nova Scotia. Ross is a common name here."

Jock smiled. "It looks great on a book jacket. Catchy, like Stephen King."

"You don't give up, Jocko." Ian gazed at his agent. "One of the traits of an outstanding agent, I suppose." He paused.

"I won't do horror, no. But I might be persuaded to do adventure. Or even fantasy."

It was difficult to resist that smile, Jock decided. It came from deep within, lighting the onyx-dark eyes with mystery and something else. Romance, probably, if the stories he'd heard about Ian's success with the ladies were true.

And they probably were, Jock thought with a twinge of jealousy. It wasn't fair for one man to have all that creative talent and those dark good looks besides. Ian Ross inspired trust and affection in everyone, male or female, adult or child.

It wasn't fair. But he was glad to be the man's agent, and even more glad to be his friend.

Forgetting his earlier discomfort, Jock smiled back at his host. "How about fantasy-adventure? You could write one for adults."

"No." The voice was even firmer. "I write my fiction for children."

Ian crossed to face his agent, folding his lean body to sit on the edge of the wide desk. "I've been thinking about taking a course on Acadian folklore this summer. The university is offering a six-week course, taught by one of the best scholars in the field."

Jock's pudgy fingers fidgeted with the sofa's nubby fabric. "It's been six months since you've sent me anything. I've worried about you. It's not like you to be without an idea for your next book." He gave his client a shrewd look, searching for any reaction to his comments.

Not as much as I've worried about myself, Ian thought, but his expression remained pleasant. "I know. I've decided to do that series of Acadian books and songs for children we discussed last year. I haven't started the books yet, but I've been working on some songs."

"Songs?" The agent's head came up. "Anything marketable?"

Ian smiled again. Jock's ability to sniff out a sale was legendary. That was why he'd hired the guy, Ian reminded himself. "Perhaps."

Jock rubbed his hands together. "When do I get to listen to these songs?"

"I'm singing tonight at the Bearded Lion. Why don't you come over?" Ian glanced down at his watch. "The show starts at nine."

Jock, who'd been facing the prospect of going to bed early in an unfamiliar bed-and-breakfast inn instead of his usual luxury hotel, brightened. "I'll be there." With an effort, he hoisted himself from the depths of the sofa.

"It's odd. We've been working together now for eleven years, and I've never heard you sing." The larger man started for the door.

A smile drifted across Ian's face. "That's because you've never been able to tear yourself away from that office in New York before to come here."

The agent gave him a curious look. "I've heard that you're almost a legend, singing your songs about magic and lonely hearts and those old folk tunes. Have you ever thought of becoming a professional singer?"

"Maybe in my spare time."

Both men grinned. Jock reached for the heavy door.

"Good. You have enough to do, especially if you start work on that Acadian series."

He paused. "Will your mother and father be there tonight?"

"No. They're in California. I finally persuaded them they could afford a vacation. Right now, I imagine they're having the time of their lives at Disneyland."

Ian's dark eyes twinkled as he remembered the long hours he'd spent convincing his parents, who were comfortably off, that they could afford to go. They were both frugal and hardworking, living simply in the smaller house on the family farm.

"Mother fussed, even while they were packing to go. Said they felt guilty about going off and leaving me with all the responsibility. I had to tell her three or four times this place practically runs itself. We have excellent hired help and a good foreman."

"Have you heard from them?" Jock asked.

Ian's smile broadened. "I talked to them last night. Dad said they're having such a good time that they may extend their vacation and go to Vancouver for a while to visit one of his cousins." He remembered the excited sound of his father's voice over the telephone wires.

"Sounds like they're having a great time. Give them my love when you talk to them again." Jock extended his hand.

"Thanks. I'll see you tonight." The two men shook hands.

Jock hummed an old Beatles melody as he left the house. Ian watched him until the rental car pulled away, then turned and went back into his study.

Had it been six months since he'd sent anything to New York? He did a quick calculation. At least six months. It was time to get back to work, time to ignore the restlessness which had plagued him for the past few months.

As usual, Jock was right. It was time to ease up. But it wouldn't be that easy, Ian knew.

Since his divorce seven years ago, Ian had been driven. He'd spent so much of his time on the farm that the place indeed almost nearly ran itself now. He'd also written numerous children's books and songs, while managing to sing several times a week at concerts, fairs, fund-raisers and other events. And since the Bearded Lion had opened earlier in the year, he'd been singing there twice a week.

He thought of Joanna for a moment. Had it been seven years? The hurt was no longer there; he hadn't been in love with her for a long time. But there was still a void, the absence from his life of something indefinable. Maybe that was why he worked so hard, Ian thought. Maybe he was trying to fill up the empty spaces.

Lately he hadn't been able to write. The words simply wouldn't come.

"Maybe I should follow my own advice," he muttered, thinking of the hours he'd spent convincing his parents that work was not all there was to life. They needed some fun and relaxation. And now maybe their son did, too.

Absently he ran his fingers across the keys of his typewriter, then frowned as he looked at the dust on his fingertips. He ought to find the dustcover and put it on the machine, but that would be admitting that he wasn't using it.

He walked toward the window and stared out at the clear skies beyond. Maybe the course on Acadian folklore was indeed what he needed.

CHAPTER TWO

"WE'VE BEEN out to the old farm, Mrs. Blanchet. It's everything you said it would be and more." How could she begin to tell this elderly woman she'd never met of the feelings she'd experienced as she'd explored the farm? Julianne wondered.

The voice at the other end of the telephone line sounded strong and sure, not at all what she'd expected from a woman in her nineties. Julianne twisted the already curly telephone cord and felt excitement rising within her. What would Thérèse Blanchet be like in person?

"My dear, please call me Thérèse. I'm old enough already. I don't need to be reminded of it." Thérèse chuckled; it was a dry sound. "I remember my first few visits out there as a child. It was so strange, as if I belonged there. I think I made up my mind then that someday I must have the place."

She paused, taking a breath. "My late husband felt the same way, you know. He was my third cousin, a Blanchet also. He told me the farm drew him like a magnet. Of course, it was years before we could buy it. The original farmlands had been broken up for decades. Since the early eighteen hundreds actually, according to what I've managed to find out. It was inherited by Blanchets for a long time, but gradually the heirs began selling off pieces of it. I'm so glad we were able to put it all back together."

"So am I. It's lovely. I'm already looking forward to seeing it again." And she was, Julianne knew. She felt a bond between herself and Thérèse's late husband. The farm was also a magnet to her.

"I would like to see you today, but it wouldn't be a good idea. I've been ill, Julianne," Thérèse continued. "A touch of flu, I think, although my companion, Miss Roberts, becomes upset if I have the least sign of any illness. She worries too much about me."

Another Dale Blanchet, Julianne thought. He didn't want anyone worrying about him, either.

Thérèse went on, her eagerness evident as she rushed her words. "I want to see you right now, but perhaps it would be best if we wait a few days. We'll have most of the summer, when you aren't in school, of course."

Julianne found it hard to keep the disappointment from her voice. She was so anxious to finally see this member of her family, no matter how distant the relationship. But Thérèse was right. They did have nearly all summer.

"That will be fine. Dad and I have some settling in to do, anyway."

They chatted for a few moments more, then Julianne went back to her unpacking. She whistled softly as she worked, determined not to pay any attention to her father's grumbling as he helped her hang the few dresses she'd brought.

After a short knock, Mrs. Hardesty bustled into Julianne's bedroom. The landlady's arms were full of towels and washcloths. She headed straight for Dale, beaming up at him as she presented the pile of linens.

"These are fresh from the dryer. I took them out myself a few minutes ago."

Julianne, her own hands filled with sweaters she'd been transferring to a dresser drawer, turned to smile at the landlady. "It's kind of you to take such a personal interest in us," she said. "You make us feel right at home."

She wondered if Mrs. Hardesty had a more than professional interest in them because of Dale. Julianne was aware that her father was used to being pursued by women.

At fifty-six, he was still an attractive man. Dale was also wealthy, which was an attraction in itself, she knew. He needed to lose a few pounds, but then, thought Julianne with a rueful glance at her hips, who didn't?

Since Lillian's death, Dale had become one of the most eligible widowers on the Gulf Coast. But thank goodness, Julianne thought, he wasn't interested. How could anyone take Lillian's place?

Mrs. Hardesty was chattering now, her eyes fixed on Dale's face. In exasperation, he signaled to Julianne from behind his back.

Time for the cavalry, Julianne decided. She closed the dresser drawer with a loud thud, then pulled some boots from another suitcase. "Dad, would you put these in that little closet in the sitting room, please?"

Dale quickly slipped into the adjoining room, and Julianne turned to their hostess. "Thank you so much, Mrs. Hardesty. I think you've left us well supplied for the evening."

Oversupplied, in fact. There were enough towels and washcloths for a month, cut flowers stood in every vase in the three-room suite, and fresh juice and snacks filled the small refrigerator. Mrs. Hardesty had even insisted on running the carpet sweeper once again over the already immaculate rugs.

"Well, if there's nothing else I can do..." Mrs. Hardesty's voice trailed away; she looked around.

"Nothing." Julianne took the older woman's arm and steered her out of the bedroom, through the adjoining sitting room or parlor toward the door to the corridor. "We'll be sure to ask if we need anything at all."

She closed the door behind the landlady. "You've made another conquest, Dad."

Dale glared. "I fail to see the humor in this situation."

"You should have seen your face. I've never seen the esteemed chairman of Blanchet Industries so flustered," she said between giggles.

"I knew coming here would be a mistake. I could have been home, playing bridge or out on the golf course. June is too busy a month to leave town." He stalked back to the suitcases that lay on two folding stands. "I should be working the fishing rodeos with my club."

Julianne smiled at him. "You've told me a thousand times you hate bridge, because it is boring. Golf 'is an aimless game,' if I remember correctly. And your fellow club members will have the fishing rodeos well under control. I think for one year they can collect entry fees without you. After all, you've helped out for thirty years now."

"Thirty-four." His words were clipped.

She looked at his stiff back with growing concern. This trip was intended to get him away from familiar surroundings, to renew his interest in living. He wouldn't get much relaxation if he didn't change his attitude. With one hand, she pushed the hair back from her face.

"Dad, look in the blue suitcase. You didn't say anything about bringing them, but I brought your wood-carving tools. Maybe when you're not doing research on our family history, you could do some carving. I also brought that chickadee you started a few months ago."

Before Mother's death, she could have added, but didn't. Dale hadn't picked up his carving tools since then. "Maybe carving will give you something to do while I'm in class at the university."

Dale's expression altered slightly as he opened the suitcase, then removed a large plastic bag. Inside was the battered tackle box containing his knives, chisels, sharpening stones and other paraphernalia.

"I suppose I could do some carving while we're here."

His daughter smiled again. "At last I've piqued your interest, you old curmudgeon."

Giving him a brief hug, she rummaged through the suitcase to find a cardboard box. From it she removed the half-finished chickadee. "My birthday is next month. You don't have much time to finish this piece."

A hint of a smile tugged the corners of his mouth. "Who says this is for you, young lady?"

With a laugh, Julianne handed him the wooden bird. "Maybe a little bird—" her father groaned "—or my infamous intuition."

Julianne looked around at the dwindling contents of the suitcases. "We don't have much left to do. Why don't we finish and then head down to the Bearded Lion? It's a combination pub and restaurant that's been open about six months. Mrs. Hardesty said it's a great place for food, and there's even entertainment tonight, some folksinger who is evidently well-known around here."

His frown returned. "She mentioned it to me, too. I wonder if our lovely landlady will be there also."

"Only if you're lucky, Dad."

JULIANNE PUSHED AWAY the remains of her dinner, then sighed. "I don't know who is more stuffed, the haddock or me. Probably me. That was delicious." She glanced around the restaurant with growing curiosity. It was small enough to have a cozy atmosphere, yet filled with patrons enjoying an evening meal.

People sat at each of the tables, while more stood at a large bar to one side. A small stage faced the diners, but allowed a good view to those at the bar. Although the room wasn't noisy, it hummed with chatter and laughter. Pleasant aromas of cooking food drifted by, occasionally punctuated by whiffs of perfume or shaving lotion. All around her she could hear a variety of accents, ranging from a musical French to the distinctive lilt of Canada's East Coast.

"Are you going to have coffee?" Dale asked, as he stabbed at a crumb of coconut-cream pie.

His question went unanswered and the lights dimmed. Chairs scraped noisily as people adjusted their positions, then a hush settled over the room.

A spotlight suddenly illuminated the stage, and several men carrying guitars came into view. There was still enough light in the room to enable Julianne to study the man in front. Like the other two, he was dressed all in black. He carried himself with regal assurance and eased his tall frame onto a chrome stool.

As the man leaned forward to adjust something on the guitar he sheltered under one arm, his eyes swept the room. Julianne was sitting too far away to see, but knew his eyes would be raven black, like the hair that stubbornly fell over his forehead.

The spotlight moved over his face, picking out dark brows, a straight nose, and high cheekbones sweeping down to a square chin. A stubborn chin, she decided. The man was handsome, Julianne conceded, all lean angles and planes. Those striking looks would be a definite asset to his career, especially if he could sing.

He caught her eye and for a moment returned her appraisal. Then a grin slowly spread across his face; he nodded in her direction.

With a start, Julianne realized that she was staring. It occurred to her that anyone that handsome was probably used to the stares of young women. The thought brought a twinge of irritation. She flushed and turned away from those probing dark eyes.

"That must be the singer Mrs. Hardesty told us about," she whispered to her father. "By the way, have you seen any sign of her tonight?"

"No," Dale shot back. "Be grateful for small miracles."

Julianne giggled. "The evening is young. She may show up later."

Dale's answer was lost. The room suddenly went dark except for the spotlight on the musicians. Three guitars came noisily to life, sending the rousing chords of a sea-chantey skittering throughout the crowded room. Several amplifiers enhanced the sound, but the music wasn't as loud as it had been at too many of the concerts she'd attended lately.

Julianne's fingers tapped the wooden tabletop as the trio hammed their way through the chantey, buoyed by the good-humored clapping of the audience. They had excellent voices, she decided. Maybe the music would be as good as the food.

The tempo slowed to a ballad, and the man in front began to sing by himself. Julianne forgot her surroundings. The liquid baritone flowed through the room, filling all the nooks and crannies. He sang of love found and lost in a voice both vibrant with joy and aching with sadness.

Forgetting her professional interest in the musical tales, Julianne sat mesmerized, hardly breathing as she listened. The man was good, she realized. Very good, indeed.

Looking over the audience, Ian felt the familiar excitement. It came before every performance, whether his audience was small enough to fit into the Bearded Lion, or made up of thousands gathered for an annual festival of traditional music. It was a good night, as he'd known it would be.

All but the closest tables were hidden in darkness. His eyes drifted about, searching unsuccessfully for Jock. He was probably out there somewhere.

His glance stopped again at the front table, where the young woman had earlier caught his eye. It was difficult to tell in this light, but she seemed to be small and slender, with masses of thick black hair cascading over her shoulders.

Evangeline. He smiled to himself. The night or maybe the music was making him fanciful. How else could a modern young woman remind him of Longfellow's legendary heroine?

With barely a pause between songs, the singer wove his musical spell over the throbbing of guitar and bass. The haunting songs of Quebec and Acadia mingled with Elizabethan ballads and Scottish chants, then changed to modern melodies.

The voice enthralled, coaxed, caressed, enchanted. Julianne recognized several tunes as those sung by her own family during the frequent reunions in Louisiana's bayou country and along the Mississippi Gulf Coast. Some were slightly altered, with a phrase changed here and there or a difference in the melody. But the songs were the same.

She knew the Cajuns were descendants of the Acadians of Nova Scotia. Every child brought up in a Cajun family had heard, time and time again, the tragic stories of deportation to the wild Louisiana Territory. Somehow the relationship she shared with the Acadian descendants of those same families had never seemed so close to her until now.

Julianne glanced around the darkened room, seeing no one in particular, only movement. Maybe some of her own distant relatives were sitting in the pub at this very moment.

Excitement shot through her, an excitement tinged with sadness for all the unexplored relationships lost over the years. She stared at the man onstage, silently thanking him for this new awareness.

The singer shifted his position on the tall stool until he faced the slender brunette at the front table. He could sense her reaching out to him; his music had somehow touched a responsive chord. The thought pleased him.

Without any conscious planning he began another song. Softly at first, then with increasing intensity, he sang of two lovers separated by the Expulsion of the Acadians. His voice trembled as he recalled the tragedy of shattered lives, of steadfast love that lasted through years of hardship. His eyes found Julianne's and didn't stray again. His song filled the room.

She stiffened, unable to move. He was singing to her. She didn't even know his name, and he was singing a love song to her. The words and music reached out and pulled her on to the stage, although she sat as if entranced, unable to move. She felt the sadness of the two lovers, lived the hopelessness, rejoiced in a love undiminished by time and distance. When the song finally ended, a curious sense of loss made her long for more.

The words reminded her of other words, written long ago by a man separated from the woman he loved. She could almost see the faded writing on the letters penned by Gaston Blanchet, her own ancestor, to his beloved Anne.

Today I planted the last of the seed, wondering even as I did so if you would be here to share the harvest. I think not, and I am filled with sorrow. But there will be other plantings and other harvests for us, my dearest Anne, if only we have the courage to be steadfast and true.

Brave words, she thought. Along with the seeds pressed into the soil of Nova Scotia, Gaston had planted hope. Although the singer couldn't possibly know about the letters between Gaston and Anne, he'd distilled the essence of their story into his song.

Slowly, as if he were reluctant to end the beautiful ballad, the man turned away and began a lively Irish pub tune. A sigh seemed to go about the room as the pace changed. With tireless energy, he beguiled the audience with song after song.

In his own way, the singer was as much a storyteller as she was, Julianne realized. His words came out in melody, with the guitar and other instruments enriching the sounds, but the tales were told in the music.

Julianne relaxed only as the last haunting strains of "Nova Scotia Farewell" died away. The audience came to its feet, demanding more, but the singer laughed and waved them back into their seats. In a French-accented voice he announced that there would be a second show later in the evening.

The houselights came on. Julianne blinked, tearing her thoughts away from the singer. "Dad, have you ever heard that song before?"

Searching his plate for any leftover crumbs of pie, Dale sighed. "That pie was incredible. I'm tempted to order another piece."

"Dad." Julianne couldn't help but smile. Her father's weakness for sweets, especially pie, was a standing joke between them. "The song?"

"Which song?"

"The one about the two lovers separated when the British forced the Acadians from Nova Scotia. I thought I knew most of those old Acadian ballads, but I've never heard that one. It was lovely."

Julianne searched her memory, but could not recall the song. "It reminded me so much of what happened when Gaston and Anne Blanchet were separated during the Expulsion."

Dale shook his head. "Funny. I don't remember the song either. I thought my mother taught me all those old tunes. Why don't you ask the singer? He may know the song's origins. Didn't Mrs. Hardesty say his name is Ross? Ian, I think."

Ian Ross. The name suited him. A Scots name, of course, but she knew the man had an Acadian soul from the way he sang. Ross was a common surname in Cajun country as well as in Acadia.

She took a deep breath, then walked over to the stage. Ian Ross was nowhere to be seen, but the other musicians paused from tuning their guitars as she neared.

"I'd like to speak with Mr. Ross," Julianne said to the man nearest to her.

"Hey, Ian, you've got another visitor." The young man smirked and pointed at Julianne with his guitar. "This one's good-looking."

Julianne winced. The man's tone implied what she already knew. Ian Ross probably was constantly pursued by young women infatuated with his voice and the mystery that seemed to swirl about him. She set her jaw as he placed his guitar on an amplifier, then turned to face her. A groupie she wasn't.

"I apologize for Antoine's remark. He sometimes gets carried away when he is performing." Ian glared at the young musician.

"Hey, I'm sorry, too." Antoine grinned at her, his face wrinkling like a puppy's fur.

Julianne smiled back. Antoine's huge grin was difficult to resist. Then she turned back to Ian.

"Could you tell me the origin of the song about the two Acadian lovers?" She paused, flicking her tongue over her lips in a nervous gesture as his attention focused completely on her. "The one you sang about five songs before 'Nova Scotia Farewell.'"

Ian studied her for a moment. Now that he could see her up close and in the light, the girl was striking. No, not a girl, he amended. She had to be in her late twenties.

Black hair, thick and lustrous under the artificial light, framed a heart-shaped face. The hair fell past her shoulders, tumbling into fat curls on the ends. He nearly smiled as he wondered how long it took her to achieve that careless look. Or maybe it was natural.

Thin brows arched upward over eyes so brown that they were nearly black. Those eyes, wide now with some indefinable emotion, would trap a man as easily as the great blue herons snatched unwary fish from the ponds near his home.

She was also small, he realized. At six feet two inches he was at least a foot taller than the slender woman standing before him. She looked somewhat uncomfortable, he decided. He backed up several inches and leaned on his stool, hoping to relax her.

"I wrote the song. Some of my ancestors were dispersed in the Expulsion of the Acadians. I've been fascinated by the stories for as long as I can remember."

He paused, as if hesitant to say more, then continued. "I don't sing it often. The emotions it stirs inside me are very powerful."

Powerful, indeed, Julianne thought. No one who heard it could fail to be touched by the tale of lost love.

"It's a very moving song, much like some of the old legends that traveled from Acadia to the Louisiana Territory. It reminded me very much of something that happened in my own family," she said. "And your emotions showed in the way you sang."

So she was American. It was difficult to tell with that faint accent, he mused. She sounded almost like a French Canadian. For reasons he couldn't name, the thought pleased him.

"Thank you," he replied. " 'Song for Acadia' is special to me. I'm glad you liked it, miss."

He was so formal, she thought, calling her "Miss" with an old-fashioned courtliness. Then she remembered. She hadn't told him her name.

"I'm Julianne Blanchet. My father and I will be visiting Wolfville for several weeks while I take a course at the university. Mrs. Hardesty, the owner of the inn where we are staying, recommended the Bearded Lion, especially since you were singing tonight. She said you are outstanding, and I agree with her. You're a talented songwriter, as well."

If that made her a groupie, then so be it, Julianne determined, lifting her chin slightly as she silently dared him to be amused. She was telling the truth, giving him praise he deserved.

"Thank you again." He smiled, but there was no trace of condescension in his manner.

"But you aren't French-Canadian, are you?" he went on. "Your accent is similar, but I would guess that you are from somewhere else."

"I'm a Cajun," she replied, oddly pleased that he cared anything at all about her origins. The man seemed to be in no hurry to get away from her, although she was certain he was tired. He probably needed something to drink, as well.

"Ah, from Louisiana."

"No, South Mississippi, right next to Louisiana. It gets rather complicated down in that part of the world," she explained.

"Most people think of Louisiana when they think of Cajuns, since most Cajuns settled there. But there are true Cajuns in Texas, Alabama and Mississippi as well as other states, Mr. Ross." His interest was genuine, she noted, rewarding that interest with a smile.

Her smile reminded him of sunrise over the Bay of Fundy, wide and sparkling with promise. Ian stood up and took her hand.

He gently squeezed the fingers as he enfolded them with his own. "Please call me Ian. I've never met a Mississippi Cajun before. I hope I will see you again before you leave."

Conscious only of the hand holding her own so gently, Julianne had difficulty finding her voice. She had to be tired, she thought, for this man to affect her so much. It *had* been a long day, with the flight from New Orleans and the drive from Halifax. She would have to go soon, if he ever let go of her hand.

"Do you live near here?" She could not imagine anyone with such a magnificent voice living in a town the size of Wolfville. He should be in a large city, singing to thousands, rather than the small audiences he would attract in this little town.

"Yes. I have a home here in the Annapolis Valley, not far from Wolfville at all. I'm a farmer as well as a folksinger. I also do some writing." Slowly, as if reluctant to do so, he let go of her hand.

Julianne paused, wishing she could think of a way to prolong their meeting. But it was time to go.

Suddenly she became aware of the busy restaurant around them. Waitresses scurried about the room, handling orders, so that all the patrons would be served before the next show. On the stage, Ian's backup musicians were eyeing them with curiosity.

Her father would be getting very restless, she thought. He would be tired, too, from all the traveling. Dale probably wanted to go to bed rather early tonight, she realized. Yes, it was time to leave.

"Thank you for the concert, Ian."

The name came easily off her tongue. She liked the sound of it. "Your song is lovely," she repeated.

He surveyed her, his face grave. "Thank you, Julianne. Having such an attentive listener makes the song mean much more to me."

Ian watched as Julianne made her way back to her table. She walked with the natural grace of a dancer, her movements sensual without being obvious. Several other male heads turned to follow the woman as she gave a brief hug to the older man seated at her table.

Within a minute both Blanchets were gone. Despite the crowds that surrounded him, the room seemed strangely empty.

What was it about her? he wondered. Of all the many women he knew, why was this one so intriguing?

Then he knew. She reminded him of Joanna, his wife. He frowned, correcting himself. Joanna was his ex-wife. How could Julianne Blanchet remind him of that elegant person?

The resemblance was subtle. Joanna was a tall, green-eyed blonde, watchful as a tawny lioness. With claws to match, he recalled. No, there was little to remind him of Joanna, except for the grace of movement, the way both women watched his face as he talked, as if hungry for his next words.

"It's time to warm up for the next show." Henri Fontenot, one of the backup musicians, clapped a friendly arm around his employer's shoulders.

"That little one you were talking to, she is beautiful, yes?"

Shaken from his reverie, Ian laughed. Trust Henri to notice any woman. Tall or short, thin or chubby, young or old, it mattered little to Henri. He loved them all, and they loved him back.

"You're right, Henri. She's beautiful. But we have a show to do. It's time to get ready." He walked back to his guitar and pulled the strap over his shoulder.

As he sang during the second and final show, Ian found it difficult to concentrate on the music. His thoughts kept returning to brown eyes, and the small fingers so recently entwined in his own.

CHAPTER THREE

"COME ON, DAD. Can't you eat a little bit faster? If registration at Acadia University is anything like registration at Southern Mississippi, I need to get there early." Julianne sighed, knowing her entreaty was useless.

Her father was in one of his gloomy moods, moods that came all too frequently lately. Dale wasn't going to hurry, no matter what she said. Her fingers smoothed away a nonexistent wrinkle in the embroidered white cloth spread over the small table. It would be a long morning, she thought, resigning herself to standing in endless lines. It was enough to put her in a grouchy mood, too.

As she knew he would, Dale dawdled over the light breakfast supplied by Mrs. Hardesty. He buttered another warm croissant with unconscious precision, then gave his daughter an arch look.

"I'm in no hurry. At my age, why hurry? What is there for me to do here anyway, but putter around some dark library, looking through musty records for details about strangers?"

He popped one end of the croissant into his mouth and began to chew with deliberate slowness. "Besides, you kept me out too late last night. I'm already tired this morning."

Julianne hid a smile. "You're working hard at being grumpy, aren't you? If you recall, we went to the early show so you could get to bed early."

Dale merely grunted, his mouth still full of croissant. But his fingers drummed the table.

There were times, Julianne thought, when she wished her father had stayed in South Mississippi. She folded her hands to keep from clenching them, then took a deep breath. She was not going to lose her temper with her father, no matter how obstinate he became.

"I thought you enjoyed yourself last night. Don't you remember telling me how wonderful the music was, how much you enjoyed the haddock and, of course, the pie?" Especially the music, she thought, remembering Ian, clad all in black, and the voice throbbing with emotion as it caressed the audience.

Her father shrugged. "Maybe, but I'm paying for it this morning. I can't take these late nights anymore."

Despite her best efforts, Julianne felt her temper beginning to rise. "You're not exactly on your last legs, Dad. Anyway, I can remember when you and Mother would stay out all night during Mardi Gras, then sneak into the house like two adolescents, hoping I wouldn't be awake to catch you. That wasn't so long ago."

The memory brought a smile to her face, and she momentarily forgot her exasperation. "Mother always said you wore her out, dancing till dawn."

For a moment Dale's eyes lighted with happiness. "I remember the last Mardi Gras we had together, when your mother went dressed as a pilgrim. She was so beautiful."

The costume had suited her mother, she remembered. Julianne sat still for a moment, letting her thoughts roam back through the years of Mardi Gras parties. A sigh from her father brought her back into the present.

"So many memories. Those happy times are all gone now." The sadness came back to his face. He reached for another croissant.

"Dad." Julianne tried to keep the irritation from her voice. "It's time to go, or I'll never get through registration. I don't know how many students will sign up for summer courses here. It could take all day."

Dale replaced the croissant on the china dish, his expression regretful. "Okay, okay. But what is it I'm supposed to look for at this library?"

They had been over this at least ten times in the past several days. Julianne silently counted to ten, aware that her father knew exactly what he was to research.

"I put the copies of all the letters between Gaston and Anne Blanchet in your briefcase." She reached down and handed it to Dale.

"I think the best place to start would be with Gaston," she said. "From what I pieced together at home, he probably died in the early 1760s. Maybe you can find some record of his death there."

She paused, thinking about the letters. "I've always wondered why the British authorities allowed Gaston to stay and care for his mother. Even though she was ill, Governor Lawrence wasn't so lenient with the other Acadians during the Expulsion. From what I've read, he forced everyone to go, whether they were young or old, sick or infirm. Even pregnant women were crowded into the deportation ships."

"There had to be a reason Gaston and his mother were allowed to stay, while his wife was forced to go," she continued. "But I've never found it in any of the letters."

"Charles Lawrence must have been a monster to cause so much human misery and suffering. Maybe I'll do a little research on him, too." Dale finally stood up, stretched and yawned, then reached for the briefcase.

With a silent prayer of thanks, Julianne followed her father out the door. Maybe he would become interested in researching the family history, after all.

"REMEMBER, DAD. Getting started is the hardest part of doing research." Julianne waved a cheerful goodbye, then eased the rented car away from the curb.

Dale watched her, his expression morose. Then he headed up the sidewalk to the university library.

The drive through the shady streets of Wolfville had failed to cheer him, although he would normally have taken great interest in the houses—some of which appeared to be over a hundred years old—and the well-manicured lawns. Even the grand old elms and other stately trees his daughter had taken such pains to point out brought only a momentary interest, although he loved trees.

No matter that the air was clear and pleasantly warm, or that a breeze scampered through the trees surrounding the library; it was going to be a terrible day. He had decided that much already.

Dale clamped his lips together to keep himself from grinning at his own stubbornness. Then another thought hit him. If he didn't do the research, or at least get a good start on it, Julianne would scold.

He shook his head. How could the respected board chairman of a prosperous company worry about his daughter's scolding? But Julianne, once she got an idea in her head, was as obstinate as any mule.

The mental picture of mule's ears peeking through Julianne's long hair brought the glimmer of a smile to his face. His daughter came by her stubbornness honestly enough, he reminded himself. He had earned a reputation for obstinacy over the years.

At least he would be away from her watchful eye for a few hours; the thought lightened his steps a bit. Her concern for his well-being was touching, but Julianne fussed over him too much. He knew she was trying to ease the pain of her mother's death by shaking him out of his rut, but sometimes she drove him crazy.

Heading through the library's double glass doors, he found himself in a small lobby. Straight ahead was the main reading area, while stairways at each side of the lobby led both up and down. A literature rack, covered with posters and pamphlets, caught his eye and he ambled over.

Dale browsed through several pamphlets that advertised local attractions, then noticed a poster nearly at the bottom of the rack. The simply drawn poster announced that Fiona Graham, a local wood carver, would be demonstrating in the university's student center, wherever that was. He checked the date. The demonstration was today.

Fiona Graham. The name seemed familiar. Then he remembered. She had written one of the manuals he used in his own wood carving. Dale whistled softly, remembering the detailed and precise instructions it contained. The woman was more than a local carver. She was recognized throughout the United States as well as Canada. All thoughts of research on the Blanchet family history fled from his mind.

With instructions from a friendly librarian, he headed downstairs to a long hallway. At one end was another set of double doors. He pushed one open.

A crowd, evidently made up of students, judging by their ages, had gathered around one table at the room's far side. Dale made his way through the group until he was standing next to the table.

He had the fleeting impression of hair, masses of flame-colored strands floating about the head of the woman who sat behind the table. He couldn't see her face; the thick hair shielded it from view.

But he wasn't interested in her face, only in her carving. His attention was quickly drawn to the object she was working on.

It was a hawk, about one-fifth scale, if his eyes judged correctly. It probably was a red-tailed hawk, he decided, noting the broad, somewhat rounded wing the woman was carving, as well as the raptor's stocky build.

Her knife made quick strokes into the basswood, and Dale's trained eye recognized the skill in the slender fingers. The woman was good, very good, he acknowledged in silent admiration. She was indeed a master carver.

Around her, the students watched in silent awe. She seemed unaware of anyone as she concentrated on the outstretched wing that was coming to life in her hands.

Dale observed her for a few moments, his respect for her abilities growing at a rapid rate. Then he noticed something awry on one of the wings.

He leaned forward. "Excuse me, ma'am. That wing isn't exactly right. You need a more gentle round to it."

The woman ignored him. Several of the students standing close by grinned.

Dale flushed. Even in semiretirement, his comments usually drew respectful attention. Except from Julianne, of course, but she at least listened most of the time.

He decided to try again. "If that's a red-tailed hawk you're carving, the wing isn't quite right. You need to curve it more on the down side."

The carver said nothing, but her knife moved faster through the wood. Somebody snickered.

Dale's irritation mounted. He didn't like anyone interfering with his own carving, but if something was incorrect, it needed to be fixed. Master carver or not, the woman could still learn a thing or two from another carver.

He leaned even farther forward, causing a shadow to fall across the carving. "All you need to do is take a little off here."

His fingers touched the smooth wood. "See, right here?"

Fiona slapped down her knife onto the table and looked up, her eyes harder than any of the sharpening stones that lay strewn about the table. "If you think you can carve this any better, do it yourself." With one swift motion, she held out the nearly finished hawk.

Dale stepped back, stunned by his first glimpse of Fiona's face. He judged her to be about fifty, although it was difficult for him to tell.

She was beautiful, a real knockout with eyes the color of Scottish tarns. The hair drifted about her face, its strands red and gold under the fluorescent lights. Her almost translucent skin was lightly dusted with freckles. Red-gold brows slanted over those wide-set eyes, while her thin nose sloped down to a generous mouth. She wasn't smiling, but he knew instinctively that Fiona's smile would melt icebergs, maybe even solid rock.

A student shuffled his feet. Dale willed his gaze away from Fiona's face, finally noticing the curious stares of the onlookers.

He took a deep breath. He'd probably never see that smile now. Why had he opened his big mouth, anyway? Only another experienced wood-carver, or maybe an ornithologist consumed by the study of raptors, would have noticed the wing's curvature. Fiona had challenged him to do better. He would have to correct the wing or leave in shame.

It was too late to do anything about it now. He took the bird from Fiona's grasp. She had small hands, he noticed absently, warm to the touch.

"Uh, if you're sure you don't mind..." His voice trailed away as the midnight-blue eyes frosted over. "I didn't mean to interrupt."

"Well, you did." She stood up and motioned for him to come around the table. "Now, let's see if you know what you're talking about."

Stung by her dare, Dale moved into position. Maybe he wasn't in her class of carving, but he was good, too. And he knew the proper shape of the red-tailed hawk's wings.

Without another word, he picked up the knife and began to carve, haltingly at first, then with increasing confidence. The wood came away from the wing. The knife, its blade as sharp as a surgeon's scalpel, felt good in his hands. It had been a long time, too long since he'd last carved, Dale thought. He forgot about his audience.

Fiona watched impassively as Dale's knife began to fly through the wood with sure strokes. Gradually the bottom of the wing took on a more rounded appearance.

He was a real carver, she acknowledged. It surprised her. Usually the people who gave her unwanted suggestions knew little about carving. This man was doing an excellent job on the hawk's outstretched wing.

Dark hair fell over his face as he worked. The man looked about fifty-five or so. He was nice-looking, too, although judging by his intervention and the set of his chin, he was someone used to getting his own way.

Fiona almost smiled. She was doing it again, analyzing people she didn't know. Her late husband had often called her a witch, she recalled—meaning it as a compliment to her powers of intuition.

She said nothing until the stranger put the carving knife back onto the table. He looked up at her, his eyes locking with hers in silent challenge.

"Well, it seems you were right." She tried to make the words sound grudging, not wanting him to become smug, but they came out as honest praise. "You did very well with the wing, better than I was doing."

To her surprise the man smiled at her, his pleasure obvious. The smile lighted up his face, crinkling the corners of his dark eyes. She found herself thawing.

"Thank you," he said. "That's high praise coming from you, Fiona Graham. I have a well-thumbed copy of your songbird manual sitting on my carving bench at home."

Surprised, she dropped her eyes to the wooden bird. "Thank you. I'm proud of that manual. It took a long time to get it just right."

Dale watched as pink tinged the porcelain skin. Then she smiled. He nearly lost his hold on the wooden bird. As he'd known it would be, her smile was dazzling.

"You're not from around here, are you?" she asked. "I've never seen you at any of the local carving clubs or workshops."

Red-gold lashes, their tips darkened with a hint of mascara, fringed her eyes, some part of him noted. Her eyes were spectacular.

Someone coughed. Drawn back into his surroundings, Dale looked up, remembering where he was. One by one, the students drifted away from the table. Obviously the lesson was over for the day.

"No. I'm from the United States. Ocean Springs, Mississippi, to be exact." He wiped the carving knife clean with a soft towel Fiona had placed nearby, then set the tool on the table.

"I didn't recognize your accent as American, or southern American, for that matter. I thought everyone from Mississippi had a pronounced drawl." Red-gold brows narrowed in question as Fiona began wrapping the hawk in a large cloth.

He laughed. "Not all of us. I'm a Cajun, so I guess I've picked up the speech patterns of my parents and grandparents. I don't really notice it until someone else points it out."

"It's familiar, like that of our own Acadians, and yet different. I like your accent." One by one, Fiona placed her carving tools in a plastic tackle box. She snapped the lid shut, then looked back at Dale.

"I guess it's time to go." She gestured around the empty room. "I seem to have lost my audience."

Because of me, Dale thought. "I'm sorry. I shouldn't have intruded. But since I've scared away all the students, the least I can do is treat you to lunch."

He stopped short. He hadn't invited any woman to lunch in a long time.

Surprise registered on Fiona's face. "Thank you, but I have to go to the student center. I've run out of sandpaper and need to pick up some there." She glanced down at the watch she wore on one slender wrist. Her smile reappeared. "Besides, it's a bit early for lunch."

Her voice was incredible, he thought. Low and throaty, it promised and invited, even when she was turning down his offer. He looked at his own watch. She was right, but he didn't want their meeting to end.

"It is too early for lunch. I guess I lost track of time watching you carve. So how about some coffee? Student centers usually have some place to eat, a coffee shop or cafeteria. Why don't we stop in there, then you can pick up the supplies you need afterwards?"

He picked up the heavy tackle box. "I'll carry this for you."

The man was persistent. And very nice, she decided. Why not? The idea of coffee was enticing. She tucked the cloth-wrapped hawk under one arm. "That's a good idea. In fact, it's a wonderful idea. Shall we go?"

JULIANNE HURRIED UP THE STEPS, taking them two at a time. Thanks to her father and the unfamiliar streets of the campus, she was late. But then she'd expected it, she told herself.

A bewildering array of signs, written in both French and English, gave directions to the crowds of students milling about. As with most university registrations, everyone seemed confused. The lines were too long already, she noticed.

"Thanks a lot, Dad," she muttered, pulling the requisite sharpened pencils from her purse. Now she had to decide where the seminar registration would be. From experience, she knew she would have to go through a process of elimination.

"College registrations are alike, no matter where you are," she said to no one in particular. Around her several students, clad as Julianne was in denim jeans and sweatshirts, grinned. With a sigh of disgust she peered at the signs, trying to figure out where to go first.

"Let's see, I don't need financial aid or scholarships," she said, quickly eliminating one possibility. "Or student housing or a job on campus." Deciding that she didn't need the area set aside for senior citizens either, she walked over to where most of the students were gathering.

One sign announced lines for undergraduates, while another pointed to several queues for graduate students. She headed in that general direction, then stopped short as a hand took hold of her shoulder.

"May I help you find the right table, Julianne Blanchet? Registration is always confusing in a new school."

It was a voice she would recognize anywhere. Despite the noise all around, the liquid baritone sounded as good as it had the night before in the Bearded Lion. Confused, she looked up—into the dark eyes of Ian Ross.

Dressed in faded denim jeans and an old chambray shirt, he looked every bit as imposing as he did in black. The blue shirt accentuated the color of eyes that studied her with obvious interest, while the denim hugged his long legs.

Suddenly Julianne felt shy; it was an unaccustomed feeling. Even in this large, brightly lighted room, far away from the Bearded Lion's stage, Ian still had an air of mystery, a charisma that attracted notice.

"What are you doing here?" *What an inane question,* she berated herself. He had as much right to be at registration as she did. She smoothed the front of her old sweatshirt with nervous fingers.

Ian's smile broadened. "I was about to ask you the same question, but I remember now you told me you'd traveled here to take a course."

Relaxing, she returned his smile. "Only partly. We want to do some research into our family history. We're planning to trace some information in letters written by an ancestor who lived during the Expulsion. That's where my dad is now, in fact. He's investigating old documents at the university library. At least, that's what he is supposed to be doing. With my dad, you never know."

He laughed, enjoying the rueful expression that made her wrinkle her nose. "My father is much the same. A few weeks ago, my mother sent him to the grocery store for something she'd forgotten during her regular trip. He came back with a new car and no groceries."

"I can imagine the look on her face when he showed up. Was she upset?"

Her delighted laugh enchanted him. "No, but she sent him straight back to the grocer's. In the new car, of course."

Julianne's eyes danced. "I think I'd like him."

"He would find you charming." His eyes darkened. "As I do."

Looking into his lean face, she forgot the crowds of bored students, forgot the lines and the endless registration forms she had yet to fill out.

She felt a pulse beating in her temples. "Thank you," she said, hoping her voice sounded steady.

"You're welcome." Someone jostled him, causing him to remember where they were. "So, what course are you taking this summer?"

"I'm enrolling for one on Acadian folklore. The professor is one of the world's recognized experts in the field."

"It's a small world, Julianne. We're signing up for the same course." He grinned. "It will be nice having you in the class."

Excitement surged through her at the thought of spending several weeks in the same class with Ian. *Steady*, she told herself. *It's only a summer course, and then the summer will end. We'll each go back to our regular lives in places far from one another.*

"Of course, we still have to get through registration," she said. "At this rate, we'll still be at registration halfway through the seminar."

His rich laugh caused several heads to turn in their direction. "Never fear. Acadia University is my alma mater. I can get you through registration in one piece, if you'll promise to have lunch with me afterward."

He was irresistible, she realized. Suddenly registration no longer seemed endless and boring. Even standing in line was all right with someone to share it with. Especially someone like Ian, she thought. "It's a date," she agreed.

CHAPTER FOUR

"THANKS FOR HELPING ME get through that ordeal." Julianne stabbed another chunk of lettuce with her fork, then looked at the man sitting across from her.

He was studying her, but the expression in his dark eyes was unreadable. Suddenly nervous under the silent scrutiny, she dropped the lettuce.

Even seated in the student dining area, a place noisy with the excitement of people returning to school, Ian exuded mystery, Julianne decided. What was the indefinable quality about him that caused heads to turn, whether he was the center of a spotlighted stage or simply one of many struggling through university registration? she wondered.

It wasn't merely his dark good looks, although Ian would be striking in any crowd. It was something else, something she couldn't quite put her finger on. The man had a charisma, a vibrancy that reached out to include all those who came into contact with him.

Ian's expression grew quizzical. Julianne realized that she was staring. She let her eyes fall and concentrated on her salad.

"Registration would have taken me a lot longer if you hadn't been there to help."

"I enjoyed it." Ian leaned back in the plastic chair. "Filling out the paperwork is the hardest part of any university course. I think it's a weeding-out technique, designed to keep the faint of heart from attending."

Julianne grinned. "I've often thought the same thing. It's strange to think that university registration in Canada is almost like registration at home."

She took another sip of diet soda. "Two sharpened #2 pencils and you're in business."

He laughed. "We probably would find similarities everywhere."

"You said Acadia University is your alma mater," she recalled, shifting one denim-clad leg underneath the other as she tried to get comfortable. "Have you ever lived anywhere else?"

She couldn't imagine Ian, who was so polished, his manner so cosmopolitan, living all his life in Wolfville. Delightful as the town seemed to be, it was still a small rural town.

"This has always been my home," he said. "I was born on my parents' farm, which has been in my family for generations. In fact, part of the main house was built in the early eighteen hundreds, although it's been added to from time to time. I still live there."

He paused, then focused his eyes on her face. "I've lived in several other places for short periods. Berkeley, for one. I went to the University of California for a while."

She nearly asked more about his California days, but stopped, leaving the question unasked. From the look on his face, it was not a subject he wanted to discuss in detail.

After a moment he continued. "During high school I was an exchange student. I went to France for my junior year. It was an experience I'll never forget. I traveled all over France and spent a lot of time in Brittany. I never realized how beautiful that area would be."

"Brittany is a lovely place," Julianne agreed. "I visited there once with my parents, and I've always wanted to go back. According to everything I've read, the original Acadians came from there."

He smiled. "I felt very close to the land there. There was a pull, something I couldn't quite define."

"Like a magnet," she offered. "I felt the same tugging, almost like I was returning to a place I'd been before, when it was my first visit."

How odd, she thought, that they would share the same emotions for a country far across the seas. Yet somehow the sharing seemed like the most natural thing in the world.

She took another mouthful of the cold soda and swallowed. "I'm sure you know some of the songs you sing have Breton origins. The music hasn't changed much."

"That's one of the reasons I sing," he explained. "If people like me don't preserve the old music—not only the ancient Breton songs but the later music of the Acadians— our legacy will die. It's like all of the Acadian culture. We'll need the dedication and hard work of a lot of people to preserve this heritage for our children."

Julianne stared at him, only partly aware of the passion underlying his quiet words. Unless he had sources she didn't know about, the man had no way of knowing she'd spent the last few years of her life working to save and protect the Cajun culture in the American Deep South.

He was doing essentially the same thing in his own homeland, working with music instead of stories. "But that's what I do. In fact, I've been working at it for several years now," she said. "I run a center for children in South Mississippi, where our sole purpose is to preserve our Cajun background."

Julianne's hand swept out in an encompassing gesture as she continued. "Our heritage is unique in American history. Yet until a few years ago, we were in danger of losing it all. The children wanted to be completely American, like their friends at school. They didn't want to have accents that were different, much less speak Cajun at all. There wasn't much interest in the folk dances, the music, the old stories."

Watching her, Ian sensed the depth of her feelings. She was as committed to her work in cultural preservation as he was, he realized. The thought pleased him.

He suddenly found himself intensely curious. "Have you made any progress toward changing those attitudes?"

"That's what makes the center so rewarding," she said. "I can see real gains. We started with only a handful of children, mostly dragged in by their parents."

"Now, the Cajun Cultural Center, or—" she grinned "—as my staff has dubbed it, the CCC, has made tremendous gains. We're crowded every day during the summer, after school, even during Christmas break. And it's not just children. Parents, even older brothers and sisters are coming in. There's so much interest now."

Her eyes were lovely, Ian decided, especially when they sparkled with such passionate intensity. He wondered briefly what it would be like to be the focus of such passion.

Then he forced himself to concentrate on her words instead of her face.

Julianne shifted in the hard plastic chair, still trying to make herself more comfortable. "Of course we use music, but we also tell stories, using the old Acadian legends as well as more modern Cajun lore. We tell the children about the Indians and how their way of life influenced our ancestors."

She laughed. "As you may have guessed by my wordiness, I'm the chief storyteller. I tend to get wrapped up when I talk about the center."

"I can see why it is your profession. Please go on," he requested.

Encouraged by his interest, she continued. "We teach the old crafts, such as basketry and weaving. We even have a fiddler who comes in to give lessons. He has one of the most popular classes at the center. Several of the older boys are turning out to be accomplished fiddlers.''

It was Ian's turn to stare. Then he laughed. ''Even fiddlers. What you're saying should surprise me, but it doesn't. Not at all.''

His eyes darkened. ''You don't know this, but the first time I saw you, sitting so quietly at the table near the stage, I thought of Evangeline.''

Evangeline. Julianne caught her breath, needing no other explanation.

How often she'd read Longfellow's epic poem herself, caught up by the magic tale of steadfast love found, lost, then found again. The tragic romance between the two young Acadians had always been one of her favorite stories.

Someone near their small table dropped a plastic tray, scattering dishes and cutlery. The noise startled Julianne back into reality.

''Thank you for the compliment. Evangeline is my favorite heroine.''

''Mine, too.''

She caught a glimpse of something in his face, a strange intensity, but his expression changed too quickly for her to read it. Was Ian a man of complex moods, she asked herself, a man whose passions ran deep? The question intrigued her. Trying to imagine the depth of those passions, Julianne shivered.

''Are you cold?'' Ian reached across the table and enfolded her hand in his. ''Your hand feels like ice.''

Now the dark eyes reflected concern, Julianne noticed. His hand felt warm around hers, causing tingling sensations up and down her arm. She tried with little success to suppress another shiver.

"No. I guess I'm not used to summer temperatures in Nova Scotia yet." That wasn't quite true, she knew. Her shivers came as much from her reactions to Ian as they did from the temperature, but he didn't need to know that.

She tried to relax, although with Ian making no attempt to take his hand away from hers, relaxation was difficult. "In South Mississippi right now, the days are already steamy hot."

"Sometimes the weather is hot here also, although the humidity isn't high usually. I like it, especially if I'm out working cattle. It feels good to ride along in warm breezes, with the sun touching my face and arms." He squeezed her hand gently.

Julianne formed a mental image of Ian on horseback, surrounded by cattle, in rolling pastures like those she'd seen surrounding the old Blanchet farmhouse. "I didn't realize you are a cattle rancher as well as a singer."

Somehow she'd thought of him only as a professional singer. With his charisma and the talent that had been so evident at the small club in Wolfville, he could be a major pop star, she thought. The man was full of surprises.

"Singing is only a small part of my life, unfortunately. I run our family cattle farm." He gave her a warm smile. "We call ranches farms here."

"Lately our staff has been so well trained, I've been able to delegate more of the responsibility," he continued. "My parents are semiretired. At least my dad says he is. Most of the time, he can't keep his fingers out of running the place."

That sounded rather like Dale. Julianne grinned.

"I know exactly what you mean," she said. "My father is a lot like that. He is supposed to be retired, but he can't resist going to his office every day."

She wondered briefly where Dale was, then concentrated her attention on Ian again. "Maybe now that you can turn over some of your farming responsibilities to your staff, you'll be able to do more singing. From what I've heard, you have incredible talent.''

He inclined his head, regarding her from behind thick black lashes. "Thank you. But I'm content with the amount of singing I do. I do it as my contribution, however small, to Acadian culture. The farm is beginning to run itself, leaving me more time for what I love most.''

He traced tiny circles in her palm. "I'm really a writer.''

Ignoring the electricity his touch generated, Julianne pushed away the remains of her salad with her free hand. "You mentioned that before.''

She tried to imagine him with his head bent over a typewriter in some dusty office but couldn't. "What do you write?''

His smile was lazy. "When the ideas come, I write children's books. I try to deal with the serious side of life, thinking of ways to help children handle the problems that face us all. Only lately, I haven't been able to come up with anything new. My agent thinks I've gotten too serious, that I need to write something lighter. So I thought I'd tackle some Acadian legends for children.''

He increased the pressure on her palm. "Which is why, Julianne Blanchet, we're taking this course together. Our reasons seem to be much the same.''

A children's writer. Her eyes widened with recognition as his words sank in.

Of course he was. The name Ian Ross printed on book covers flitted across her consciousness. He'd won several major awards for children's literature. She'd seen his books in the hands of the youngsters who came to the cultural center in Ocean Springs. She'd even read one herself.

"I can't believe I didn't recognize your name. One of your books helped me through a difficult adjustment last year when my mother died. It was the book on dealing with the death of a parent. I found it as helpful for someone my age as I'm sure kids find it."

Had only a year gone by since her mother's death? She fell silent, her thoughts far away.

His fingers stopped moving, and he gripped her hand tightly. "I'm sorry, Julianne. Your mother's death must still be very painful for you."

Grateful for his expression of concern, she squeezed his hand. "Sometimes it's still hard to believe she isn't coming back. She was so alive, intense in her quiet way.

"My mother was always there for both my father and me," she continued. "Not that we didn't have our differences, especially when I was a teenager. I'm sure I made her life miserable. But she never complained. When I grew up a bit, we became very good friends. I miss her terribly."

She stopped, wondering why she was confiding her innermost thoughts to a man she barely knew. Julianne knew her reputation for being reserved. She rarely shared her private thoughts with anyone, especially now that her mother was dead. Unconsciously she began to fiddle with her fork.

"And your father? Has he been able to cope with the loss?" Ian prodded gently. With his free hand, he took a drink of iced tea.

Julianne shook her head slowly. "They were very close. My father adored my mother. It was difficult not to, she was so kind and gentle to everyone. He took her death very hard."

"This past year he's spent moping about, dropping in at his office occasionally, spending time with his civic organizations, playing a little golf," she continued. "He's shown little enthusiasm for any of it, saying it all bores him. My father tends to be hardheaded some of the time."

"Actually he's hardheaded most of the time," she amended. "I know it's one reason why he's so successful in business, but his stubbornness can be tough to deal with in family matters."

She frowned, remembering her occasional exasperation with her father. "So, when I read about this course on Acadian legends and folktales, I talked him into coming up to Nova Scotia with me. He didn't want to come at first, but this time I wouldn't take no for an answer. I'm hoping the change in scenery, as well as involvement in a project, will get him interested in life again."

"But he didn't sign up for any classes, did he?"

"Heavens, no. My dad wouldn't set foot inside a classroom that smacked in any way of history. He hated the subject when he was in school, unlike his daughter. No, Dad is supposed to do some research into our family background. Our ancestors came from around here."

"Isn't that history?" Laughter glinted behind Ian's eyes, belying his bland expression.

It took Julianne a second or two to catch his meaning, then she laughed. "You're absolutely right! I suppose we never connected doing research on our own roots as history. Of course it is history, the most personal kind. Let's hope Dad doesn't figure that out, or he might quit doing any research at all."

"You may have distant relatives up here," he said. "I know there are Blanchets living in Wolfville."

Julianne's face lighted up. "I know. I've been corresponding for some time now with a woman named Thérèse Blanchet. We have a common ancestor, Gaston Blanchet. I'm supposed to meet with her soon, so we can compare some old letters we have."

"Thérèse Blanchet? I've known her for a long time. She's been a family friend for years. That's a wonderful start, to already have a contact here. Tell me about the letters you mentioned.''

"There are actually two sets.'' Her voice dropped to almost a whisper as she recalled the story she'd told so many times.

"Gaston and his young wife, Anne, owned a farm around here. Evidently they were hardworking, prosperous and had some education. They were separated when the Acadians were expelled from Nova Scotia. They hadn't been married very long when it happened. Anne went to the Louisiana Territory, taking their infant son with her. His name was Paul Gaston.''

Julianne's fingers trembled. Ian felt rather than saw the emotion mirrored in her eyes, eyes as dark as his own. "So, then what happened?''

"I don't understand all the reasons why, but evidently they never saw each other again.''

Julianne swallowed with difficulty, feeling again the impact of the old tragedy. "Of course, they did write letters. Miraculously, the letters Gaston wrote to Anne survived and were passed down for generations in my family.''

"That's remarkable,'' he agreed. "Most of the time people throw away old letters, not realizing the value to future generations.''

"Ah, but that's not all.'' Her smile was nearly conspiratorial. "Anne wrote letters back to Gaston. The Blanchets who settled back in Nova Scotia in the late seventeen hundreds saved those letters. So now we have two sets.''

"Have you seen the letters Anne wrote?''

She shook her head. "No. Thérèse has them. She's promised to show them to me when I see her. I'm very anxious to see them. I hope I'll find the answers to some of my questions in those letters.''

She hesitated, wondering if she should go on. Encouraged by the warmth in Ian's eyes, she continued. "There's even a family mystery, which the combined letters may help solve."

One eyebrow quirked up. "A mystery? Acadians always love a good mystery."

His grin was contagious. Julianne responded with one of her own.

"Just a little mystery, you understand. Gaston refers several times to their treasure, which he put somewhere for safekeeping. He obviously expected Anne to return."

She smoothed back a few unruly strands of hair from her face. "Of course she didn't get back to Nova Scotia, and neither did her son. Paul Gaston had two sons. One stayed in the United States, but the other came back to this area and settled here. I'd like to find out more about him."

"Gaston's letters never indicate what happened to his treasure," she continued. I'm hoping Thérèse's letters may give us a clue."

"Perhaps there will be something valuable hidden around here somewhere."

She laughed. "I doubt it. I'm sure anything of value was found long ago. It's the idea of finding out what it was that intrigues me."

Her expression became serious. "No, the real treasure is the letters. To me they are extremely valuable, because they can help me learn more about my family's history. I can't wait to see the ones Anne wrote back to Gaston."

Her eyes found his as she wondered if Ian would understand her next thoughts. She plunged ahead. "It's odd. Gaston lived in the seventeen hundreds, in a time and country far from me, and yet, from the words he wrote so long ago I feel like I know the man. I'm sure if he walked into this student center right now, I'd recognize him instantly.''

To her surprise, Ian nodded. "I understand. Sometimes when I'm singing, I can feel the thoughts of the songwriter, the emotions that caused the song to come into being.''

For a moment they stared at each other in complete understanding. What a contradictory man Ian was turning out to be, Julianne thought. So obviously masculine, with his strong, lean body and a face handsome enough to turn heads, and yet Ian radiated sensitivity—one born of a quiet inner strength, of a confidence in himself.

He was, she thought, a very complicated man. For some reason the thought was unnerving.

A firm tap on her shoulder interrupted her musings. "The tough life of a graduate student, I see. Sitting around the student center in the middle of the day, eating...''

Julianne looked up in surprise. "Dad! I didn't expect to see you in here.''

Then she noticed the woman standing beside her father. Petite, with red hair that glowed, backlighted by the fluorescent bulbs overhead, the woman possessed a beauty dramatic enough to stun. Her perfect mouth, lightly touched with pink gloss, curved into a smile that reminded Julianne of a sated ginger cat.

Several dozen questions went through Julianne's mind, all at the same time. Who was this knockout? What was she doing with Dale? And why did her father look so pleased with himself?

Dale grinned. "I'm glad I ran into you. Fiona, this is my daughter, Julianne, and uh—'' his brow furrowed for a moment "—Mr. Ross. Ian Ross, if my memory serves me.''

Ian stood up and extended his hand. "It serves you well. Please call me Ian, Mr. Blanchet.''

Dale beamed. "Please call me Dale.''

He pulled the woman forward a bit. "This is Fiona Graham." He touched his daughter's arm. "Fiona's a wood-carver, one of the best working today, in fact."

Julianne found the older woman hard to resist. Fiona's smile lighted her entire face, dancing about eyes that were a remarkable shade of blue. Nearly navy, Julianne judged, and rimmed by long, thick lashes.

Recovering her voice, Julianne smiled back. "A wood-carver? That's wonderful. Dad is quite a good wood-carver himself. He brought his tools with him to Nova Scotia, in fact." Knowing he would have protested she refrained from adding the fact that she'd slipped the wood-carving paraphernalia into her father's luggage at the last minute.

"Won't you join us for lunch?" Julianne indicated the small table.

Dale glanced pointedly at the empty plates. "Thanks for the invitation, but you're already finished. Fiona and I are going to do some exploring in Wolfville. There are some artists' shops and craft stores I'd like to visit."

Julianne tried to keep the surprise from showing on her face. Had Dale forgotten they were supposed to go back to the Blanchet farm that afternoon? He knew she wanted to spend more time in the ruined farmhouse.

Anyway, she reflected ruefully, she knew from experience how much her father hated poking around in stores of any kind. His distaste for shopping malls had always been a family joke. It was hard to imagine he'd volunteered to squire Fiona around any shops in Wolfville.

Unless one looked at those midnight-blue eyes shining so expectantly at Dale, Julianne thought. With a jolt, she realized that her father's interest in the lovely red-haired woman probably had little to do with wood-carving.

Something wrenched in her stomach, then she looked back at Dale, seeing again the eagerness, the relaxed lines around his eyes. Dale hadn't looked this happy in a long time. Was Fiona responsible? She already knew the answer to that. *Yes.*

Julianne buried the protest she'd been about to utter. "That's a terrific idea, Dad. Maybe you'll find that special chisel you've been hunting for."

Watching the play of emotions across Julianne's face, Ian wondered at the struggle he saw there, then remembered her account of her mother's death. The tragedy was still fresh in her mind.

He reached for her hand. "I was about to ask you to spend the afternoon with me. I'd like to do some exploring also."

"Shopping?"

Ian laughed. "No, although that would be fun to do sometime, too. Actually, I wondered if you would like to go up to Cape Split with me."

He looked down at her leather tennis shoes. "Good. You're set for some walking. There's something there I'd like to show to you."

She recalled the place-name from the literature she'd read before coming to Nova Scotia. "Cape Split? Doesn't that overlook the Minas Channel?"

A tendril of land curling out into the wild channel, Julianne remembered. Something else about the place flitted about the edges of her memory, but it eluded her. What else had she read?

Her father's brisk voice settled the matter. "I'll see you this evening then, Julianne. Nice seeing you again, Ian. Take good care of my daughter." With a friendly wave, the pair headed toward the doors.

CHAPTER FIVE

MINUTES LATER, JULIANNE found herself sinking into one of the leather seats of Ian's inky-black Ferrari. The shining machine was a surprise, although Julianne realized she hadn't thought about the kind of car he would drive. Another facet of the man's unpredictable personality, she concluded. Somehow that unpredictability made her nervous.

But then, she admitted as the engine throbbed to life, she liked the complexity, the sense of inner depths unprobed. What thoughts lay behind those eyes, now completely hidden by dark driving glasses?

His hands seemed relaxed against the leather-clad steering wheel, but she saw determination in the set of his chin. Ian was the kind of man, she surmised, who usually knew what he wanted and how to get it.

A comfortable silence stretched between them as the powerful car crawled through the streets of Wolfville. Julianne felt any lingering tenseness disappear as she watched the shops and city houses give way to less populated areas. Now farmland rolled by as the automobile traveled through the countryside.

"No wonder my ancestors loved it here. This is lovely country." Julianne folded both hands over her knees. "I'd love to see this area blanketed with snow."

Without taking his eyes from the road, Ian nodded. "Our winters are cold, but enchanting. There's something about the contrast of all that white against the dark of tree limbs and shadows.''

Ian slowed the auto as they entered the small town of Port Williams. "This is charming, really more of a village than a city," Julianne observed.

"Port Williams was first settled by the Micmac Indians, our native people," Ian told her.

"The Micmacs were nomads, weren't they?" Julianne asked. "Hunters and fishermen? I read about them when I was getting ready to come up here."

Ian nodded. "Port Williams is a good place to buy fresh produce, including wonderful apples and strawberries.''

Several pedestrians looked up and waved as the Ferrari rolled by. Julianne smiled.

"Do you always get a response to this car?" she asked. "It is beautiful," she added hastily, hoping he wouldn't take her question as a criticism.

He smiled. "And a bit out of place? You're right, of course. There aren't many Ferraris in Wolfville. Getting service is sometimes a problem, but luckily, I haven't had to do much."

He smiled. "Owning this was a dream I had. I think my dream started somewhere in California. It seemed like everyone had luxury sports cars and I was young. I wanted one, too. So when I'd sold several books, I bought this. Actually I don't drive it a lot. I'm usually in one of the farm trucks or four-wheel-drive vehicles."

An image formed in her mind, that of a much younger Ian laughing on a sunlit California beach. Somehow he seemed out of place in her fantasy, as if he didn't belong in a land of eternal sunshine. Ian would thrive better, she knew instinctively, in an environment of many moods and seasonal contrasts.

"My parents were scandalized, of course." He chuckled. "But they got over it. Even Dad, who tends to be very conservative, drives it every now and then, especially when he's taking his best girl out to dinner."

"Your parents sound like fun." She tried to keep the wistfulness out of her voice, but it was difficult. "Still very much in love, as my parents were."

Ian reached for her hand as he slowed the car again. "We're about to come to Old Wellington Dyke. It's one of the dykes built by the Acadians to reclaim the marshlands from the sea as well as hold back the Bay of Fundy tides. There are dykes all around the area."

Julianne noticed several more signs as the car eased along the roadway. Several, such as Lower Canard and Canning, a village filled with well-kept colonial homes, she remembered from her research.

It seemed like only minutes later when Ian again slowed the car, then stopped. With a few short strides he came around to the passenger side and held open the car door.

Julianne shaded her eyes against the sunshine. Spread out before her was a crescent of beach. Sunlight glittered from the smooth surfaces of millions of rocks, while beyond the beach, whitecaps danced along the surface of the water.

Ian took her hand as they walked down to the water's edge. For a moment he studied the wide expanse of water. Then he turned back toward the road.

"The tide is beginning to come back in. Where we are standing now will be covered in no time at all," he cautioned. "Let's find a better vantage point."

As they headed back to the parked car, he bent down and picked up a small stone. "If you look down as we walk, you may find some of Glooscap's jewels."

Julianne glanced at the shining pebble in Ian's free hand. "Glooscap? Let me see now. Wasn't he the great god of the Micmac?"

She stroked the red stone with gentle fingers, admiring its deep luster. "His anger became thunder and when he smiled, the sun came out, if my memory serves me well."

Ian nodded. "His footsteps can still be found along the Cape Blomidon cliffs not too far from here. Legend tells that Glooscap scattered precious stones here for his friends."

"I've found agate, amethyst and—" he held up the stone with two fingers "—jasper. This is a pretty one. It would go well with your dark hair." His fingers brushed her cheek as he held the stone next to her skin.

For a moment, both pairs of dark eyes held each other. Julianne barely felt the breeze lifting the ends of her hair. Somewhere a bird cried, the sound harsh against the rustling noises as waves broke along the shoreline. A sea tang tantalized, promising rain-swept nights as it whispered tales of the ocean.

She held her breath, feeling only the touch of Ian's fingers against her cheek. Even in bright, afternoon sunshine on a rock-strewn beach, she sensed the timeless mystery of wild, forgotten places, places where a man like Ian would fit in well.

Ian broke the silence. "Why don't we move on? I've got another place to show you."

Julianne turned for a last look at the beach. The spot where they had stood minutes before was already covered by water. She hurried to catch up with Ian.

"I've heard so much about the incredible Bay of Fundy tides, but I guess a person has to experience them to understand how quickly the water can come in. Tides on the Gulf Coast are much slower," she said as Ian started the car.

"I'd like to see them with you."

She glanced at him, but he kept his eyes on the road. "I'd love to show you the Gulf Coast," she replied.

Ian drove in silence for a few minutes, then pulled the car off the road at a finger of land jutting out over the Minas Basin. Except for a lone farmhouse several hundred yards distant, the treeless area was uninhabited.

"This is private property," he explained, "but the people who own it are old family friends. They won't mind if we watch the tides come in from their cliffside. I'll get something for us to sit on."

As Ian opened the car trunk, Julianne walked to the end of the narrow gravel pathway. She took a deep breath. Below, spread out as far as she could see, was water.

But these were not the placid, warm waves she knew from the Gulf of Mexico and the Mississippi Sound. These waters swirled and leaped as if alive, flinging spume high into the air. She could almost feel the droplets.

"Impressive, isn't it?"

Ian's baritone came from behind. She turned slightly to smile at him. "I hate to repeat myself, but I've never seen anything like these tides."

He spread a red plaid blanket on the rocky ground, then motioned for her to sit. Making sure she could still see the roiling waters below, Julianne eased herself onto the soft woolen surface.

"These tides are the highest in the world," Ian commented as he stretched out beside her. "They vary from about three meters at Yarmouth to over sixteen meters at Burntcoat in the Minas Basin."

Julianne did some rapid calculations. "But that's over fifty feet."

She glanced down at the steadily rising water. "I never knew tides could come in so fast, except during hurricanes."

For a while, they sat quietly as the tides rolled in far below. Seabirds called overhead, swift-moving shadows against the clear blue of the sky.

It would be easy to fall in love with this windswept part of the world, Julianne thought as she hugged her knees. This rugged part of Nova Scotia was nothing like the coast of Mississippi that she knew so well.

In her mind she could see the gentle Gulf of Mexico, with deep blue waters contrasted against the sugar white of man-made beaches. Right now, she knew, tall-masted shrimp boats would silhouette the line where sky met sea, taking advantage of the opening of shrimp season.

"You're far away from here."

Ian's low voice startled her. She looked down at the lithe frame stretched across the red plaid. His head was cocked to one side, his expression quizzical.

"I was thinking of home, actually. June is one of my favorite months there. With the beginning of shrimp season there are lots of fishing rodeos."

She turned her face to catch a stray breeze. "And the weather is usually good, not as steamy as it is in July and August."

He propped his head on one hand. "You feel a strong sense of home, don't you? I imagine it would be difficult for you to live anywhere but South Mississippi."

Would it? Julianne realized she'd never thought about leaving her home before. Could she live away from the live oaks hung with gray Spanish moss, the curve of white sand beach along the Gulf, the vibrant colors of the lush tropical foliage that bloomed most of every year?

Home was memories and familiar people, things and places. Home was the Cajun Cultural Center, invested with years of her hard work. What would it take to get her to leave, if indeed she ever wanted to?

She shook her head. "I don't know. I've never really thought about it before."

"At least you'd think about it."

She looked down, surprised by the bitterness in his voice. "I try to keep an open mind, although it isn't always easy." She wondered what had triggered the emotion she'd heard.

Ian stared up at the sky, ignoring the patches of white clouds. "Not everyone keeps an open mind. My wife certainly didn't."

Wife? She glanced at his bare ring finger. It hadn't even occurred to her that Ian would be married. The thought jabbed at her temples with a sharp pain.

"My former wife," he continued. "She was a California girl, born and bred. A golden girl, just like the stereotype. She was tall, a willowy blonde. Joanna."

Julianne exhaled, only then aware that she'd been holding her breath. A former wife was not a present wife, she thought, then wondered why it mattered so much.

"I met Joanna at the university I attended," he said. "She was a freshman, too. We were both nineteen and reckless. Without even thinking about what it would be like to spend the rest of our lives together, we eloped to Las Vegas one weekend. We got married in one of those tacky wedding chapels along the Strip. Both sets of parents were upset, although there was nothing they could do about it."

He sat up, leaning his elbows against his knees. "Our parents were wiser than we were, but you couldn't have told either one of us at the time, of course."

Julianne could see Ian at nineteen, tall and handsome, with all the brash confidence in his own abilities that youth usually bestows. For a fleeting moment, she wished she had known him then.

"I know," she said slowly. "I think of all the times I resented my mother's advice when I was a teenager. She usually was right. I'd give anything to have her back, giving me her wonderful suggestions."

Ian nodded. "Once they got used to the idea, our parents were very supportive. As long as we lived in California, Joanna and I were happy. We didn't have any responsibilities. Everything was school and surfing, an eternal summer, just like in the movies."

His voice dropped. "But our movie didn't have the usual happy ending."

Moved by the sadness in his voice, Julianne touched his shoulder. "You don't have to tell me about this."

He shrugged. "It's been a long time since I've been able to talk about it. After a year we moved to Nova Scotia. I liked California, but after a while I needed something stronger, tougher, a place with responsibilities for me. Looking back with the wisdom of a few more years, I suppose I was homesick. At twenty years of age, it never occurred to me that Joanna would get homesick, too."

Julianne could see a tall, tanned beauty pining for the California sunshine. She sympathized with the woman she'd never met.

"But she did," Ian continued. "Joanna couldn't adjust to Nova Scotia. She hated the chilly spring and fall weather, and despised winter. She grew to hate the people here, too. They weren't as open as her friends in California. Not that Acadians aren't friendly. They are, but it takes longer to develop friendships."

"I know. Cajun hospitality is legendary. We are among the warmest people anywhere, but with each individual it takes a while to get to the person inside."

She ran her hands through the stubby grasses next to the blanket, feeling the coolness of each blade. Then she glanced over at Ian. The tenseness had disappeared from his face, as if talking about his long-ago hurt had eased some of the pain he still felt.

"Joanna left Nova Scotia during one of our tougher winters. I drove her to the airport in Halifax. She said she was going to visit her family, that she'd be back. But she never came back." He shaded his eyes from the sunlight.

"The next word I had from her was through her parents' legal firm. The divorce didn't take long at all. Just a few short weeks to wipe out what was supposed to be a lifetime commitment."

"I'm sorry," she murmured. The words slipped out automatically, but Julianne realized she meant them.

She was sorry as well as surprised. If she had been married to Ian, she would have stayed with him, despite the uprooting to a new land and people, she told herself.

How could any woman ever leave someone like Ian? she wondered. Instinct told her he would be a faithful and devoted husband, loving and passionate.

Her stomach knotted as she thought of the passion. What would he be like as a lover? Had Joanna found his lovemaking inadequate? Looking at him, studying his strong chin, the sensual lines of his mouth, she couldn't imagine that being the problem.

She wasn't being fair, she knew. What if she had been in Joanna's place, very young and far from home? How would she have reacted?

Her own roots ran deep in the soil of South Mississippi. Her family on both sides had lived there for generations. All her aunts and uncles, the numerous cousins and close family friends lived there, bound by ties to the land, the ocean and to each other.

Then there was her father. Dale's grief over his wife's death was profound. He was slowly accepting her loss and gradually making his way back into life's mainstream, but he still had a long way to go. Although Julianne had her own home and busy career, he depended upon his only child for support.

The Cajun Cultural Center was another strong tie. She'd spent years nursing her "child," sheltering it past the first few uncertain years of life. The center was thriving now, but it still took hard work and much dedication. How could she leave it for an unknown life in a new country?

What *would* her own reaction have been? Julianne asked herself again. The question was unsettling.

"I've asked myself many times what I could have done to change things," Ian said quietly. "I suppose life is full of what-ifs."

Did Ian blame himself for the breakup of his marriage? Julianne hesitated, reluctant to say anything. But it wasn't fair for him to take the blame, she thought.

"It takes two to make any relationship successful." She paused, wondering if she should continue. But his face seemed relaxed, his look expectant, as if he wanted to hear more. "Both people have to work hard. My parents had a very strong marriage, but they both gave totally of themselves."

For a while he said nothing. His fingers stroked the smooth surface of a pebble, and the seconds slipped away.

"You're right," he said finally. "I had an excellent example of commitment with my own parents' marriage. They had some difficult times, but no matter what the problems, they worked together to solve them."

He lapsed into silence again. Had she said too much? Probably, she decided, but Ian had listened. If he didn't want her comments, Ian would have said so.

Beside her Ian stretched, then got to his feet. "I didn't realize we'd been here so long. It's too late to go up to Cape Split. We'd still have to drive up to Scots Bay, then hike the eight miles up to the cliff. I'm sorry I didn't pay more attention to the time."

When had the afternoon turned to evening? Julianne wondered as she helped Ian fold the blanket. He tucked it under one arm, then draped one arm casually about her shoulders as they made their way back to the car.

Both were quiet as they drove back to Wolfville. Julianne wondered if Ian regretted talking about his marital history with her. He seemed like the type of man not used to sharing inner thoughts, she decided. She realized she was pleased that he'd chosen to tell her about his past.

Ian pointed out several historic landmarks as they drove, including old churches and cemeteries, but Julianne only half listened. Her thoughts centered on Ian.

He was so unlike any man she'd ever known, very masculine and sure of himself. For his country, especially Nova Scotia, Ian possessed a depth and passion she'd seldom encountered in anyone. Without turning her head, she glanced at him, wondering if his passion applied to everything. As before, the thought caused a shiver to run down her back.

She quickly looked toward the window. Water droplets touched the smooth glass exterior. The air outside was colder, she noticed. Mist settled around the automobile as it cut through the evening shadows.

The mist made her nervous, although Ian drove with a sure caution. Julianne breathed easier when the streets and buildings of Wolfville came into view.

Ian stopped the car in front of the inn where Julianne and her father were staying, then came around to open the passenger door. He extended one hand to help her out of the low-slung vehicle.

"You don't have to walk me to the door," she said as he slipped an arm through hers. His old-fashioned courtesy was very nice, she thought.

"But I'd like to," he answered.

They walked up the wooden steps in silence. Ian stopped in the doorway, then turned her to face him.

"Thank you for sharing this afternoon with me." His eyes found hers. "And thank you for listening."

Julianne couldn't look away. "Thanks for my first look at the Bay of Fundy."

"The first of many such trips, I hope," he said.

He paused for a few seconds, then his hands found her shoulders. Gently he pulled her close, then looked at her upturned face. "Perhaps we'll even get to Cape Split one day."

He was going to kiss her, Julianne knew, right out on the front porch, where the innkeeper and the rest of the world would see them. But she didn't care, she realized.

She felt the pulse throb in her temple as his lips brushed hers, softly at first, then with a firm pressure that took her breath away. When he released her, his hands still clasped her shoulders.

"I've been wanting to do that all afternoon." He touched his fingers to her face, stroking gently. "Will you have lunch with me tomorrow?"

Slowly, not wanting to disturb the fingers gliding along her cheek, she nodded. "That sounds wonderful. We can go right after class."

He drew his hand away from her face, as if reluctant to end the caress. He turned to go, then stopped suddenly. One hand reached into his pocket.

"I almost forgot. A gift from Glooscap—" he held out his hand "—so you'll return to see him again." In his outstretched palm was the small piece of jasper.

"Thank you. I have the feeling Glooscap and I are going to be good friends." The stone felt cool against her skin.

Ian pulled away from the curb and Julianne waved, then went inside. The innkeeper was nowhere to be seen and she made her way upstairs.

Inside the sitting room she shared with her father she stopped short, her heart pounding wildly. Dale lay prone on the floor, his face red and beaded with sweat.

"Dad! Stay still and I'll call a physician." She turned to run back down the stairway.

"No, no!" Her father's voice stopped her in her tracks and she turned back.

"What happened?" She knelt beside him. "Is it your heart?"

"Of course not," he reassured her. "There's nothing wrong with me. I've been doing a few exercises, that's all."

Julianne wasn't sure she'd heard him correctly. "Exercises? Dad, aren't you the same person who hates anything that even looks like it's designed to produce physical fitness? I've heard you dozens of times expounding on the evils of jogging and aerobics, not to mention simple calisthenics."

She eyed him thoroughly, alert for any signs of overexertion. "What's come over you?"

Dale grinned. "Times change, my girl. I've realized how wrong I've been."

He took a deep breath, then sat up. "I've let my body go to ruin. But it's not too late. No sir, it's not too late to reverse the damage I've done."

He patted his stomach, which drooped a bit over the waistband of his sweatpants. "It's time for this man to get in shape."

What had come over her father? Dale despised exercises, saying busy people had no need for such artificial methods.

Now here he was, resplendent in new gray sweats and leather aerobic shoes. He even had a plastic exercise mat spread out beneath him.

For some reason, Fiona's svelte shape popped into her mind. *Of course,* Julianne realized. This was Fiona's influence.

She studied her father carefully while he rolled up his exercise mat. Dale hummed a merry song as he methodically completed his task.

Was it possible that Dale had a new interest in life, namely the flame-haired Fiona Graham? Yes, it was possible, in fact probable, Julianne realized. For reasons she couldn't yet explain to herself, she found that thought very disquieting.

CHAPTER SIX

WHISTLING PENETRATED the foggy remnants of sleep. A happy tune, Julianne noted half-consciously as she burrowed deeper into her pillow, trying to shut out the sounds.

Whistling, she thought, reluctantly allowing herself to be drawn further out of sleep. Who was whistling in the middle of the night? Her eyes opened, and she was fully awake.

The only person who could be whistling in their suite of rooms was Dale, who hadn't whistled for a year. For a moment she simply listened, hearing a happiness that had been missing since her mother's death.

The melody, a 1940s big-band tune she remembered her mother humming, brought back memories she would have expected to be painful. Instead, the cheerful sounds wrapped themselves around those memories, easing the lingering hurt.

What was her father doing up so early? She glanced at the clock radio on her nightstand. The alarm, set for six-thirty, because her class started at eight o'clock, hadn't even gone off yet.

Lately Dale had been sleeping in. "What's there to get up early for?" he would mutter when Julianne called from her own home. She'd heard him say those words far too often during the weeks before this trip to Nova Scotia.

With a regretful look at her pillow, Julianne swung her legs out of bed, touching the alarm button as her feet found her slippers. Grabbing her terry robe, she quickly donned the garment and made her way into the sitting room.

It took a few moments for her eyes to adjust to the sunlight streaming through the windows. A coffee aroma quickened her senses.

"Well, I was wondering if you were going to stay in bed all day. Remember the old proverb about 'Early to bed and early to rise'?"

Comfortably seated in a rocking chair, Dale took a sip from a large blue mug. "I've already been for a walk this morning. There's something wonderful about the air here, all brisk and clear."

"I don't believe those words are coming from your mouth, Dad. I've never known you to even consider taking an early-morning walk, much less actually do it." Julianne couldn't help staring.

Dale was already shaved and dressed in khaki chino slacks and a brilliant cerise plaid shirt. New slacks and a new shirt, she noted with surprise.

Her father's wardrobe was notoriously conservative, even outdated. It had always taken the combined cajoling and pleading of mother and daughter to get him to try anything new. He usually preferred navy or gray slacks with pale oxford shirts and wing tip shoes. At work he always wore gray or navy suits with solid color ties.

Today he'd completed his outfit with brand-new loafers. He looked positively trendy. The leather shone with newness. Julianne's mouth nearly dropped open. To her knowledge, her dad had never worn a pair of loafers in his life.

His face was alive with good humor, while his old smile, the one she'd missed so much since Lillian's death, twinkled from his dark eyes. The air of excitement about him was unmistakable. Julianne couldn't help smiling.

Dale set his coffee cup on the table, then poured some steaming liquid from a thermal carafe into another cup. "Here," he said, handing her the mug.

"Mrs. Hardesty brought it up a while ago, along with breakfast. You look like you could use some."

Ignoring his remark, Julianne accepted the mug and took a mouthful of the hot brew. The coffee was as good as she'd expected it to be.

She took another sip, then looked back at her father, who waited expectantly. He wanted her to comment on his outfit, she knew.

"You bought some new clothes, I see. A bit different from your usual style," she said dryly. Then she grinned. "You look wonderful."

He really did, she thought. The cherry red contrasted with his black hair and eyes, bringing a healthy glow to a face that had lately spent too much time indoors.

Dale beamed and smoothed the already immaculate creases in the slacks. "I thought you'd like these. Fiona and I went shopping yesterday. You know, that woman has an amazing eye for color. I never thought I'd look good in red, but she insisted that I try this on."

Fiona. Of course.

Easing into the companion rocker, Julianne cradled her mug, concentrating on the heat radiating from the pottery as conflicting emotions assailed her.

"Spiff up your image, darling," Lillian had for years implored Dale, with little success. It had only taken Fiona a few hours.

But that wasn't being fair, she knew. Lillian and Fiona were different people, and this was a different time. Her father had loved Lillian and always would, but it was time for him to get on with his life. His joy and excitement this morning were all the proof she needed of that, Julianne told herself.

Mentally thanking Fiona for her good taste and powers of persuasion, she turned back to her father. He was studying her, his expression anxious. She wondered if he guessed some of her thoughts.

"Tell Fiona she's a miracle worker. She accomplished in one afternoon what Mom and I tried for years to get you to do." A warm smile accompanied her words.

His expression grew sheepish. "I guess I have been a bit stubborn about clothing."

"Stubborn, Dad? Oh no, not you."

Father and daughter grinned at each other, then Dale, with a final swallow, set down his mug. "Speaking of clothing, young lady, perhaps you should consider getting a new robe. That one certainly has seen better days."

Julianne looked down at the yellow terry cloth. It was true. The robe was threadbare, but she loved the garment. "Do you remember when I got this?"

Her father shook his head.

She fingered the worn material. "Mom gave it to me the Christmas of my senior year in high school. I saw it in a magazine and mentioned it to her once. I told her I liked it, but I knew I would look terrible in yellow. Mom said yellow was a good color for me, if it was the right shade. That Christmas, the robe was under the tree."

"Mom was right. That shade of yellow is wonderful for you."

For a moment they were both silent as they shared happy memories. Then the telephone rang.

Startled by the sound, Julianne quickly reached for the receiver. "Hello. This is Julianne Blanchet."

"Julianne, my dear. It's so good to hear your voice again."

Thérèse Blanchet. The strong, sure voice was unmistakable. "I've been hoping to hear from you. Are you feeling better?"

"Yes, yes."

The woman's tone was slightly irritated, as if Thérèse disliked any mention of illness. "Would you and your father be free for lunch today? I'd like you to come for a visit."

Lunch? Finally she would meet this very distant relative. Julianne was eager to trace the relationship, as well as to become acquainted with Thérèse.

Then she remembered Ian's invitation and hesitated. She hated to turn down Thérèse, but she'd already committed herself to Ian.

Besides, she admitted to herself, as much as she wanted to see her elderly friend, she wanted to see Ian more. Thoughts of the previous night came to her mind, thoughts of Ian's mouth on hers, firm but gentle. Their embrace had been a magical finish to a wonderful afternoon.

"Julianne? Are you still there?"

"Yes, I am. Let me check with my father." Julianne covered the mouthpiece with one hand and turned to Dale.

"It's Thérèse Blanchet. She's feeling better and wants us to come over for lunch today. I already have plans. What about you?"

Dale shook his head. "No. I've already planned to spend lunch and the afternoon with Fiona."

Julianne's eyebrows rose. Her dad was going to spend two afternoons in a row with Fiona? This was very unlike him. She would have to sort this out later, she thought, turning back to the telephone.

"I'm afraid Dad and I both already have plans. I'm going to the university for the first day of my class, and then to lunch with a friend who is also taking the course. Could we set it up for another time?''

"Is this some young man you're going to lunch with?''

Julianne smiled. The lady certainly was blunt. She thought for a moment. Ian probably fitted into the category of "young man," although she judged him to be in his mid-thirties.

"Yes. His name is Ian Ross.''

There was a small silence. "Why don't you bring him with you, then? That name sounds familiar, anyway. I think I know him.''

Julianne wondered how Ian would feel about having lunch with Thérèse. He'd probably love it, she thought. "Let me check with Ian. If it's all right with him, then I would like very much to come. May I call you right after class gets out?''

"That would be fine,'' Thérèse answered. "It's been a while since I've had any handsome young men over for lunch.''

They talked for a moment more. Julianne was still smiling as she hung up. "That lady is an absolute charmer. It's impossible to say no to her.''

"She reminds me of you,'' her father retorted between mouthfuls of pastry. "Have a Danish?''

Julianne gave the pastry a look of regret. "I'd better not. Did Mrs. Hardesty bring anything else, maybe cereal?'' Her tone was hopeful. "That's about all I'll have time for. I've still got to bathe and get dressed. I want to get to class on time. I wouldn't want to be late, especially on the first day.''

"If you'd gotten up when I did, you wouldn't have to worry about being late.'' Dale's expression was totally innocent as he ignored her mock glare.

Julianne was still chuckling as she slid into the seat of one of the vacant desks in the seminar classroom. She looked at her watch. Five minutes to eight, she read with a small sigh of relief.

"I was almost afraid you weren't coming. But it was worth the wait."

Julianne turned to her left. Ian Ross was looking at her with evident appreciation, making her glad she'd taken the time to dress with care in a silky, royal-blue shirt and linen skirt. The outfit was one of her favorites; she knew she looked good in it.

"Thanks." He looked pretty good himself, she thought, very relaxed and masculine in a striped rugby shirt and navy slacks. She wondered if he'd thought about the kiss they'd shared such a few hours before.

Her face suddenly felt warm. "I misjudged the driving time, I guess. Tomorrow I won't cut it so short."

Ian grinned, but the arrival of the professor forestalled any comment he might have made. Julianne hurriedly opened her notebook and retrieved her ballpoint pen, then straightened in her seat. The professor, with barely a glance at the assembled faces watching him, launched into a full-blown lecture.

The next few hours flew by. Despite the distraction of Ian sitting so close, Julianne found herself enthralled by the discussion of Acadian folklore. She wrote furiously as the professor lectured. When the first day's class drew to a close, she knew her decision to come all the way from South Mississippi to Nova Scotia to take the class was a sound one.

"What do you think of our first day?" Ian questioned as they walked from the classroom into the noon sunshine.

"I'm glad I was smart enough to sign up for this class," she answered. "Professor Godfrey is brilliant, one of the best lecturers I've ever heard, as well as one of the most knowledgeable. If the rest of the course goes like this first class, this will be time and money well spent."

"I agree, although anyone who drops their pen will miss a hundred years of folklore, at the rate he talks. I guess I've been spoiled by the computer. I rarely take notes in long-hand anymore." Ian flexed both his hands. "The muscles are screaming at me."

She laughed. "You aren't kidding. So are mine."

"What I need is some good food," he said as he led the way to a rather shabby pickup truck. "I hope you don't mind riding to lunch in this. I had to check some fences at the farm before I came to school this morning."

First her father with his early-morning burst of energy, and now Ian checking fences at the crack of dawn. Perhaps she was becoming lazy. Julianne hid her smile.

"Speaking of this morning, Thérèse Blanchet called to ask Dad and me to lunch. He already had plans and begged off, but when I told her you and I already had lunch arrangements, she insisted that I bring you over."

She hesitated, wondering again if he would mind lunch with Thérèse. "Would you like to do that?" she asked.

"I'd like it very much, as a matter of fact." Ian opened the truck door and helped her up.

"I remember her," he continued, "although she may not remember me. Thérèse has known my parents for years. When I was a child, I visited her home several times. It's a grand old place, filled with all kinds of antiques, if I recall. You'll love seeing it."

"She said your name sounded familiar. I think she may remember you." Julianne belatedly remembered her promise to let Thérèse know if they were coming. "I forgot. I need to call her to confirm our plans."

"That's no problem. We can stop on the way."

"THAT MAN LOOKS like a refugee hippie," Fiona whispered. "Don't you think so?"

With an effort, Dale turned his gaze away from Fiona, who looked wonderful in a mint-green jumpsuit. A belt of pewter squares encircled her slender waist. Long pewter earrings, half-hidden by masses of red hair, dangled from her ears. A light scent of roses drifted around her.

He glanced sideways at the proprietor of the little wood-carver's shop. The man, sitting cross-legged on a worn rug in the middle of the floor, wore flowered denim jeans, a pair of decrepit sandals, several ropes of wooden beads, a vest embroidered all over with the word Love, and a bright red bandanna around his shoulder-length hair.

He was chanting. The effort caused the tiny, wire-rimmed reading glasses perched on the end of his nose to bob up and down.

"Except for the graying hair, he looks like he stepped right out of the sixties," Dale agreed. "He also looks like he doesn't take much interest in his business."

Fiona glanced around the shop, which was barely stocked. The shelves held a few tools, some wooden blanks, carrying cases, sharpening stones and a lot of dust. Several of the glass-fronted showcases contained nothing but a few wood carvings strewn haphazardly on their shelves. The place looked tired and neglected.

"He doesn't," she confirmed. "It's a shame. He is an excellent wood-carver, but he usually makes odd pieces that don't sell well. He neglects the shop. That keeps all but the most dedicated carvers from buying things here."

She put one hand on Dale's arm, pulling him closer as she dropped her voice. "I've thought a lot of times about buying him out. I never have, though."

Fiona paused. "I guess it's because I've never run a business before, and I don't have enough confidence in my ability."

Dale resisted the growing urge to run his hands through the shimmering strands of her hair. Her nearness, the scent of roses and the ivory glow of her skin, the vulnerable expression in her eyes all distracted him. It was difficult to concentrate on her words, but he forced himself to listen.

Fiona was sharing some of her hopes and fears with him, he realized. The thought touched him. Even on such short acquaintance, he realized Fiona was an independent soul, with a free spirit much like those of the birds she carved so well. She probably was used to making her own decisions without consulting anyone.

He could reassure her, he knew. His own business was conducted on an international scale. Dale found it hard to imagine what was terrifying about operating a tiny shop, but he was sensitive to Fiona's distress.

"Running a business isn't hard," he said. "I suspect you have a good business head. That, a good product and hard work are what it takes to be successful."

Absently she brushed dust away from a hideous wooden gargoyle that was sitting in lone splendor on a shelf. "I'm willing to work very hard," she said. "I wonder, though, if I could operate a shop and do my wood carving. I don't want the carving to suffer."

Dale watched her hands, wondering again how such small fingers could achieve such magic with blocks of wood. A few freckles on their backs highlighted the creamy whiteness of her skin. He shifted his glance back to her face.

"You wouldn't have to run it all the time. Once the shop was well stocked and—" he ran an index finger through the grime topping one of the counters "—clean, you could hire someone to work part-time. With the college so close, I'm sure you could find a couple of students more than willing to work. Maybe even some who attend your seminars."

Fiona's eyes searched his face. "Do you really think I could do it?"

Without waiting for a reply she continued, her words tumbling out as her excitement grew. "You know, I've thought I could even sell some of my own wood carvings, as well as those from other carvers in the region. We could offer private classes as well as stock supplies. There are several rooms in back that would work well as classrooms. There's even a private office, which I could use as a carving area for me."

Pleased that Fiona was heeding his advice, Dale grinned. "Of course I think you could handle it. Do you want to talk to him about it right now?" He glanced over at the still-chanting proprietor.

"No. I'd like to give this some more thought before I approach him." She began to walk toward the shop door.

With a wave to the oblivious owner, Dale followed. As they left, Fiona slipped one arm around his waist, smiling up at him with wide blue eyes.

Stunned by her action, Dale held his breath. Although he and Lillian had loved each other dearly, they had rarely shown each other affection in public. By tacit agreement they'd preferred to keep their shows of physical affection private.

But with Fiona it seemed like the most natural gesture in the world when he put his own arm around her shoulders. She fitted perfectly against his side, he thought.

Without a second's hesitation he drew her close and hugged her, right on the sidewalk in front of the shop. It felt good, Dale thought. Very good indeed.

Fiona smiled at him. They walked back to his car in a happy silence.

CHAPTER SEVEN

"I CAN'T BELIEVE I'm finally going to meet Thérèse." Julianne stared at each house along the quiet Wolfville street, wondering which one of the well-kept old homes belonged to her friend.

"Even though our relationship is distant, she's still tied to my family by blood. Where I come from, family relationships are of major importance." She smiled, thinking about all the aunts, uncles, cousins and kissing cousins whose bonds were forged of love.

Ian pulled the pickup to a stop. "Well, you're about to get your wish. If my memory is correct, this is where Thérèse Blanchet has lived for more years than you or I have even been alive."

Julianne could hardly contain her excitement. The frame house was one of the largest on a street filled with big homes. Painted a pristine white with forest-green trim, the house exuded friendliness, right down to the wide porch that seemed to beckon visitors. The spacious lawn, shaded by magnificent oaks and other hardwoods, was trimmed to perfection.

"This looks like something right out of a painting," she said. "It reminds me of antebellum mansions in Mississippi, big and generous and friendly."

Ian studied the house as if he'd never seen it before. "You know, I've often thought that houses reflect the personalities of their owners. Some are all closed in and dark, stingy with any amenities. Others, like this, invite people to come right in.''

"That's odd. I've felt that way many times about houses." Julianne smiled, pleased by his understanding. "You'd like visiting Mississippi. There are lots of wonderful old homes there.''

"I may just do that.''

Catching an odd undercurrent in his voice, she turned. His eyes gave away nothing, however. She was imagining things, Julianne told herself.

She almost skipped up the walkway, noting with delight the chintz-cushioned wicker sofa and chairs grouped around a small table on the porch. Hanging baskets filled with cascading red petunias added to the charm.

She knocked firmly on the carved wooden door, then turned to Ian. "I'm in love with the house already. I hope I feel the same way about the owner," she whispered.

"If Thérèse is the way I remember her, I'm already envious," he replied, his voice low.

A funny, warm feeling flowed through her as Ian smiled.

The woman standing in the doorway was nothing at all like Julianne had imagined. Plum-colored material draped her stocky figure, starting at the neck and going nearly to her ankles. Iron-gray hair framed a face rendered quite unattractive by its unfriendly scowl.

"Yes?"

Julianne hid her smile. This certainly was not Thérèse Blanchet. The woman looked like something out of a Gothic novel. She half expected winds to howl through the doorway and lightning to flash across the sky. She had to stifle the urge to giggle at her own melodramatic thoughts.

"I'm Julianne Blanchet and this is Ian Ross," Julianne said. "We were invited to lunch with Mrs. Blanchet."

The woman's mouth relaxed a bit, almost but not quite forming a smile. "Oh, yes. She told me. I'm Miss Roberts, her companion. Please come in."

They entered a wide foyer and Julianne wondered about Miss Roberts. Was she an impoverished relative, living on her elderly sponsor's generosity?

That would definitely be out of a Gothic novel, she thought as her eyes adjusted to the artificial light. But any curiosity she had about the companion was forgotten; Julianne stopped short on the black and white tile, entranced by the interior.

An old-fashioned, teardrop chandelier illuminated a setting that looked the way it must have done seventy-five years ago. Julianne had fleeting glimpses of a carved banister leading up to another story, a large oval mirror framed in gilt and a gleaming walnut chest. A massive arrangement of yellow roses stood out against the blue of a willow vase.

She had no time for further inspection; Miss Roberts briskly ushered them into another room. *The parlor,* Julianne thought.

A Queen Anne sofa covered with silk damask faced the carved walnut fireplace that dominated the room. Oriental rugs graced the hardwood floor. The wide, irregular planks reflected the mellow patina of countless polishings. The light was filtered by lace curtains that draped two floor-to-ceiling windows.

A quilt covered the wall opposite the fireplace. The timeless wedding ring pattern, Julianne realized, as she scanned the still-vibrant colors. She knew without even studying the quilt further that each piece was hand-dyed and -stitched. The quilt was a work of art, one she would have been proud to have in her own small collection.

Scattered everywhere were baskets of various shapes and sizes. Julianne, immediately recognizing split white oak,

willow, grapevine and other woods used by Cajun craftspeople to make similar baskets, pointed out several outstanding examples to Ian.

"What a lovely room, Miss Roberts. Are these baskets
Acadian?"

Miss Roberts finally permitted herself to smile. "Of
course. Mrs. Blanchet has one of the finest basket collec-
tions in this area," she said with evident pride.

"They are all over the house," she continued. "I believe
a few are American, but most were made in Nova Scotia and
New Brunswick. Some of these are several hundred years
old."

So the old dragon could smile, Julianne thought. Perhaps she was merely shy. Spotting a particularly fine white
oak specimen, Julianne picked it up and ran her fingers
along the weave. "Mrs. Blanchet must have an excellent eye
for good craftsmanship. This is exquisite."

"Thank you, my dear. The 'excellent eye,' as you put it,
comes from many years of studying baskets. You must be
Julianne and Ian."

At the sound of the beautifully modulated voice, Julianne and Ian turned simultaneously. A woman who could
only be Thérèse Blanchet was entering the room.

Julianne's first impression of her relative was one of great
age and equally great dignity. Thérèse was at least ninety.

She walked slowly into the parlor, her carriage erect although one hand held a carved wooden cane. An elegant
print dress gently outlined her slender body. Julianne knew
the material was silk.

A Battenburg lace collar matched her snowy hair, which
curled softly about a face creased by decades of living. A
still-beautiful face, Julianne decided, for all its age. Thérèse
had been blessed with good bone structure.

Intelligence sparkled from dark eyes, eyes that were alive with curiosity. Julianne had an overwhelming impression of graveness tempered by good humor. She knew instinctively that she was going to like Thérèse Blanchet.

Thérèse openly returned Julianne's scrutiny. The younger woman stood quietly as the dark eyes inspected her face and form, wondering if Thérèse liked what she saw.

Finally, as if satisfied, Thérèse remarked, "There seems to be a family resemblance. You have the same black eyes and hair, of course. You also have a red undertone to your skin and a stubborn chin. It's a Blanchet trait, you know. You come by it honestly."

Julianne thought fleetingly of her father. He had the "Blanchet trait" in abundance. She grinned. "That explains a great deal to me."

"I thought it might. Parents have a tendency to blame upbringing for things heredity is responsible for. You can't help who your ancestors are."

Returning Julianne's smile, Thérèse walked to the damask sofa and, her back still straight, quickly sat down. She patted a spot beside her. "Come and sit beside me, my dear. We have a lot of acquainting to do."

She turned her attention to Ian, who stood watching the exchange between the two women. "You, too, young man."

One slender hand indicated an upholstered Queen Anne chair. "Sit there, please, so I can have a look at you, too."

"I hadn't expected you to be quite so good-looking," she continued, gazing at Ian. "Although you did show great promise as a child." Her dark eyes gleamed with good humor as she continued.

"As I recall, you also showed an inordinate fondness for apples. Specifically my apples. Does Julianne know you broke your arm, falling out of one of my trees?"

Thérèse went on without waiting for a reply. "Let's see now, Ian. You would have been about nine, if I remember correctly."

"Nine exactly," Ian replied as he eased himself into the chair.

Then he smiled. "It was my birthday and you invited us over for tea. I still have the soccer ball you gave me, although it's a bit worse for wear."

The look he gave Thérèse was frankly appraising. "You have an astounding memory. I'd forgotten that entire incident until this moment."

"At my age, memory is about all that's left. Well, maybe not all," Thérèse replied.

She winked at Ian. "You were an appealing child, but I must say, I much prefer you all grown-up. Much more handsome. I haven't seen your parents in some time, Ian. Are they well?"

Julianne followed their conversation with only partial attention, preferring to study Thérèse. The old lady flirted shamelessly with Ian, her face as animated as a young girl's.

In turn, Ian showed a gentleness that touched Julianne. He really cared about this woman several generations removed from himself, she thought. The more she got to know him, the more she realized he was a man of great depth and understanding.

"Lunch is ready."

Startled, Julianne turned. Miss Roberts stood in the doorway, her attention focused completely on Thérèse. "May I help you into the dining room?"

Thérèse waved her away. "No, not when I have a young and handsome escort." Her carriage still erect, Thérèse rose from the couch and held out her arm to Ian.

With courtly gentleness, Ian took Thérèse's arm and led her into an adjoining room. Julianne followed.

An array of crystal, china and silver glittered on a lace-draped Queen Anne table. Tempting aromas wafted from several silver dishes, each topped with a scrolled lid, which had been placed at intervals along the length of the table.

Miss Roberts excused herself and the others took their seats. She returned with a bottle of wine and poured the ruby liquid into each glass. Then, with quiet efficiency, she served the contents of each silver dish.

"This is a lovely home," Julianne said to Thérèse, who had taken her place at the head of the table. "Do you know how old it is?"

Thérèse beamed. "This house was built in 1822, according to a plaque in my bedroom. My great-grandfather designed it and had it built. He did much of the finish work himself. My family has lived here ever since."

Her smile faded. "Of course, the house probably will be sold when I die. My husband died years ago," she said, her eyes focused on some faraway place, "and none of our children lived past childhood."

Julianne felt the emotion of the woman sitting next to her. She touched Thérèse's hand with her own.

Thérèse returned the sympathetic gesture. "That's all in the past, where all memories are supposed to be."

Her face lost its faraway look, and her voice took on a brisker tone. "My closest relatives are my two nephews, Jean and Marc Blanchet. I had hoped one of them would want this place, but I guess that's asking too much. Neither has shown much interest in my home, or in me, for that matter. So I imagine this home, which has seen so many Blanchets come and go, will be sold."

She brightened. "Perhaps a family with children will buy the place. There are three staircases, you know, with banisters made for sliding."

Thérèse's smile was impish. "Not to mention apple trees just made for little boys to climb when they're stealing fruit."

Ian grinned. "But no broken arms, please."

Lunch proceeded. Julianne, listening to the affectionate teasing between Thérèse and Ian, marveled at the easy rapport the two had developed so quickly.

Thérèse told them stories of her own parents, grandparents and great-grandparents, telling about people long dead as if they were about to walk through the wide dining-room doors at any moment. The woman was a natural historian, Julianne thought; Thérèse told them how she had used old letters, diaries, land records and other documents to reconstruct her family's past.

This distant relative was filled with information about Acadian history, too, especially about the Blanchets. Julianne made a mental note to bring her pocket tape recorder to any future meetings with the old lady.

Julianne took a last bite of strawberry pie. "I hate to see this end."

Thérèse laughed. "I can hear the regret in your voice. I'll send the recipe home with you."

Miss Roberts reappeared to clear away the lunch dishes, and Thérèse led the way to a glassed-in porch just off the dining room. "We'll be more comfortable out here. It's the coziest room in the house."

Julianne immediately liked the sun porch. Here there was more of the wicker furniture she'd already seen in the house, and Oriental rugs were scattered about, while overhead a brass ceiling fan kept the room from becoming stuffy on this warm afternoon. Huge ferns were suspended in each corner. The fronds formed graceful patterns on the charcoal slate floors.

She sank onto a chintz cushion, feeling strangely pleased as Ian sat next to her in the love seat. Thérèse, with an inscrutable smile for both of them, picked up a large, white oak basket, then seated herself in a wicker rocking chair.

From the depths of the basket she drew out a blue silk envelope. Untying the ribbons, she took out a stack of papers and handed them to Julianne.

"These letters were written by Anne Blanchet to her husband, Gaston, our common ancestor. These are the originals, so they are extremely fragile," she added.

Gingerly opening one of the delicate pages, Julianne found a flowing script. It seemed almost like an intrusion to scan the faded letters, written by a loving wife to her husband so long ago.

She hesitated, then smiled at herself. Somehow, Julianne thought, Anne Blanchet would understand.

"It's incredible to be reading letters written in the eighteenth century," she said slowly; her fingers traced the patterns of the writing. "It's even more incredible to realize that this woman was one of my ancestors."

For a moment the room was silent but for the low hum of the fan blades. Julianne handed a page to Ian, who took the aged sheet with care.

He scanned it quickly, then looked up. "This script is beautiful, but it sure is hard to decipher. It's like trying to read old music."

Thérèse chuckled. "Maybe if our ancestors had known we'd still be reading their papers hundreds of years later, they would have taken more care to be legible."

"But take heart," she continued, still smiling. "Reading that handwriting gets easier with practice, believe me. I've spent years working on old documents."

Thérèse took another stack of papers from a small wicker end table. "I'm afraid the original letters are too delicate to take much handling, so I've had these copies made."

With a last regretful look at the original letters, Julianne handed them back to their owner. Then she took the copies.

"I know you're right about making copies, but holding the originals, touching the words actually written by her own hand, seems like a link with Anne." Would Thérèse understand? she wondered.

The older woman held the letters for a moment before encasing them again in their silk container. Then she sighed. "You're right. Every now and then I can't resist taking them out for a brief look."

Julianne thumbed through the copies and felt her excitement growing. She itched to begin reading them, but as she opened the first, she caught Ian's eye. His grin reminded her of their surroundings. There would be plenty of time later to study the letters.

"There's a lot of information in those. The copies are for you. I have another set." Thérèse leaned back in the rocker, then put both feet up on a small, needlepoint-covered stool.

"I've never been able to determine why Gaston was permitted to stay in Acadia, when all the other Acadians were forced to leave during the Expulsion. There isn't a clue in the letters Gaston wrote to Anne," Julianne said.

Thérèse folded her hands, then looked at her young relative with bright eyes. "Ah, now there's a story. You'll piece part of it together by reading Anne's letters to her husband. I've done enough research into other documents to fill in the gaps."

She settled back even farther into the rocker. "The tale begins with one Lady Sarah. I wouldn't be surprised if the family stubbornness doesn't come straight down from that headstrong young woman."

Ian winked at Julianne, who squirmed in her seat. The "family stubbornness" was becoming notorious.

"Lady Sarah was the only daughter of the eighth Earl of Strath-Huntington, who was a hero in the Battle of Ramillies," Thérèse said. "In fact, the earl was given a grant of land by the queen, who was grateful for his services during the war with the French."

Thérèse dug into a pocket in the skirt of her dress and brought out a small, round object. "This miniature is the only surviving likeness of Lady Sarah." She handed the tiny portrait to Julianne.

"She was a real beauty, wasn't she?" said Julianne after studying the portrait for a few minutes.

She handed the painting to Ian. "All those raven-black curls must have taken hours to arrange," she said.

"Lady Sarah has the look of someone born to command," Ian commented. "Proud and very aware of her beauty, I would guess," he added.

Thérèse nodded. "You're both right, of course. She was lovely, proud, headstrong, and fifteen years old when that was painted, according to some records I dug up."

"Her father was an extremely wealthy and powerful peer," Thérèse continued. "The grant added vast landholdings located in the New World to his estates. These new lands were given to the earl and his family in perpetuity. But unlike his lands in England, these lands were not entailed. This meant, of course, the lands did not have to go to the oldest male heir when the current lord died. This particular property could be willed to anyone, even females, although that was unusual in that day and time."

Thérèse frowned. "I'm glad times have changed in that respect."

She folded her hands again. "Lady Sarah was the earl's youngest child, born when he was quite a bit older," she said. "Evidently he doted on her. He gave her many gifts, including a lot of jewelry. He also gave her a large tract of land in the New World, prime farmland in what is now the Annapolis Valley."

Ian whistled. "It seems our Sarah was a spoiled and wealthy young heiress."

Thérèse shook her head. "Not everything was so wonderful for her. The earl, like other noble fathers of the time, contracted for a powerful and wealthy husband for his daughter. He married her off to a much older man, a former soldier and a baron from one of England's most prominent families. Unfortunately, the baron was also much older than his new bride. She was only seventeen."

Miss Roberts bustled into the room, carrying a silver tea tray. "I thought everyone might like some tea about now."

Thérèse gave her a grateful smile. "Thank you. I would love some tea. Julianne? Ian?"

A few minutes later, happily fortified by the strong brew, Thérèse continued. "Lady Sarah, from the few reports I've managed to find on her, was a high-spirited young miss. Evidently she didn't love the baron, although he loved her. I've read correspondence between them. Hers is scrupulously polite, while his is almost shy, as if he wasn't quite sure of her."

She took another sip of tea, then went on. "Almost as soon as they were married, the baron was sent to the New World colonies. He was an excellent soldier, according to old military records. They no sooner arrived here, when he was sent to help quell some disturbances on the frontier. Lady Sarah was, of course, left behind. Her husband installed her in the main house on her property in the Annapolis Valley, then left. He was gone for over half a year."

"Uh-oh. I can almost imagine what happened," Julianne commented.

Thérèse smiled. "It seemed inevitable. While her husband was away, his new wife fell in love with the young Acadian farmer the baron's agent had hired to work their lands. Unfortunately, they were indiscreet. Lady Sarah became pregnant." She picked up her teacup again.

"How sad," Julianne said. "For all that she was spoiled, Lady Sarah was awfully young to have been married, uprooted from her country and family, then left alone among strangers. She must have been very lonely."

"Ah, the distance of many years certainly softens the harshness of what must have been a horrifying situation." Thérèse's hands moved as she talked. "But Lady Sarah was a brave young woman."

"When her husband returned from the military campaign, she confessed her liaison with the Acadian farmer and her pregnancy. She refused to name the father, knowing full well her husband, not to mention her father, could have had the man put to death immediately. As for Lady Sarah, she faced disgrace and certain ruin. Not a good fate for a young woman of such impeccable breeding."

"Surely this story doesn't end unhappily," Ian said with a smile. I prefer love stories with happy endings." He draped one arm around the back of the love seat, brushing his hand against Julianne's hair.

Julianne searched his face, but his expression was unreadable. What was he thinking? she wondered, recalling his failed marriage to Joanna. *That* story had ended unhappily enough.

"Don't rush me," Thérèse admonished him. She smoothed her skirt with both hands, then continued.

"The baron loved her dearly. No matter what his wife had done, he forgave her. He was an unusual man for his day and time, I might add. He decreed that they would remain married. However, she had to give up the child as soon as it was born."

"How awful," Julianne murmured. "Forcing that young woman to give up her child."

"Times were different then," Thérèse pointed out. "I'd say Lady Sarah realized the outcome could have been much harsher indeed. At least the baron allowed her child to live."

"So what happened to the baby?" Julianne asked. "Did it have the chance to grow up? So often babies born then didn't make it out of infancy."

"Of course, or else we would have to end the story right here. It was a boy," Thérèse said slowly. "Lady Sarah arranged to have it adopted by her lover's brother and his wife, who were childless. They were to raise the boy as their own. The baron, of course, had no idea who exactly the adopting couple were, or he might not have permitted it."

She shrugged. "Who knows? He must have been a very enlightened man. He insisted that the Annapolis Valley land be given to the child. I suspect it was to make sure this child of his beloved wife's wasn't left penniless. Officially, he declared that he wanted no reminders of his wife's indiscretion. As soon as Lady Sarah could travel, her husband took his somewhat wiser wife home to England."

"Quite a gift for the baby, wasn't it?" Ian's fingers played with the tips of Julianne's hair. "A tract of fertile farmland here must have been worth a lot, even then."

"Yes. It made the child quite prosperous by Acadian standards, although the land was only a minor part of Lady Sarah's holdings," Thérèse commented.

Aware that Ian's arm was resting casually along her shoulders, Julianne leaned forward slightly. "This is much better than any fiction I've ever read. Did Lady Sarah ever come back? Did she ever find out what happened to her son?"

Thérèse smiled. "Now we're coming to the good part of the story. Yes, although her husband never did make it back. Interestingly enough, Lady Sarah became devoted to the baron. She was devastated when he was killed in a freak hunting accident."

"Not more tragedy. That poor woman," Julianne remarked. She felt a wave of sympathy for Lady Sarah.

"Many years afterward, Lady Sarah, who was now a very wealthy widow—thanks to her husband and her father, who both had died—returned to Canada for a long visit. She brought one of her other sons, the young baron."

"She didn't come back in disgrace, did she? She already had enough problems for one lifetime," Julianne said.

"Gracious, no. Our Lady Sarah, because of her vast wealth, was a powerful woman with many political connections. She had great charm and influence. She was also a friend of Governor Lawrence."

Julianne remembered the name immediately. "He was governor of the province when the Acadians were expelled, wasn't he?"

Thérèse nodded her agreement. "Lady Sarah immediately set about finding her first child, who was now an adult. His name was Gaston Blanchet."

The name reached across the years, pulling Julianne even further into the tale. She smiled. "I should have realized long before now that Lady Sarah was his mother."

Thérèse continued, looking somewhat smug. "Even though she had three legitimate sons and a daughter, Lady Sarah still cherished this first child. Gaston, who'd always known about his beautiful English mother, although he didn't know her identity, was betrothed to a young Acadian woman. As a wedding gift, his mother gave them two gold rings."

Julianne let out her breath. "It must have been very touching."

She could see the entire scene in her mind, the mother and son reunited after being forced apart when he was an infant. Then she remembered a passage in one of Gaston's letters to his wife.

"Gaston refers to those rings in a letter. His mother's gift evidently touched him profoundly. He said they were the only material reminder, besides the land, of his birth mother," Julianne interjected.

"That's right," Thérèse agreed. "Anne mentioned how Gaston's mother was unable to come to their wedding. Because of propriety, I'm sure," she added. "But he felt her presence in the rings. Anne did also."

Miss Roberts, who had whisked away the tea service, came back with a light blanket. Without a word, she began tucking the blanket about her employer's legs.

"Quit fussing," Thérèse responded with a testy note in her voice. "I'm not cold. The sun is streaming through those windows."

Ignoring the old lady, Miss Roberts finished her task, then stood up. "There. Now you'll be comfortable."

Thérèse irritably waved her away. "Now, where was I?" she asked.

"You were telling us about the wedding between Anne and Gaston," Ian prompted. "What happened then? Did they live happily ever after?"

"Unfortunately, no. Those were difficult times for the French-speaking people of Acadia."

She kicked the blanket away from her ankles, frowning after her companion. "I can't stand fussing. Let's see now."

Julianne watched Thérèse with concern. The older woman seemed to be tiring. "We can finish this story some other time, if you'd like."

"No, no," Thérèse shot back. "I'm fine. Miss Roberts thinks I'm an invalid. I want to finish this."

She gave the blanket another kick, then continued. "Like the rest of the Acadians, Gaston and Anne were caught up in the political situation. The relationship between the English and the Acadians deteriorated. There was much uncertainty."

"Then, as it often does, fate intervened. Lady Sarah became ill. She had consumption. To make matters worse, the young baron had already gone back to England, at his mother's insistence."

"Leaving her alone again in a strange land," Julianne continued. "That poor woman."

"Without realizing the Acadians were on the verge of being expelled from Nova Scotia, Lady Sarah asked Gaston to stay with her during her illness," Thérèse said. "She fully intended to recover, of course."

Her voice shook with emotion. "Governor Lawrence set about deporting the Acadians, because they refused to take an oath of allegiance to Britain. He was determined to root them out of all Nova Scotia. When the Acadian men were taken hostage at the church in Grand-Pré, Gaston was not among them. He was with his mother."

"But Lady Sarah determined it was only a matter of time before English troops would come for her son. She used some of her power and influence. From her sickbed she went to Governor Lawrence, asking for permission to keep Gaston with her until she recovered. She wanted to live in the farmhouse Gaston built for his new bride. The governor, because of Lady Sarah's position, granted her request."

Thérèse's voice dropped to a whisper. "But only Gaston could stay. Anne and all the rest of the Blanchet family had to go. Lady Sarah used all her wiles, but on that point, Lawrence was inflexible."

"What a terrible time for the Acadians," Thérèse continued. "They had to leave everything they knew, everything they'd worked for, to face an unknown future. They didn't even know where they would go."

Julianne felt the sadness in the room. "There are so many stories of heartbreak resulting from the Expulsion. It was a terrible time."

"Like the story of Evangeline," Ian added. "The effects of a people forced to leave their homes went on for many years after the actual Expulsion." His arm tightened around Julianne's shoulders.

"Gaston, of course, wanted to go with Anne and the rest of their families," Thérèse continued. "But Anne, who must have been a very generous woman, insisted that he stay with Lady Sarah. At the time she must have thought the Expulsion would be temporary."

"Or maybe she thought Gaston could join her in a few months, after Lady Sarah recovered," said Julianne. "No one could predict what would happen in such unsettled times."

Thérèse nodded. "You're right, my dear. Lady Sarah, for all her indomitable stubbornness, did not recover. Her illness dragged out for months, and then for several years. During this time, Gaston and Anne wrote letters of hope to each other as they waited faithfully for their day of reunion."

"The letters that we have now," Julianne said, her voice soft; her hands tightened their hold on the copies. "They didn't give up hope while Lady Sarah was alive, did they?"

"No," said Thérèse. "But Gaston's faithfulness to his mother drew a terrible penalty. When Lady Sarah finally died, Gaston realized that he, too, had consumption. The government allowed him to stay in Acadia, right in the farmhouse he'd built. He stayed there until his own death some months later."

Thérèse's voice quavered as she ended the tale. Julianne looked at her with concern. Then she realized that Thérèse, who'd studied her family's history for many years, felt close to these long-ago ancestors.

It wasn't surprising, Julianne told herself. She herself could almost see those first Blanchets, could feel their love and faithfulness during the years of separation. She glanced at Ian. His dark eyes shone with emotion. He felt the tragedy, too, she realized.

As if he heard her thoughts, Ian put one hand on hers in a reassuring gesture. "This all happened so long ago," he said, "but their love, the sadness and joy of it, seems to be right in this room."

He smiled at Thérèse. "You made the story come alive."

Her answering smile was gentle. "I've studied these people for a lifetime. They are as real to me as my own family, as you are, sitting here with me in my sun room."

For a comfortable moment no one said anything. Long streams of sunlight puddled on the charcoal floor, bathing the wicker in gilt.

It was late afternoon, Julianne realized. Where had the time gone?

"In Gaston's letters to Anne, several times he mentioned a family treasure. I've always been curious about that," Julianne said. "Gaston was prosperous because of his landholdings, but I can't imagine what treasures the family would have had."

Thérèse shrugged. ''Who knows? I'm sure anything of value is long gone by now. The Blanchet lands passed out of the family's hands after Gaston's death. It wasn't until several decades ago that my husband and I were able to acquire all of the original holdings. With so many owners over the years, I'm sure any treasure would be long gone by now.''

''Except we still have the letters,'' Julianne said. ''Those are the real treasure, our links with the past.''

''Still,'' she couldn't help adding, ''I love mysteries. While I'm in Nova Scotia I may do a little treasure hunting.''

CHAPTER EIGHT

"IT'S TIME for you to rest." Miss Roberts's voice broke the silence. "You've tired yourself out."

She pursed her lips, standing in front of Thérèse with arms akimbo and legs planted firmly on the slate floor. Her disapproval was almost palpable.

Julianne looked at her watch. It was nearly five. The afternoon had disappeared while they'd been talking. Had they tired their hostess too much?

"I'm sorry, Thérèse. Until just a moment ago, I had no idea it was so late. I guess it's difficult to come back into the twentieth century after your marvelous storytelling," she said. "I feel like I've been in another time all afternoon."

The older woman scowled as Miss Roberts readjusted the blanket covering her thin legs. "Sorry? This has been the most fun I've had in a long time."

She pushed away Miss Roberts's hands. "Leave that blanket alone. Quit fussing!"

Miss Roberts's mouth tightened; she removed her hands. "You know you're supposed to rest now."

Ian and Julianne stood up simultaneously. "I really need to go, anyway," Julianne said. "I have some reading to do before class tomorrow. I don't want to get behind when the course's just getting started."

"I've got work to do, too," Ian chimed in.

"Oh, all right," Thérèse grumbled. "I suppose I do need to rest a bit. The story of Lady Sarah, Gaston and Anne is a long one, both to listen to as well as tell."

With one hand on her cane, she stood up, ignoring the blanket, which crumpled around her ankles. She extended both hands to Julianne.

"I'd like you to come back soon, especially after you've had a chance to look over the copies of Anne's letters," she said.

"Thank you," Julianne replied, giving Thérèse's hands a gentle squeeze. The skin felt papery and dry.

Julianne frowned and thought about their hostess's advanced age, as well as her recent illness. They had stayed far too long.

"I'd like that very much," Julianne said.

Thérèse turned to Ian. "And you, too. The invitation extends to you both."

She eyed him thoughtfully, then winked. "You remind me very much of my husband. He was a handsome devil, just like you."

Miss Roberts cleared her throat for the third time.

"Yes, yes, I know." Thérèse slowly made her way to the door. "I'll let you see yourselves out."

"I hope we didn't tire her too much," Julianne said as they pulled away from the house. "She seems so sturdy. It's difficult to believe she's over ninety."

"Maybe we did," Ian replied, "but she enjoyed every minute of it."

"I suspect Thérèse doesn't get much chance anymore to share her stories with anyone except Miss Roberts. And I'm not sure how good a listener she would make," he added.

Julianne chuckled. "She's a character. I kept thinking of the Brontë novels. Miss Roberts would fit right into some moldering old mansion lost on an English moor. Although in all fairness, she does seem devoted to Thérèse.''

They lapsed into silence during the drive back to the inn. Julianne reflected on the story she'd heard that afternoon.

Such love and faithfulness, she thought, trying to conjure pictures of Anne and Gaston in her mind. Somehow, Gaston kept reminding her of Ian.

Would Ian display the same loyalty and faithfulness under similar circumstances? she wondered. Deep inside, she knew that he would.

WHAT WOULD IT BE LIKE to be loved so selflessly? Ian asked himself silently as he maneuvered the auto along the streets. Anne had showed so much devotion to Gaston, remaining faithful throughout the long separation. *Unlike Joanna,* he thought.

Not that Joanna had been seeing anyone else. No, she had been unfaithful in her commitment to her marriage vows, ending their union before it really had a chance to get started.

Now why was he thinking of his former wife so much lately? he wondered. He'd thought her memory was safely buried, a forgotten part of his past.

He glanced at Julianne, who sat quietly, evidently lost in thought, her small hands folded in her lap. He wondered how she would have handled the terrible circumstances Anne and Gaston had had to face. The question intrigued him.

He pulled up in front of the inn. Julianne started to open her door, then stopped. Ian wondered why.

"It's hard to rejoin the real world after listening to Thérèse," she said.

"I know. I've been thinking a lot about Anne and Gaston. The Expulsion wasn't merely something to fill up students' history textbooks. It was a horrifying nightmare to so many people."

He gripped the steering wheel with both hands. "I don't know that I'll ever think of the Expulsion the same way again."

The seconds ticked away; neither spoke. Julianne finally opened her door. "Thanks for taking me over there."

"I enjoyed renewing my acquaintance with Thérèse. She's quite a lady."

"This time you got away without breaking your arm."

"Only because I didn't get outside to that infamous apple tree."

Julianne lingered for a moment more, then got out of the car. "I'll see you tomorrow." She waved once, then headed up the walkway.

Ian watched until she closed the front door. He sighed, wanting to be with her, but aware that he had pressing responsibilities. He watched until she entered the inn, then he moved away from the curb.

LATER, as she was studying, Julianne found her thoughts wandering to Ian. Her neck still tingled where his arm had rested during the long afternoon on the sun porch.

She was very drawn to him, she realized. And Ian was attracted to her, she knew. The chemistry between them was clear enough.

Julianne sat back in her chair, absently drumming her fingers on the small writing desk. At this point in her life, she wasn't ready for a serious romantic relationship.

She sighed; the sound echoed in the quiet sitting room. Then she sat up straight. Thinking about Ian was keeping her from studying, and 8:00 a.m. would come all too early, if she wasn't prepared.

She forced her attention back to the book and soon found herself lost in the legends of Acadia, so much so that she had to consciously remind herself to take notes as she read.

An hour or so later, the sound of whistling cut into her concentration. She knew Dale was back before the door to their suite opened. His timing was excellent, she thought, rubbing her temples with both hands.

Although the subject was fascinating, she hadn't studied so intensely since her days as a college student. She needed a break.

Still whistling, Dale entered the room. He stopped short as he caught sight of Julianne, then gave her a wide smile.

"Hitting the old books, I see. This brings back memories of your college days."

Julianne returned his smile. He looked happier and more rested than he'd been in ages, she thought. This trip to Nova Scotia was good for him.

"Hi, Dad. You're in time to share a cup of hot chocolate with me. I was just thinking about making some." She stood up, stretching and yawning at the same time.

"I can see you're fascinated by whatever it is that you're reading." He made a wry face. "History, no doubt."

Julianne laughed and made her way across the room to the tiny fridge, microwave oven and sink that served as a makeshift kitchen. "No, but almost as bad in your eyes, I imagine. I'm studying some Acadian legends. Actually, it is fascinating. The problem is me. I'm a little tired tonight."

"Maybe jet lag is finally catching up with you."

"Jet lag of a different sort, Dad. I spent all afternoon in the eighteenth century." Briefly she described the meeting with Thérèse and recounted the long story she'd heard.

"Despite my notorious lack of interest in history," Dale said finally, "I have the feeling I'm going to like this distant cousin of ours."

He filled a pottery teapot with water and placed it in the microwave while Julianne measured cocoa mix into two large cups. "No marshmallows," she said, frowning.

Dale patted his stomach, then turned the microwave dial. "That's all right, I don't need any. I'm dieting."

Her eyebrows shot up. "Dieting?" She put one hand to her forehead in mock amazement.

"Dieting?" she repeated. "I may have to sit down on that one. I've heard your views on dieting countless times—" she rolled her eyes "—and none of them were positive."

"As I've told you only recently, times change."

"Then I guess you don't want any hot chocolate," she shot back. "I'm sure it's not on your diet."

His expression grew mournful. "I said diet, Julianne. I said nothing about fasting."

She chuckled. "I thought you'd change your tune when hot chocolate was involved."

When the microwave signaled, she poured water into both cups, watching as the sweet-scented steam rose into the air. Then she slipped into a chair beside the small dining table.

"Were you able to do some research on family history today?" she asked, sipping the hot liquid.

Dale hesitated, then grinned as he sat down in the chair across from her. "My intentions were good, I suppose. But I didn't even get to the library. I spent the afternoon with Fiona, looking at a wood-carving shop in Wolfville."

He looked at his watch. "In fact, we're going out tonight. We're going to a lecture on the fishing industry in Nova Scotia. It probably won't be as exciting as hearing about Lady Sarah, but would you like to come along?"

"Thanks, but I'm sure Fiona wouldn't want a third party." She stirred the hot chocolate, watching the swirls form patterns. Was Dale becoming more serious about Fiona? It certainly looked that way.

Although she'd often teased her father about all the women who pursued him, she'd never expected him to show any real interest in anyone. Not that she opposed the idea.

Opposition never did any good with her father, anyway. It only caused him to dig in his heels, as many of his business associates had learned to their dismay.

No, Dale's life was his own, and she had no intention of interfering. But the idea of her father becoming seriously involved with any woman besides her mother would take some getting used to, Julianne knew. It would also take time.

"Actually, Fiona suggested that I ask you. She'd like to get to know you a little better. We could get a bite to eat, then go on to the lecture. Fiona is going to bring her car. That way, if you don't want to stay with us after the program, you'll have your own transportation."

He set his cup on the table. "Unless you'd rather stay here and study." He wrinkled his nose.

Julianne glanced at her book of legends, still open on the desk. Then she laughed.

"You sure know what buttons to push, Dad. I'd love to come."

As they waited for the lecturer to take his place on the auditorium stage, Julianne studied Fiona. It wasn't hard to see why her father was so attracted to the lovely woodcarver.

Dressed in a slim skirt, shirt and cardigan sweater, Fiona had turned several male heads when she entered the auditorium. The heather-green she wore suited Fiona perfectly, Julianne knew, but it wasn't the contrast of the green to that flame hair that caused a stir, although the results were spectacular.

No, beautiful though Fiona was, the attraction wasn't merely physical. Fiona exuded a radiance, a strong presence that quietly demanded attention.

Somewhat like Ian, Julianne realized. They both had charisma, that indefinable quality.

Even now, sitting in the university auditorium and surrounded by people, she could still feel the force of his personality, still feel the weight of his arm around her shoulders. Was he studying now, she wondered, or had some problem on the farm taken him away from his books?

The appearance of the lecturer interrupted her thoughts, although not for long. She normally would have found the subject of interest, but this night Julianne found it difficult to concentrate on commercial fishing in Nova Scotia.

Instead she watched Fiona, who sat, hands folded in her lap, listening intently. Every now and then, Fiona leaned over to say something to Dale, causing her red-gold hair to ripple about her head.

Fiona was so different from Lillian. Julianne tried not to compare the beautiful Canadian with her mother, but the comparisons came, anyway. Fiona seemed vibrantly alive, an exuberant contrast to Lillian, who'd always maintained a cool reserve to everyone but her family and close friends.

Although their personalities were different, Fiona possessed the same graciousness Lillian had had, and the same warmth. Julianne swallowed. It was difficult to think about her mother without grief.

Her father leaned forward to catch something Fiona said. His face radiated happiness as he answered.

Since Lillian's death, Dale had been pursued by several women, but he'd been wary, and nothing serious had developed. Watching her father now with Fiona, Julianne knew this relationship would be different.

Suddenly she felt a curious vulnerability. Was it too soon after his wife's death? she wondered. It had been about a year. Was Dale looking for a substitute for Lillian?

A smattering of applause interrupted her thoughts. She looked at the stage, surprised to see the lecturer gather up his papers and leave. She checked her watch. The lecture had lasted exactly one hour, and she'd missed it all.

"That was positively scintillating." Dale grinned at both women.

Fiona punched him gently in the ribs. "I could tell how much you enjoyed it. I don't think you heard two words the man said."

"Yes, I did," Dale countered. "I heard him say 'Good evening' at the beginning and the end of his talk."

He winked at his daughter. "Although I liked it better at the end."

Fiona smiled, then turned to Julianne. "I made a carrot cake this morning. Why don't we go to my house for cake and coffee? I also promised to show your father some of my wood carvings."

Julianne debated for a moment. Fiona seemed sincere, but she didn't want to intrude on their privacy. She also had a lot of thinking to do about the relationship between this woman and her father.

"Thank you, but I really have more studying to do. My professor is cramming a lot of information into a few weeks." Despite her best efforts, she knew the words sounded cool as she spoke.

Fiona regarded her silently for a moment. "I understand," she said at last.

As if unsure of herself, she hesitated, then put one hand on Julianne's arm. "Maybe some other time. You are always welcome in my home."

With rigid control, Julianne kept herself from pulling away. The woman meant nothing by the gesture, she knew. It was simply more evidence of Fiona's genuine warmth and caring. The problem lay within herself. It would take time for her to adjust to seeing another woman with her father.

"I'll see you later, Dad." With a small wave, Julianne left the nearly deserted auditorium.

Fiona watched as Julianne, with back still stiff and chin held high, walked away. Then she turned to Dale, her eyes full of concern. "I think I handled that badly."

Dale observed his daughter's retreating figure. "It's not you. I should have realized this might be difficult for Julianne. She took her mother's death very hard."

He took her arm and began walking toward the exit, choosing his words with care. "Julianne was very close to her mother. Oh, I'm not saying they didn't have their differences."

He grinned. "Especially when Julianne was a teenager. Lillian had her hands full. They did a lot of arguing and a lot of compromising. Unfortunately, Julianne inherited a great deal of my personality."

"She certainly seems to be a fine young woman." Fiona spoke with sincerity.

Dale gave her a grateful look. "Thank you. I think so, too," he said. They got into Fiona's car, and he lapsed into a thoughtful silence as she turned the ignition key.

During the drive to Fiona's home, he recalled Julianne's face as she'd left the auditorium. It wasn't like her to be so reserved. She was upset, and he knew the reason.

Another woman, he thought. The term sounded strange. His interest in Fiona *was* more than just friendship, he realized for the first time. Julianne had already figured it out. She was struggling with her feelings about seeing her father with someone new.

It occurred to him that Julianne might even think he was trying to substitute Fiona for Lillian. He smiled to himself and glanced at Fiona. Masses of hair hid her face from view as she drove through the quiet streets of Wolfville. Fiona would never be a substitute for anyone, just as Lillian could never be replaced.

Lillian would have understood, he knew. His love for her would always be a part of him, like breathing. His interest in Fiona was actually a tribute to his wife. He missed the warm and loving relationship he'd shared with her.

Dale liked being around Fiona. The feeling was one he hadn't had with any woman since Lillian's death. Yes, Lillian would have understood, he told himself again. She probably would have encouraged this new relationship, because she would have wanted him to be loved and cherished.

What if Julianne, after she'd struggled with her initial reactions, objected to his interest? The thought was disquieting.

Julianne had been his heart, the apple of his eye ever since the first time he'd seen her fighting the ubiquitous pink blanket in the hospital maternity ward. Now that Lillian was dead, his relationship with his daughter was the most important part of his life, and he didn't want to jeopardize it.

Thoughts of Julianne and her reaction to this new relationship continued to swirl in his head. Then he took a deep breath and sat up straight in the seat.

He couldn't worry about it, he decided. He loved Julianne more than anything else in the world, but he had his own life to lead. He would always be close to his daughter, but they were both independent souls. Independent, stubborn and entirely too much alike, he acknowledged.

Yet if he knew his daughter as well as he thought, she would respect any decisions he made about his own life, just as he would for her.

"You're smiling to yourself, so lost in thought you haven't noticed I turned off the motor several minutes ago."

The warm voice curled around his thoughts. Startled, he looked at Fiona.

She smiled at him. "Do you still want some carrot cake?"

"Of course." He came around to the driver's side and opened the door. He extended his hand, and Fiona slid out.

"I didn't mean to ignore you," he said. "I was thinking about Julianne. In my own grief I tend to forget sometimes that she lost her mother, too. This past year has been very hard on Julianne. It's one of the reasons I agreed to come up here with her. I thought a change of pace and scenery would do us both some good."

"Not that she's been moping around or dwelling on her grief," he added. "Julianne isn't like that. She's a very positive person. I think she just needed some space."

Fiona stopped on the wide porch, stretched and kissed him on the cheek. "I understand. It's so hard to lose someone close. When my husband died, I thought my entire world had collapsed. He was a wonderful man, so kind and loving."

A breeze ruffled the red-gold hair as she searched for something in her handbag. "But I survived. The first year was the hardest. I didn't realize how hard until my sister talked me into going on a cruise. I came back so refreshed, with such a different outlook on everything."

She pulled out a set of keys and held them up. "My house keys. I never can find them."

Dale touched his hand to the spot her lips had brushed. He could still feel them, soft against the rough texture of his own skin.

He twined his fingers into her hair. The strands felt silky and cool. "I've wanted to do this since this afternoon." Even in the darkness, he could see her eyes deepening to a midnight blue.

"Let's not stand out here, when we could be comfortable inside." With a twist of her hand, Fiona opened the door and walked in.

IAN STARED at his old manual typewriter. The machine was his good-luck charm. They'd been together through many manuscripts, some published and some that would never move again from their place, deep within his office closet.

But even the old typewriter wasn't working its familiar magic this night. He stood up and began to pace again, his dissatisfaction so intense that he could almost touch it.

What was Julianne doing? Probably studying, he thought, as he needed to be, but wasn't. He could envision her as she had been that afternoon, those liquid brown eyes shining with eagerness as she listened to Thérèse.

What a story Thérèse had told, he thought again. How could anyone fail to be touched by the tale of faithfulness and courage under such terrible conditions?

Love and faithfulness. The two words went around and around in his mind. When had he stopped believing in both? Or had he ever?

The restlessness continued. He opened the private door to his office and stepped onto the small side porch he'd built several years before. Hooking one leg over the railing, he leaned back against the side of the farmhouse and looked up, his thoughts as faraway as the view.

It was time to sweep out the cobwebs of the past, he thought. For the first time since his divorce, he realized he'd been mourning his relationship with Joanna.

Not that he still loved her. That had been over years before, he knew with an unshakable certainty.

It was the breaking of a lifetime commitment, her unfaithfulness to the marriage vows, which had devastated him. No matter that those vows had been said in the hearts and flowers atmosphere of a Las Vegas wedding chapel. He had taken them seriously.

What was it Julianne had said, when he told her about his failed marriage? For a moment he tapped a booted heel on the wooden railing, listening to the sounds of insects in the clear night air. Then he remembered.

Both people need to be committed to any lasting relationship, she'd said. One person alone couldn't make a marriage work. Joanna had never been committed, he realized at last.

Ian swung his leg back over the railing, feeling an ease he hadn't known in a long time. It was time to get on with his life. High time.

He strode back into the office, letting the door slam behind himself. He ignored the noise.

With growing excitement, he lifted the old plastic cover off the typewriter and sat down at the desk. It was as if he had opened some long-shut door in his mind. He inserted a fresh sheet of paper into the machine and began tapping at the keys.

CHAPTER NINE

"I CAN'T BELIEVE it's Saturday. No classes, and I'm all caught up with my studying. I suppose I should work on the term paper Professor Godfrey assigned, but I don't feel like it."

Julianne spread a piece of toast with marmalade, slathering it on in thick chunks. "Maybe today I'll be able to do some exploring."

Dale lifted one eyebrow. "Have some toast with your marmalade?"

She grinned. "It's the weekend, Dad. Calories don't count, remember?"

"Mrs. Hardesty evidently doesn't think so, either. Look at all this stuff."

He pointed to a basket piled high with croissants, English muffins, and bread in various shapes and sizes. Beside it stood a rack that held several types of jams and preserves. "This is enough for ten hungry people, not two."

Julianne swallowed the last of her toast, then took another drink of her tea. "This strong tea takes some getting used to after a lifetime of morning coffee, but I'm beginning to like it."

She took another sip, wondering as she did what Ian was doing. A picture formed in her mind of Ian sitting at a desk, his long legs propped against it as he bent his head over a book or a pile of notes.

Maybe she would see him during the weekend, Julianne told herself. With a jolt, she realized she'd been hoping to see him again after class, but they'd both been too caught up in classes and studying for any after-school meetings.

"I'm looking forward to exploring the Blanchet farmhouse this morning." She reached for a croissant, then stopped herself. Even if calories didn't count on weekends, she'd had enough.

"I set up a meeting with Thérèse's nephews for this afternoon, so we'll have plenty of time this morning at the farm. But you'll probably want to change," she continued, looking at Dale's tailored slacks and crisp linen shirt, then at her own comfortable blue jeans and cotton pullover. "The farmhouse is full of cobwebs."

Dale's eyes widened in surprise. "I forgot all about going to the farm this morning, *chère*. I've already promised Fiona I'd take her to the opening of some new art gallery she's interested in. Can we postpone the trip to the farm? Maybe tomorrow? Fiona is really looking forward to this gallery opening."

He looked at his watch. "In fact, if I don't hurry, I'll be late picking her up."

Julianne swallowed her disappointment. Of course Dale would want to spend time with Fiona. "That's fine, Dad. I probably ought to spend some time at the library, anyway."

"Do you know anything about these nephews?" Dale stood up, then reached for the empty plates and cups. He carried them to the tiny sink and began rinsing.

"No. They both were very agreeable when I called to set up the meeting. In fact, they seemed excited about getting to meet us."

The cousins had sounded very much alike over the telephone, Julianne recalled. She tried to remember if Thérèse had said anything about her nephews, but nothing came to mind.

"I'll finish those dishes, Dad. Why don't you go? You don't want to be late for Fiona." She stretched, then got up from her chair.

"Thanks." Dale tossed her the dishcloth. "Although why I'm in a hurry to go to some art gallery opening, I'll never know."

Later, as she dried the last plate, Julianne smiled to herself. Her dad had never been interested in any kind of art, despite her mother's best efforts to the contrary. Now he was going to the opening of an art gallery. This trip to Nova Scotia was having more of an impact on her father than she'd ever dreamed it would.

Pulling back the lace curtain that draped the sitting-room window, Julianne sighed. A few stray clouds scurried across the morning sky, a vivid contrast to the intense blue. From her vantage point in the second story, she could see breezes ruffling leaves in the garden below, causing only the slightest sway in Mrs. Hardesty's shrubs and flowers.

Another sigh escaped her. It was too pretty a day to spend inside a library, especially since she was completely caught up with her studying and course work.

There were some Acadian customs she wanted to research, Julianne reminded herself. Now was as good a time as any. Besides, there was still the term paper lurking at the back of her mind. Sooner or later she would have to get started on it. *Sooner will be better,* she thought.

With a last glance at the tempting garden, she let the lace fall and headed for the small coat closet. Even though the breezes were slight, she knew a jacket was in order.

The gentle tap on the door startled her. Had Dale forgotten something?

Probably. He'd been in such a hurry to meet Fiona that he'd probably forgotten his car keys or something equally vital.

But she was greeted by the ever-smiling Mrs. Hardesty. "Ah, Julianne. I thought I saw only one of you leave. There's a man downstairs asking for you. Says his name is Ross. Ian Ross. I think he's that singer at the Bearded Lion."

Ian. Excitement tingled through her. Maybe she wouldn't have to spend the morning in the university library, after all.

The landlady dropped her voice to a whisper. "I didn't want to tell him you were here, until I made sure you wanted to see him."

Julianne almost smiled at the conspiratorial tone in Mrs. Hardesty's voice, but not wanting to hurt her landlady's feelings, she kept her face poker-straight.

"It's all right. I do want to see him," she assured the older woman. Very much, she added silently.

Grabbing a lightweight jacket, Julianne hurried down the short flight of stairs. Ian stood in the sunlit foyer, his back to both women.

The man seemed to fill the space, Julianne reflected, allowing her eyes to roam the muscular triangle formed by the broad shoulders that tapered to his narrow waist. The snug denim of his jeans hugged his lean hips in a way that caused her to inhale sharply.

He turned suddenly. "Hi. I tried starting work on my term paper this morning, but my mind kept going outside. It's too nice out there to waste the day inside, studying what life was like hundreds of years ago."

His eyes traveled over her with frank appreciation. "I'd rather study life as it is today."

Julianne felt her cheeks go pink with pleasure; Mrs. Hardesty, with an almost audible giggle, shook her head in agreement.

"That's right," said the landlady. "Don't spend the day with your noses buried in books. Get out and enjoy the morning sunshine."

Ian grinned. "My sentiments exactly. Well—" he turned his gaze back to Julianne "—can you be tempted?"

"I certainly can." She held up her windbreaker. "As you can see, I was just waiting for someone to come and take me away from here."

With a wave to the still-beaming Mrs. Hardesty, Julianne and Ian set off. "That was easier than I thought," he said as he opened the car door. "I was afraid I'd have to drag you away from studying."

"I think I've changed a lot from my undergrad days," she said with a laugh as she got into the car. "Then I would have stuck to the books, no matter what the cost in lost sunshine. These days I don't need any arm-twisting at all to play hooky."

She looked over at him as he started the engine. "Actually, I thought you would be snowed under with studying as well as the farm chores."

"I get up early." He turned off the quiet street onto a busier thoroughfare, then headed east.

"I thought you might like to visit Grand-Pré today. Then maybe you won't feel any guilt at all about not studying, since so much Acadian history happened right there."

Grand-Pré. The words seemed to hover in the air. She hugged an inner vision of the Great Meadow, wondering if it would be desolate and windswept, or if time had altered the scene of so much tragedy.

"I'd like that," she replied, choosing her words with deliberate slowness. "I feel almost like this is a pilgrimage of sorts, a time for me to see where my roots are, to learn where I came from.''

He glanced away from the road for a moment. "That's really important to you, isn't it?"

She thought about his question, unconsciously rubbing the leather upholstery with one finger. With two parents who loved her dearly, she'd never been insecure, Julianne knew. All her life she'd been sheltered, surrounded by affection.

Then why did it matter so much who she was? she wondered. Why was there this need to search back in time, digging into the lives of people long dead?

"I don't really know," she said, thinking out loud. "I don't know that I've really given it a lot of thought."

He returned his attention to the highway. "I've always wanted to know the history of my family. I've spent a lot of time studying old family documents, pictures and other records. My parents' attic is filled with stuff that's been saved for generations. Even when I was small, one of my favorite rainy-day activities was exploring the attic, looking for family treasures.

Julianne could easily see him, a dark-haired imp of a child, rooting through old trunks, perhaps sneezing from stirred-up dust as he sought out his "treasures."

"I've often wondered," he continued, "if my need for family history came from a feeling of being different."

"Different?" She looked at him with curiosity. "How would you ever feel different?" She couldn't imagine Ian, who seemed so self-assured, so full of confidence, ever feeling out of place or different in any situation.

"After the Expulsion of the Acadians, some of these lands were settled by New England planters," he explained. "And many Americans loyal to the British during the War of Independence settled here in Canada. But you knew that.''

He gave her a half-apologetic look. "I don't mean to be giving you a history lesson."

Julianne smiled. "I like hearing my own country's history from a different perspective." Especially Ian's, she realized, wondering why his knowledge of her country suddenly seemed so important.

"Even though I don't agree with them, even from the vantage point of over two hundred years later, I've always thought the New England planters who left the United States were very brave souls," she said.

"They left everything they had because of their loyalty to their king." She knew that some of these Tories, as they were called, had left voluntarily, while others had been driven out during the war and its aftermath.

"That's right," he agreed. "Today, most of the people here are descendants of those New Englanders. Many Acadians came back to Nova Scotia following the peace of 1763, but the few who settled right around here were a minority. Of course, they've continued to be a minority."

Understanding began to dawn in Julianne's mind. In South Mississippi, she'd sometimes felt like a minority, too.

"My family spoke French, of course. Many of our French customs have been handed down through the years," he said. "Sometimes, as a small child whose native tongue was French, I felt left out in an English-speaking environment."

He stopped for a moment, letting his thoughts clear before he continued. "Things have changed, of course. Now that I'm an adult, I realize these cultural differences contribute to our uniqueness as Canadians. But I wouldn't have bought that explanation when I was twelve or fifteen."

"I've felt the same way," Julianne commented. "Although I'm an American, I'm very much a product of my Cajun Heritage. For a long time I equated that with being different, with being against what was normal for kids from small towns in South Mississippi."

"I think the situation is funny," she continued. "It's very 'in' to be Cajun now. Food is a good example. It seems like every American restaurant I've been in lately carries jambalaya or gumbo on its menu. But my family has been eating highly seasoned food, especially seafood, for generations."

She leaned back against the leather seat, shading her eyes from the sunlight. "For a long time, especially when I was in my early teens, I didn't want to be different. I wanted my mother to serve hamburgers or fried chicken and potato salad when my friends came over, not jambalaya or crawfish bisque."

Remembering, she shook her head. "My parents were not very happy with me for a while. Now I can see why. I refused to speak French, and I absolutely would not go to any family reunions. I knew they'd drag out those fiddles and start singing Cajun songs and playing washboards."

She rolled her eyes dramatically. "Sometimes they even made me sing with my cousins. It was awful."

He laughed. "I can see you now, digging in your heels and refusing to budge. A charming picture."

"Now I love to go," she said. "From a historian's point of view, it's like working in a living laboratory. I've even become very fond of washboard and fiddle music."

She paused. "But I still hate to sing with my cousins."

"I'm glad you understand," he said. "It's hard to put into words sometimes."

She felt a small thrill of pleasure. Again, as he had when he'd talked about his former wife, Ian was sharing some of his most private thoughts with her.

Ian pulled onto a smaller roadway, going past a sign announcing Grand-Pré National Historic Park. "The park marks the actual site of the Expulsion of the Acadians back in 1755," Ian noted.

Expanses of grass were punctuated by huge oaks and other hardwoods. Julianne caught glimpses of gardens and tall willows as the automobile neared a parking area.

Within minutes they were walking along a stone pathway between an old stone church and the statue of a woman.

Julianne walked to the stone pedestal and looked up. Caught forever in weathered metal, a young woman gazed skyward, as if searching the clouds overhead for her beloved. She was simply dressed in what would have been the homespun cloth of the period, Julianne knew, and her hair was pulled away from a careworn face. *Evangeline.*

Julianne stood quietly, absorbing the sounds of birds twittering in the clear air, feeling the sun's warmth on her shoulders, aware of the breeze that was doing its best to lift the metal fringe of Evangeline's skirt.

With gentle fingers she touched the stone base of the statue. The rock was cool.

She felt Ian's hand on her shoulder and turned. He looked down at her, his face reflecting her own inner serenity.

"I always feel a profound peace here," he said, his voice low. "It's as if I can read the thoughts of those first Acadian settlers as they tilled the earth each year, making their living from this fertile soil."

"It's difficult to believe they ever had to leave," Julianne added. "I know the Expulsion took place over two hundred years ago, but there's no sense of disruption—only a deep peace."

She thought for a moment. "I've often visited the National Military Park at Vicksburg in Mississippi. It's a beautiful park, full of rolling hills and spectacular views of the Mississippi River. There's an abiding sense of history, of the great battles that raged between North and South in our Civil War. But it's serene, too, a place of peace. I have the same types of feelings here at Grand-Pré."

"I've never been to Vicksburg, or to Mississippi for that matter," he said. "Now that I know you, I'd like to go there someday."

Ian took her hand into his own. Odd, Julianne thought, how comfortable she felt with this man she'd known for only a few short days.

"I'd like that," she said, meaning every word. "I'd love to show you my home."

Together they stood for a while in silence, each lost in thought. Then they walked the stone pathway to the small church.

Like the pathway, the church was built of gray stone. A simple steeple reached high into the air, drawing the eye ever upward.

Julianne recognized the French design of the structure. "This isn't the original church, is it? I thought all of Grand-Pré was burned by the British troops."

"This is a replica," he said. "Inside are historical displays about the Acadians and also the New England planters, since they formed so much of this area's history. Would you like to go in?"

"I'd like that," she said. "Places like this are like bookstores to me. My dad always says I never can pass one without going in."

For a while they walked around the church, exploring the exhibits and enjoying the simple beauty of the building.

Then, following a helpful suggestion from a park employee, they took a tour.

"I'm glad we took the French version of the tour," Julianne said some time later. "It made everything seem so much closer, hearing about these people and the way they lived in the language they spoke."

"I've enjoyed this very much, but it's getting close to lunchtime," Ian said after a look at his watch. "Are you hungry?"

Julianne looked at him. "Now that you mention it, I'm very hungry. I didn't realize how long we've been walking around the park."

"Well, we'll have a little bit more walking to do." He chuckled. "But I promise you a feast afterward."

Ian was true to his word. He rescued an old-fashioned picnic basket from the trunk of his car, then they set off for the shady picnic area.

Minutes later he unfolded a large quilt and spread it beneath a wide-limbed oak. Then he began pulling an assortment of bundles and dishes from the basket's depths.

Julianne took the cover from an insulated dish containing still-warm chicken. A delicious aroma curled into the air.

"Mmm. Smells like Parmesan cheese," she said as he handed her several containers of salad, condiments and fresh fruits. There was even one dish full of plump strawberries.

Julianne eyed the strawberries with delight. "Did you make all this?" If he had, the man was truly talented, she thought silently as she sniffed the salad.

He laughed and pulled a dark bottle of wine from the hamper, then proceeded to open it. "No. Emphatically no. I'm afraid my talents as a cook verge on woeful. Mrs. Pruden, our cook, is responsible for this wonderful stuff. She's been cooking for my family since I was six years old."

With a flourish he poured wine into two tall glasses. Then he gave her a devilish grin. "I can't cook, but nobody's perfect. Besides, I have other talents."

Julianne returned his smile. "I wouldn't touch that opening."

They both laughed and soon were munching away on the chicken and the other foods. Finally Julianne reached for another strawberry.

"This is my last one. Absolutely. I think." She took another fat berry and popped it into her mouth. "Well, maybe one more."

He gave her a lazy smile. "Those are local strawberries. There are pick-your-own farms all over the place. My car is trained to stop at all of them, I'm afraid."

He reached out with one hand and touched a finger to her mouth. "You have strawberry juice on your lips. I wonder what it tastes like."

Before she could blink, Julianne found herself in Ian's arms. His mouth came down on hers, he pulled her close and increased the pressure on her lips. His mouth felt firm. He tasted of wine and strawberries.

Somewhere in the back of her mind, Julianne decided that she could never feel the same about strawberries again. Now she would always associate them with the blue skies of Nova Scotia, the occasional calls of songbirds, with the feather touch of breezes against her face.

And always, she knew, the brilliant red berries would remind her of the man who was holding her so close. She relaxed in his arms and felt him pull her even tighter against the rock wall of his chest.

She could stay here forever, Julianne thought, caught securely by strong arms promising warmth and much more. For a moment—or was it hours?—the rest of the world faded from her consciousness.

"You remind me of legends I've heard, the ones about wild faerie creatures of aching beauty," he whispered; she slipped both arms around his neck. Together they stretched out upon the soft fabric of the quilt.

Ian never relaxed his grip. "I'm afraid you'll slip away, maybe disappear into some forgotten legend."

She touched her fingers to his face, feeling the smooth area of his temple give way to the beard-roughened expanse of cheek and chin. He kissed her fingers one by one, sending shivers of delight racing through her body.

A cry pierced the stillness. "Amelia! Amelia, come back here right now!"

With a vague sense of returning to reality, Julianne gently withdrew from his embrace and sat up. The sky was still a vibrant blue, and she still heard birds calling to each other. The world was the same and yet, she knew, nothing would ever be the same again. She had changed.

A little girl about five years old, Julianne judged, came running from a small grove of trees. Behind her scampered a small, furiously barking dog. The youngster shrieked with delight as a woman tore after her, calling out "Amelia!" over and over again.

Amelia ran straight to Julianne, throwing her chubby arms around her neck and holding on tightly. "Hide me quick," she said, her little chest rising and falling rapidly with the effort of her sprint. "Hide me so Mommy won't see. Hide Jazzy, too," she said, scooping up the dog.

Julianne caught a whiff of baby powder mingled with the scent of chocolate as the tyke wriggled in her arms. Then she heard the little girl giggle.

Amelia's mother, red-faced from running, puffed to a stop. "Oh, Amelia. You've spoiled this nice man and lady's picnic. Do apologize and come back now." She grabbed the child and hugged her tightly.

With Amelia on one hip, the young mother turned to Ian and Julianne, her face split by a broad smile. "We're having a picnic through those trees over there. Amelia wanted to play hide-and-seek, and I'm afraid we've run right into you. I'm very sorry."

"I won, Mommy, I won," Amelia crowed, waving her little arms in an attempt to get her mother's attention. "I won," she announced again, in a much louder voice this time.

"Hush, Amelia," her mother soothed, pecking Amelia on one rounded, rosy cheek. "Of course you won. Now say goodbye and we'll go find Daddy. I'm sure he's searched the entire park for you by now."

"You come, too, Jazzy," Amelia said to the little dog, which Julianne recognized as a dachshund. The dog wagged its tail in reply.

With friendly waves, mother and daughter set off at a brisk trot. The dachshund trotted behind them. "Goodbye, goodbye," Amelia cooed.

Ian laughed. "Just watching that child is tiring."

Julianne chuckled. "I can't remember ever having that much energy."

For a moment they looked at each other, each shaken by the depth of their feelings during the one kiss. Neither spoke, but they both knew the afternoon's interlude was over.

But there would be more, Julianne told herself, as they began to gather up the empty dishes. She began to fold the quilt, while Ian stashed utensils and dishes back in the hamper. It was time to go.

FIONA SQUEEZED DALE'S HAND again as they strolled through the gallery. Splashes of bright color filled the canvases large and small that lined the walls in the spacious rooms.

Dale linked arms with Fiona, feeling a sense of satisfaction when she moved closer to him. He shifted the briefcase he'd been carrying all morning to make it more comfortable.

The more he was around the beautiful Canadian, the more entranced he was, Dale knew. Besides her obvious beauty, what was it about her that made him feel like an eighteen-year-old again?

They were such opposites, he knew. Dale was precise, organized almost to a fault, as his daughter frequently reminded him. He liked everything in his life neatly planned, with few surprises.

Fiona on the other hand was a free spirit. She drifted lightly from one preoccupation to another. The only thing she ever seemed to be really serious about was her wood carving.

She had a great passion for life, an enthusiasm that was evident in everything she did. He suspected that she also had a fiery temper.

"I never did like all this modern stuff," he said finally. "It looks like someone threw paint directly from cans onto the canvases."

He pointed to one huge painting. "Just look at that. How can it be called art? Julianne did better finger painting in kindergarten."

"I'm sure she was an exceptional child," Fiona said, her face innocent. Then she giggled. "I'm afraid I have to agree with you. This 'stuff,' as you call it, really is terrible. I thought it would be better."

"Why don't we leave? If there's a restaurant or café close by, I could use a cup of coffee," Dale said. "Besides, I have something I want to show you."

"There's a little tearoom across the street," Fiona recalled. "We could get something to drink there."

A few minutes later, they were seated at a small table next to a window in the cozy tearoom. Dale looked down at his cup, inhaling the fragrance of the coffee.

"When you said tearoom, I was skeptical, but this coffee is great. Nice and strong," he said, taking a sip.

"Mmm," Fiona said between mouthfuls of tea. "It's one of my favorite places to come while I'm out shopping or puttering around."

Dale looked about him with interest, observing the friendly furnishings and the cheerful colors. "This place has atmosphere. It's the kind of little restaurant that people enjoy as much for the surroundings as they do for whatever is served here."

He took Fiona's hand. "That's what I have in mind for your wood-carving shop. I've worked up a few ideas during the past few days. That's what I wanted to show you," he added as Fiona raised her eyebrows.

For some reason he felt a little nervous, Dale realized. Yet he'd presented hundreds of project plans for a multi-million-dollar net-making business over the past thirty years. There was no reason to be jittery over plans for a little wood-carving shop.

With great ceremony he opened his briefcase, then began pulling out various papers. "I hope you like what I've done here."

"I've been wondering why you lugged that briefcase around all morning," Fiona replied. She leaned across the table for a better view of the papers.

Dale smiled. She would be absolutely thrilled with what he was about to show her.

Speaking with great precision, he explained each document as he laid them on the table. He included drawings of the remodeled shop, complete right down to the smallest bits of merchandise on the shelves.

Cost estimates, lists of supplies, a yearlong estimate of income and other detailed plans came out of the briefcase. He explained page after page, and Fiona said nothing. Dale found his nervousness increasing.

"I've even made an analysis of the mail-order business for wood-carvers. Here are working plans for a complete mail-order business you could run from your shop."

He beamed, rubbing his hands together. "Within a few short years you could be a wealthy woman."

Still Fiona said nothing. Alarmed, Dale put his hand over hers.

"Did I overwhelm you? Julianne says I tend to go overboard when I get excited about a project." He waited with growing anxiety.

Finally Fiona spoke. "Overwhelmed isn't the word. Stunned is more like it. I can't believe what you've done here."

Dale smiled again. At last! She loved it.

"You've taken my dream of a little wood-carving shop and turned it into a nightmare," she continued, her words tumbling out as her agitation clearly grew. "What we have here now is some corporation doing business on an international scale. That isn't what I want at all."

Now it was Dale's turn to be stunned. Perplexed, he looked down at the papers he'd spread across the table. "But I don't understand," he said.

Her eyes narrowed, flashing navy sparks in the dim lighting. "I can see that."

She pushed herself away from the table, facing him squarely. "You can't just come into my life and change it completely with some grandiose scheme for an international wood-carving conglomerate. I'm an artist, not a businesswoman. I don't want or need a lot of fancy plans, cost estimates and percentage projections."

She threw up her hands. "Oh, I know that I'll have to have some skill, running a business. I'd planned for that, but on a small scale."

Fiona stood up abruptly, nearly overturning the wooden chair. "I don't need any more money. I have quite enough for my needs."

She brushed her hair away from her face with both hands. "And I don't need all this." Her hands indicated the pile of papers.

Visibly shaken, Dale stood up, too. He scooped up the papers and stuffed them into the briefcase, paying little heed to order in his haste. How could she not understand what he was trying to do? The plans were excellent. He'd been so sure that she would love them.

He felt rejected, Dale realized. Fiona had rejected him as well as his plans.

The morning no longer seemed bright as they walked out of the tea shop, each careful not to touch the other. Within a few minutes they were in Fiona's car, heading back to town.

It was silent inside the smoothly running automobile; its occupants remained lost in their own thoughts. It was too quiet, Dale reflected. He had to make some gesture of reconciliation.

"Fiona." He glanced at her. Fiona kept her eyes on the road, her chin high in the air.

"Why don't we have dinner tonight? We could talk about this some more."

"There is nothing left to discuss about the shop. As for dinner, I already have other plans."

She seemed to soften slightly, but her tone was still cool. "Maybe some other time."

They rode the rest of the way in complete silence.

CHAPTER TEN

"THÉRÈSE REALLY DIDN'T have too much to say about her nephews, did she?" Julianne commented as Ian pulled the car to a stop in front of an imposing house on a street filled with well-kept office buildings and restored houses. "I wonder what they're like."

As they got out of the car, Ian took off his driving glasses, then shaded his eyes against the bright afternoon sunlight. "Marc and Jean are both about my age," he told her as they walked toward the house. "I went to high school with Marc. Jean went to a boarding school in England, if I remember correctly."

He took her hand, and they headed up the brick walkway. A wood and brass sign announced the office of Jean Blanchet, attorney.

"They had an intense rivalry, I remember. They both were very smart, but Jean was considered brilliant. He's done well in law, I understand. I haven't had any dealings with him myself," Ian explained. They mounted the two brick steps that led to a panelled doorway. "In fact, I guess I haven't seen him in several years."

"His office certainly is nice," Julianne said, admiring the exterior. "He's done a lot of work, turning this old home into an office building."

From the dignified brick and wood facade to the stone lions flanking each side of the porch, everything was done with style. *And a lot of money,* Julianne thought. This nephew of Thérèse's was evidently successful.

Once inside, they encountered more evidence of wealth and good taste, from the rich aroma of leather to the subtle sheen of polished wood.

An attractive blonde rose from her seat behind a Chippendale desk. Her smile was gracious.

"May I help you?" she asked in a low voice.

"We're here to see Mr. Blanchet," Julianne replied. "I'm Julianne Blanchet. I have an appointment with him at two o'clock."

She turned to Ian. "I've brought a friend along, if that will be okay with Mr. Blanchet. This is Ian Ross."

How odd to describe Ian as merely a friend she thought. He was already so much more than that.

"I'll check with Mr. Blanchet," the woman replied. "If you'd like to have a seat, he'll be with you in a few minutes." With a manicured hand she indicated several leather chairs grouped around a gleaming cherry table.

"That won't be necessary, Mrs. McGaughey. I'm ready for Miss Blanchet now."

Both Ian and Julianne turned at the sound of the rich voice. The man who had opened the oak-paneled door was tall and darkly handsome.

Handsome as a movie star, Julianne thought. Jean Blanchet extended one hand to her. *And probably just as charming,* she decided. He smiled. His grasp was firm.

As he shook hands with Ian, she studied Jean with growing curiosity. Although many generations removed, this broad-shouldered being was related to her. The well-cut suit of an obviously expensive wool blend covered a powerful-looking body. The man probably worked out every day.

Behind the charm she sensed an air of self-confidence and power. The black eyes that now seemed to be assessing Ian exuded intelligence, the same sharpness she'd found in Thérèse.

"Please come in. I've been anxious to meet you," Jean said, ushering them both into an inner office.

Like Ian he moved easily, with the grace of a man in excellent physical condition. Julianne wondered if his clients found the attorney an overwhelming presence.

"It's not every day I get to meet a long-lost relative," Jean said with an admiring glance at Julianne. "Especially one from South Mississippi."

"I feel the same way," she replied, smiling. "It's strange to think I'm related to people in another country. Until I started corresponding with Thérèse, I thought every relative I had lived in Louisiana and Mississippi."

This office was even more luxurious than the reception area. Julianne identified the carpet that partially covered the shining oak floor as an Aubusson. Oak bookcases, filled with richly-bound volumes, vied for space along the paneled walls with hunting and botanical prints. Brass and crystal fixtures gleamed from walls and desk, while a lavish chandelier—probably Waterford—cast a subtle illumination throughout the elegant room.

Julianne sank into one of the maroon leather chairs that faced the immense red oak desk. Her feet barely touched the carpet. Ian filled the other chair.

For a while the three chatted politely. Julianne decided that her earlier assessment of Jean was entirely correct. The man both asked and answered questions with quick precision. He would be a difficult adversary in a court of law, she judged, listening as Ian and Jean renewed their earlier acquaintance.

"I know I'm repeating myself, but I'm delighted to find out we're related to each other," Jean said after they'd discussed their mutual ancestor, Gaston Blanchet. "When

Aunt Thérèse told me she'd been in correspondence with you, I wondered why no one in the family had made any earlier efforts to contact the American branch of the Blanchets.''

He spread his hands. Like his secretary's, the fingers were superbly manicured, Julianne noticed. The observation bothered her.

Thérèse had hinted more than once that her nephews neglected her. Her complaints might have been the fussy ramblings of an elderly lady, but Julianne wondered if Thérèse perhaps was justified. If Jean had time for manicures, why couldn't he spend more time with his aunt?

Now she was the one being fussy, she scolded herself. Jean was a busy man, an obviously successful attorney, whose appearance was important in his line of work.

From the brass-framed photographs of a smiling woman and three handsome children on the wall behind his desk, she decided that he probably also had a family. With all the demands on his time, he probably spent as much time as he could with Thérèse.

"Ah, well. Life is so complex," Jean continued. "We all get busy and caught up in our own affairs."

Then he smiled, radiating good-natured charm. "Now that I know you, I'll be much more eager to study our family history."

He sat back in his large chair, folding his hands together on the desk. "Now, tell me what brings you to visit your Canadian relatives."

Julianne quickly told him about the course on Acadian legends, as well as of her desire to research some of the family history. She also told him of her search for the unknown treasure.

Jean listened quietly. Occasionally, as if assessing an adversary, he glanced at Ian, who sat just as quietly.

Julianne finished and also glanced at Ian. He looked thoughtful. Was he too analyzing the situation? She found herself grateful for his quiet presence.

"Family treasure," Jean said. He shook his head. "All my life I've heard the story about some long-lost family heirloom, which supposedly originated with Gaston Blanchet. Maybe even money, perhaps gold coins."

"After so long a time with no evidence, what could there be?" he asked. His glance traveled between Ian and Julianne. "I think maybe Gaston had hidden some coins somewhere in his farmhouse, but those surely were found in all the years since his death."

"You're probably right," Julianne agreed reluctantly. "I suppose it's the romance of it, the thought of finding something that was so important to Anne and Gaston that intrigues me. I wouldn't care if the treasure, if it does in fact exist, turns out to be valuable."

She smiled at Jean. "I think the real find is the letters, mine and Thérèse's."

Jean's expression altered subtly. "Ah, the letters."

He laced his hands across his abdomen and gave her a shrewd look. "Aunt Thérèse told me you had Gaston's letters. I would be interested in reading them for the historical value—" he shrugged "—but I have little hope of finding anything about lost valuables."

Feeling somewhat deflated, Julianne glanced at her watch, then rose from the chair. "Maybe not. I guess my training as a storyteller causes me to think there may be something to the legend, even after all these years. In most stories, even fantasies, there is usually some truth to be found."

She turned to Ian. "It's time to go. We have another meeting this afternoon."

They all shook hands again, then Jean turned to Julianne. "My wife and I would like you and your father to come for dinner soon. We'll contact you at the inn to make the arrangements."

Julianne found herself warming to the man. He was charming, she reminded herself.

"And of course, we'd also like you to come," he said to Ian. "It's been a pleasure to talk with you after losing track of you over the years."

As Julianne and Ian left the beautiful office, she thought about Jean. Handsome, self-assured and undoubtedly successful, he was almost too good to be true. Would his cousin Marc turn out to be the same?

PHYSICALLY, Marc and Jean Blanchet could have been twins, Julianne decided after one look at the man. A banker in one of Wolfville's oldest financial institutions Marc was as handsome as his cousin, although in a fleshier sort of way. She wondered if he would exude the same charm.

"Thank you for arranging to meet us on a Saturday afternoon," she said. "Aunt Thérèse said you normally don't come in to the bank on weekends."

His smile was genial. "Actually, I do come in sometimes to catch up on paperwork. But I try not to make a habit of it, like I did when I was just getting started."

He led them into his well-appointed office on the second floor of the small bank building. "I've been anxious to finally meet you," Marc said as he indicated a comfortable-looking sofa along one wall. "Aunt Thérèse couldn't wait to call with the news that you were coming."

Like his cousin, Marc certainly believed in surrounding himself with luxury, Julianne decided as she looked around the elegant room. Although the walnut furnishings were a little too heavy for her own taste, they gave the room a look of imposing dignity.

Her feet sank into the gray-blue carpet that covered every inch of the floor. Instead of the paneling favored by Jean, this cousin had walls covered with blue- and silver-striped wallpaper. Intricate gilt frames surrounded the several oil paintings of pastoral and hunting scenes. Heavy silk damask draped both of the floor-to-ceiling windows, shutting out the afternoon sun.

As Julianne and Ian settled into the velvet sofa, Marc took his place behind his vast walnut desk. Unlike Jean's desk, which had been immaculate, the top of Marc's was littered with folders and documents. Pens and paper clips were scattered across the surface.

She wondered if the man's mind was equally disorderly. Then she chided herself for making snap judgments. *Give the man a chance,* she told herself.

Although the men and their furnishings were different, Julianne couldn't help comparing this man with the one they'd talked with earlier in the day. Both sat behind large wooden desks in lavish offices. She wondered if they thought alike.

But as they talked, she realized that even though both cousins were articulate and intelligent, they were entirely different persons. Marc was more reserved; his replies and questions came at a slower pace. His mind seemed less organized, and he frequently tended to ramble off the subject.

He also was not a superb physical specimen like Jean. Both had the same large build, but Marc outweighed his cousin by at least thirty pounds. His face even looked a bit bloated, as if he perhaps indulged himself too much.

Julianne wondered if she wasn't being too hard on Marc. Under any circumstances, Jean Blanchet would be a difficult act to follow.

At first Marc seemed somewhat reserved, Julianne observed. Only gradually did his caution give way.

As she explained the purpose of her visit to Nova Scotia, Marc unbent even more, and when Julianne mentioned the letters written by Anne, his expression grew animated.

"Aunt Thérèse has always been fussy about those old letters," he confided. "She wouldn't let Jean or me near them until we both were settled family men. Even now she won't let us touch the originals, just the copies."

In a gesture that reminded Julianne of Jean Blanchet, Marc leaned back in his chair and folded his hands across his abdomen. "I think Aunt Thérèse always thought there was some substance to the rumors about a family treasure hidden away by Gaston."

His expression remained skeptical as he continued. "Of course, that's ridiculous. Aunt Thérèse has been getting dottier as she gets older, if you want my opinion."

Julianne bristled. If there was one thing Thérèse Blanchet wasn't, it was dotty. The woman was in complete control of her mental faculties. She glanced at Ian, but his expression revealed nothing.

"Actually," Julianne said, "I agree with Thérèse. I think there may be something to the rumors of a lost treasure." She explained how her own family had carefully preserved the letters written by Gaston.

Skepticism vanished from Marc's face. Smiling broadly, he leaned forward in his chair.

"Letters written by Gaston? But that's marvelous. I had no idea of their existence. I'd like to see them. Right away, if possible."

Now he reminded Julianne of a predatory cat. Instantly her guard came up. For reasons she couldn't explain, she did not trust him.

"I'm afraid I can't give you access to the letters myself," she said. "The letters actually belong to my father, and he has them. I'd be happy to talk with him about it, then get back in touch with you."

Marc continued to talk about the letters while they were leaving the office. He pressed his home telephone number into her hand, with instructions to call as soon as she found out anything from her father.

"He certainly is anxious about those letters," Julianne said as Ian started the car. "Didn't you think so?"

"A little too anxious," Ian agreed.

His expression was thoughtful when he looked at her. "I don't think I'd be in any hurry to let Marc see even the copies, especially until you've had a chance to do a little treasure-hunting with your father."

Julianne mulled over Ian's advice during the drive back to the inn. He was right. Marc was too anxious, but why? She wondered if he knew more than he was saying about Gaston's legacy, even though he protested the existence of any such treasure.

She was still thinking about Marc Blanchet as they entered the inn and went upstairs. The door to the Blanchet suite was slightly ajar.

Dale, his dark hair still wet, came out of his bedroom as Julianne and Ian walked into the sitting room. "I thought I heard someone talking out here," he said. "I just got out of the shower."

Something was different about her father, Julianne thought. He came to shake hands with Ian, but the spring was gone from his step. He wasn't smiling, either, and lately his smile had been much in evidence.

PLAY THE

LUCKY CARNIVAL WHEEL

scratch-off game
and get as many as
SIX FREE GIFTS...

HOW TO PLAY:

1. With a coin, carefully scratch off the silver area at right. Then check your number against the chart below it to find out which gifts you're eligible to receive.

2. You'll receive brand-new Harlequin Superromance® novels and possibly other gifts—ABSOLUTELY FREE! Send back this card and we'll promptly send you the free books and gifts you qualify for!

3. We're betting you'll want more of these heartwarming romances, so unless you tell us otherwise, every month we'll send you 4 more wonderful novels to read and enjoy. Always delivered right to your home. And always at a discount off the cover price!

4. Your satisfaction is guaranteed! You may return any shipment of books and cancel at any time. The Free Books and Gifts remain yours to keep!

NO COST! NO RISK!
NO OBLIGATION TO BUY!

FREE! 20K GOLD ELECTROPLATED CHAIN!

You'll love this 20K gold electroplated chain! The necklace is finely crafted with 160 double-soldered links, and is electroplate finished in genuine 20K gold. It's nearly ⅛" wide, fully 20" long—and has the look and feel of the real thing. ''Glamorous'' is the perfect word for it, and it can be yours FREE when you play the ''LUCKY CARNIVAL WHEEL'' scratch-off game!

◄ CLAIM YOUR FREE GIFTS! MAIL THIS CARD TODAY!

More Good News For Members Only!

When you join the Harlequin Reader Service®, you'll receive 4 heartwarming romance novels each month delivered to your home at the members-only low discount price. You'll also get additional free gifts from time to time as well as our newsletter. It's "Heart to Heart"—our members' privileged look at upcoming books and profiles of our most popular authors!

If offer card is missing, write to: Harlequin Reader Service, 901 Fuhrmann Blvd., P.O. Box 1867, Buffalo, NY 14269-1867

Harlequin Reader Service®
901 Fuhrmann Blvd.
P.O. Box 1867
Buffalo, N.Y.
14240-9952

BUSINESS REPLY CARD

First Class   Permit No. 717   Buffalo, NY

Postage will be paid by addressee

MAIL THIS CARD TODAY!

NO POSTAGE
NECESSARY
IF MAILED
IN THE
UNITED STATES

Uh-oh. Her dad was having problems with Fiona, if she read the signs correctly.

"How did the meetings with the Blanchet cousins go?" Dale asked. He opened the small refrigerator and pulled out a pitcher. "Would you like some iced tea?"

"That sounds terrific," Ian replied.

Julianne and Ian explained the day's progress over tall glasses of the frosty beverage. Dale listened, she noticed, but he seemed distracted, as if he were only half hearing about their meetings with the Blanchet cousins.

He also seemed tired, much as he had in the months following Lillian's death. She wondered if her father was all right.

"I agree with Ian," Dale said finally when they'd finished their story. "It may only be a hunch, but from what you're both telling me, I think Marc may know more than he's telling."

He took a last mouthful of tea, then got up to refill their glasses. Ian rose at the same time.

"I hate to leave this conversation, but it's getting late. I've things to do at the farm before tonight's performance at the Bearded Lion." Ian turned to Julianne. "Would you like to come?"

Yes, she wanted very much to see Ian perform again. But she was worried about her father. Reluctantly Julianne shook her head.

"I'd really like to, but I've got some things to take care of here."

She couldn't leave Dale. What if the problem wasn't Fiona? What if he didn't feel well?

Disappointment showed for a moment in Ian's face. Then he started for the door.

She gave him a wan smile. "Why don't I walk you to the car?"

As they left the inn, Ian took her hand. "Is anything wrong?"

"I don't know. My dad looks like he's upset or not feeling well. I can't tell which. That's why I can't go see you perform this evening." They reached the car and she looked at him, hoping he would understand.

"I'm disappointed," he said, still holding her hand. "I'd hoped to spend more time with you this evening. But I understand."

He laced his fingers tighter around hers. "Since you can't go tonight, why don't we plan on church tomorrow? There's an old church I'd like you to see."

So he did understand! Her relief was almost tangible. What Ian thought mattered a great deal to her, she realized, a very great deal.

"That sounds wonderful." She hesitated. "That is, if my father is okay."

"The invitation includes him, too," he replied. "I don't want him thinking I'm monopolizing all your time. After all, one of the reasons you came up here was to spend some time with each other."

She laughed. "So we did."

Then, before she even thought about what she was doing, Julianne stood on tiptoe and kissed him. "Thanks for coming with me this afternoon."

Then she turned and went slowly back up the walkway. On reaching the porch, she turned and waved as Ian drove off.

Dragging her feet, she climbed the stairway to the suite. Dale was still in the sitting room.

"That's a hardworking man," Dale said. "He always seems to be involved in something."

"I hadn't thought about it before, but you're right. He does work hard."

She smiled, pleased by her father's praise of Ian. "Speaking of working hard, are you all right? You look a little tired this evening."

Dale brushed one hand across his forehead. "I suppose I am. I spent the afternoon looking through an art gallery, which is enough to tire anyone."

He smiled for a moment. "Once I was there I remembered why I've avoided art galleries all these years."

Julianne laughed. "I was surprised Fiona was able to drag you there at all. You're not exactly the world's greatest art lover."

Dale's smile disappeared. "I won't make that mistake again," he said.

His face was unreadable; he turned toward the bedroom. "I think I may go read for a while, then turn in early."

Feeling both disappointed and concerned, Julianne watched the bedroom door close.

Maybe whatever it was would work itself out, she thought. But from the look on Dale's face, she didn't hold out much hope.

Julianne couldn't help but worry about him. Since Lillian's death he'd been vulnerable. It was difficult to think of her father, who'd always seemed much larger than life, as vulnerable.

At home he'd been able to fend off the attentions of women eager to pursue an eligible and wealthy widower. Away from home, his familiar surroundings and the things that reminded him of Lillian, he was more vulnerable.

Besides, she admitted, Fiona wasn't like most of the women who were interested in her father. Fiona was stunning, one of the most beautiful women she'd ever known. She probably could have her pick of many men.

And judging from the clothing and jewelry she wore and her expensive automobile, she also seemed to have no financial worries.

A head turner under any circumstances, Fiona was also sincere, sweet and very nice. She had intelligence and a creative drive that would attract intelligent and creative men. *Like my dad,* Julianne told herself.

She looked down at her watch, and restlessness overtook her. It was already eight o'clock.

Right now, she knew, Ian would be onstage, illuminated by a single spotlight as his voice, that fluid baritone, washed every corner of the room. For all the contact she was having with Dale, she could have been at the Bearded Lion.

Stop it, she told herself. What if her father had wanted to talk and she'd been gone? It was a chance she didn't want to take.

Maybe she could read a good book. With another sigh, strangely loud in the otherwise silent room, she went into her bedroom. She started for the small nightstand, where she knew a British mystery was stashed, then stopped.

Now was a good time to reread Gaston's letters to Anne. Maybe now that she'd seen some of the places where he might have walked, she would have more understanding about the type of man he was.

She took the letters out of the desk drawer, then plopped onto her double bed. Untying her shoes, she kicked them off.

The old letters *were* fragile, she thought, loosening the ribbons around them. Thérèse had had the right idea about making copies. She would have to do that, too.

Gradually Julianne deciphered the faded handwriting to read the words of love and longing written so many years before, and she began to feel almost like an intruder. The emotions were deep, yet they were as fragile as the paper she held in her hands.

Gaston had the soul of a poet, she decided; the descriptions of the Acadian landscape really came to life on the pages. And now she could picture the places, could feel the ground beneath her feet and see the blue sky overhead.

The tales of Gaston's struggles against nature, of his efforts to earn a living, moved her, as they had so many times. The terrible story of his mother's long illness seemed especially poignant on this night.

Maman is terribly weak. Her hands, once so proud and slender, are too thin. Her cheeks have lost the rose hue that once charmed many admirers. I fear her strength will never return and I grieve for her.

On days when the sun shines, *Maman* feels better. We sit outside underneath the trees. Then she tells me stories of her life in England, the many balls and fetes, the hunts across the wild Scottish moors. Although I have never traveled to her homeland, I feel as if I know it well. It is strange to think of a family I have never seen in a country faraway. And yet, my own beloved Anne, you also are faraway in a country I have never seen. I grieve for us all.

Overwhelmed by sorrow, Julianne put the letters aside, then hugged her knees to her chin.

A sharp rapping intruded upon her thoughts. Now who was that? she wondered. She padded into the sitting room.

Mrs. Hardesty looked around the almost dark room, her expression apologetic. "I'm sorry to disturb you, but you have a telephone call downstairs. I thought it might be that Mr. Ross."

Ian. Her spirits suddenly soared. Maybe Ian wanted to meet her after the show. Then she remembered. He had the telephone number to the suite. He wouldn't have called Mrs. Hardesty.

So if it wasn't Ian, who was it?

The voice at the other end of the line definitely wasn't Ian's. "Julianne? This is Marc Blanchet."

She tried to keep the disappointment from her voice. "Hello, Marc."

"I wondered if you had a chance yet to talk with your father about the letters. I'd like to see them soon, this evening, if possible."

A warning bell sounded in Julianne's head. "I'm sorry, Marc, but I haven't had a chance to discuss it with Dad. He was a little tired tonight and went to bed early."

Which was true, she knew, although she could have discussed it with her father earlier. She simply hadn't wanted to bother him when he wasn't feeling well.

"Oh. Well, I'd really like to see those letters soon," he said. "I'm sure your father wouldn't mind if you showed them to a relative."

Now how could he assume that? she wondered with growing irritation.

"The letters belong to my father," she said, emphasizing each word. "I really couldn't allow anyone to see them without his permission."

"Can you check with him this evening?"

"No, I can't." Despite her best efforts to be civil, the words came out rather clipped.

There was silence at the other end. "All right," he said finally. "I'll wait until you talk with your father."

At last, she thought. He'd finally understood that he would not get access to the letters that evening, if ever.

"I also wanted to talk with you about something else," Marc said. He paused again.

Now what? Julianne wondered. If this was going to be another attempt to see the letters, she would have to tell him no in no uncertain terms.

"I think you should be careful about what you say or show to my cousin Jean. He's been known to be—" he hesitated, as if unsure of what to say "—unscrupulous."

It took Julianne every ounce of control to keep from slamming down the phone. Now he was trying to discredit his cousin, of all things. Why she couldn't fathom, unless it was somehow for Marc's own gain.

"I'll keep that in mind," she said. "Thanks for calling." With that she hung up the telephone.

Maybe Marc knew more than he was saying about Gaston's legacy. The thought intrigued her. Perhaps her instincts about lost treasure were on target, after all. A small shiver of excitement swept through her as she climbed the stairs to the suite.

CHAPTER ELEVEN

"YOU LOOK WONDERFUL, *chère*. Since we've been here, I've gotten so used to seeing you in jeans or slacks, I've forgotten what you look like all dressed up."

Dale got up from his seat at the small breakfast table to admire his daughter. Julianne, clad in a simple dress of rose silk, stood in the doorway to her bedroom.

The shirtwaist dress, belted in black silk rope, fell around her legs in graceful box pleats. To complement its shimmering silk fabric she wore black leather high-heeled shoes.

A stray beam of sunlight glittered as it met her dark hair, which she left unadorned by barrettes or other ornaments. Dale smiled and walked over to her.

He brushed her cheek with a light kiss. "Sometimes you remind me so much of your mother. Rose was her favorite color. It always looked spectacular with her black hair, just like it does on you."

Her father seemed rested today, Julianne thought. He wasn't up to his usual self, but at least he didn't look so glum. She wondered if he'd spent a restless night, but decided against asking.

"Thank you," she replied, giving him a quick hug. For a moment they stood together, each recalling moments from their past. Then she remembered the time.

"Ian will be here any minute," she said. "Are you ready to go?"

"Except for this darn tie," Dale replied, fumbling with the striped knot at his neck. "I never could get one of these things right."

As if on cue, someone tapped at their door. "That's Mrs. Hardesty, I'm sure, coming to tell us Ian is here," Julianne said, quickly rearranging Dale's tie. "Let's meet him downstairs."

She stopped on the threshold. "I need to pick up that book on Cajun crafts Ian wanted to see. I also forgot Gaston's letters. I wanted to show them to him after church. Wait just a moment while I go get them."

Julianne hurried into her bedroom, grabbed the packet of letters from her writing desk, then looked around for the book. It was nowhere to be seen.

I'll have to find it after church, she decided. She emerged from the bedroom, quickly placed the letters in her purse and followed Dale out the door.

They found Ian in the foyer, watching as they came downstairs. He caught sight of Julianne and his eyes widened.

"You look lovely," Ian said. His smile underscored the compliment.

Pleased, Julianne murmured her thanks. "You look nice, too," she replied.

And he did, she thought. It was the first time she'd seen him in a coat and tie, she realized. The blue-gray lightweight wool contrasted effectively with the lighter blue of his shirt and the navy slacks.

They headed into the crisp sunshine, and Ian reached for her hand. Julianne felt a surge of happiness as his warm fingers encircled hers. Although she'd seen him only the day before, she'd missed him.

"Which church are we going to?" Dale asked as they all got into his car. "Is it the one at Grand-Pré?"

"No," Ian replied from the rear seat. "We're going to the church my family has attended for many years. It's not in Wolfville, so I'll give you directions."

With Ian navigating, the drive from Wolfville to the old church seemed short. As they walked along the flagged footpath leading to the stone church, Julianne could see in her mind the child Ian, skipping along the irregular pathway on Sunday mornings.

He probably was a handful for his parents, she decided. The thought made her smile. Thinking of the kiss they'd shared at Grand-Pré, she decided he still was a handful, but in a very different and adult way.

The service itself was quiet. Julianne found herself moved by the centuries-old traditions of the rites, which were conducted in French. Light, filtering many-colored through the stained glass windows, cast stray shadows into each nook and corner of the old church.

Julianne, absently tracing the carvings of the wooden pews as she listened, found her attention wandering. She glanced at Ian.

He sat quietly, his head proudly high as he concentrated on the priest's words. Occasional shafts of sunshine highlighted his cheekbones and trailed along the sides of his classic nose.

Julianne held her breath; she realized he was one of the handsomest men she'd ever seen.

As she watched, he turned toward her. He caught her eye and smiled, then drew his arm through hers.

Surrounded by the timeless beauty of the simple church, Julianne slowly became aware that a question was nagging at her. Had she fallen in love with Ian?

The thought shook her to the core. The sermon melted into the background. She mulled over the situation, although it was difficult to think with Ian so close beside her, his strong arm around her own.

She couldn't fall in love with Ian, she told herself firmly. There were simply too many problems.

Distance was a major difficulty. Remembering Ian's first failed marriage, she knew he would never leave his home in Nova Scotia. It was something she would never even consider asking him to do.

But her work was too important to her, the Cajun cultural center too much a part of her life, for her to leave South Mississippi. Her family ties there were very strong, too. She especially had to consider her father, who'd lost his beloved wife only a year before.

One of them would have to leave their own country, if they were to have more than a long-distance romance. That in itself presented major difficulties.

Not that it couldn't be done. She'd read and heard about several long-distance marriages involving television celebrities and other famous people. Those arrangements seemed to be working.

But that type of relationship wasn't for her, Julianne decided. When she fell in love, especially if marriage followed, she wanted to live with her husband. She was, Julianne saw with increasing clarity, a modern woman with traditional ideas about home and family.

The priest concluded his sermon, and Julianne was still lost in thought. Only when several people stood up around them did she realize that the service was over.

"That was a wonderful service," Dale said as they left the cool interior of the church. He blinked several times to help his eyes adjust to the sunny brightness outside.

"I liked having everything in French," he continued. "It reminded me a lot of the Cajun churches I've attended in Louisiana."

"My family has attended this church for several generations," Ian said with pride. "Of course, it wasn't here before the Expulsion of the Acadians. All those structures were razed."

"But it's very old, isn't it?" Julianne asked, looking back at the church as they headed for the automobile. "It looks like it could have been here in the mid-seventeen hundreds."

"Oh, it's old," Ian answered. "This church was one of the first built by the Acadians who returned here in the years following the Expulsion."

As they reached the car, Ian turned to Julianne. "Why don't the three of us go out for lunch? I'd like to treat you."

"What do you think, Dad?" She turned to Dale, hoping he would agree to go. "Do you have any other plans?"

His face clouded for a moment, as if he were thinking of whatever had been bothering him the night before. Then he brightened. "No, I don't. Lunch is a good idea, but it will be my treat, Ian."

As the two men argued good-humoredly over who would pay for lunch, Julianne hid a smile. Ian and her dad got along very well, she decided. The thought brought a surge of pleasure. She realized it was important that her father like Ian and vice versa.

The restaurant turned out to be a small family business that catered to locals and tourists alike. Bright cotton cloths covered each table in the dining room. Tiny crocks of what looked like applesauce rested beside vases of fresh-cut summer flowers. The paneled walls were lined with baskets and other antiques, giving the entire room a cozy, homelike atmosphere. Julianne liked the place immediately.

"It smells wonderful in here." She took another whiff. "A very fresh smell, like apples."

Ian grinned. "This place is famous for its apple dishes. No matter what you order, some kind of apple concoction comes with your meal. And it's all delicious."

Ian was absolutely right, Julianne concluded some time later, polishing off the remains of a pork chop and apple casserole. "That was wonderful," she said as the friendly waitress cleared away her plate.

"Would you like dessert?" the waitress asked. "We have apple pie à la mode, apple parfait, apple brandy ice cream, apple dumplings, apple mousse, and apple cake."

She bent and whispered, "If you're tired of apples, we also have fudge pie and spumoni."

Julianne laughed. "Mmm. Apple dumplings. I can just about taste that wonderful pastry crust with an apple baked inside."

She wrinkled her nose in mock disgust. "It all sounds delicious, but not for me, thanks. I'm too full, as it is. I would love some coffee, though."

"Well, I'm not shy," Dale interjected. "Bring me one of those apple dumplings, please."

He beamed at the waitress. "Any chance of getting some vanilla ice cream on top of that?"

"There certainly is," the woman answered.

She glanced hopefully at Ian, but he shook his head. "Just coffee, thank you."

As the waitress hurried to fill their orders, Julianne remembered the parcel in her purse. She turned to Ian.

"I brought Gaston's letters for you to look at," she said. She withdrew the thick packet from her purse and handed them to him.

Slowly he untied the ribbons confining the papers and took out one letter. He read several pages, then carefully refolded them.

"These are too fragile to withstand much handling, I'm afraid. Why don't you let me make copies, like Thérèse did? I could make three copies, one for each of us."

Julianne nodded. "That's a good idea. Then we could all study the letters for Gaston's references to the countryside. Maybe from any clues in the letters, we can piece together some idea of what the treasure was. Maybe we could even locate it," she said.

"Three heads are better than one, to paraphrase an old saying," she continued. Then she laughed at herself. "Ever the optimist."

Ian shrugged. "You never know. Why don't I take these and bring the copies tomorrow?"

Julianne looked at her father. Although she trusted Ian, she felt strangely reluctant to let the letters out of their possession.

"That's fine with me." Dale grinned at Ian. "But don't hold your breath, waiting for some kind of treasure to appear. I know my optimistic daughter thinks there's something to all this, but whatever this precious secret was, I'm sure it's long gone by now."

"Probably," Ian agreed. "But I guess I'm optimistic, too. Any sort of mystery compels me."

The waitress reappeared. With a flourish she produced a bowl heaped with apple dumpling and topped with a glistening mound of ice cream.

She chuckled as Dale's eyes widened. "It was the biggest dumpling I could find."

As Dale struggled through the fragrant mounds of ice cream, apple and pastry crust, Julianne reviewed with Ian several of the landmarks mentioned in Gaston's letters. "I've read and reread these letters so many times that the words have become too familiar," she said. "I'm probably overlooking the obvious. I'm glad you're going to read them.''

Ian looked at her with such warmth that Julianne for a moment found it difficult to breathe. If looks like that could be bottled and sold on the market, she thought, the results would be devastating.

"I can't eat another bite," Dale said and put down his spoon with a sigh of regret. "Would either of you like some of this?''

"No, thanks." Julianne laughed. "I'm going to have to haul myself up out of this chair, as it is."

"None for me, either," Ian added. He smiled at Dale. "I've eaten desserts here before. They can be habit-forming."

The three were still laughing about the apple dumpling à la mode as they drove back to the inn. Julianne, listening to her father and Ian developing an easy camaraderie, relaxed. Dale seemed much happier now. Maybe whatever had been bothering him earlier was gone.

"I have to practice this evening," Ian said as the car drew to a stop in front of the inn. "The university is having a special benefit show next week for handicapped children. In fact—" he looked at his watch "—I'm due at rehearsal in an hour or so."

"Do you have time to come in for a moment? I misplaced the book on Cajun crafts you wanted to borrow, but it would only take a minute for me to find it," Julianne said.

"I'd forgotten all about it," Ian admitted. "Somehow the aroma of apple dumpling drove all thoughts of studying right out of my head."

Julianne was still chuckling when they entered the inn. She stopped abruptly as they walked into the foyer.

Mrs. Hardesty stood just inside, sobbing and looking down at something she held cradled in her hands. She caught sight of her boarders and relief filled her face.

"Oh, I'm so glad you're back," the landlady cried, hiccuping between sobs. "The most terrible thing has happened!"

Alarmed, Julianne put her arms around the distraught woman. "What's wrong, Mrs. Hardesty?"

"A burglar," the landlady sobbed. "Someone came in while I was at church and ransacked your rooms."

She held up a small object. "Broke the arm off my little dancer."

Julianne recognized one of the figurines that stood here and there about in their suite. The porcelain ballerinas, flower girls and other graceful figures were part of an extensive collection she knew Mrs. Hardesty treasured.

Ian took the steps two at a time. With a quick glance at each other, Dale and Julianne followed right behind him. He opened the door to their suite.

The sitting room was a mess. Mrs. Hardesty's sofas were overturned. The pretty rose floral chintz coverings were ripped; stuffing from the comfortable cushions littered the room.

Pictures torn from the walls were strewn about, mingling with dishes and flatware emptied from the small cupboard. Even the tiny refrigerator had been hit. Milk mixed with coffee grounds puddled in several spots on the carpet, while the few apples and oranges Julianne had bought for snacks had been thrown at the walls.

Mrs. Hardesty came in, wringing her hands as she surveyed the litter. "This is awful, just awful. Nothing like this has ever happened here before."

"Have you called the police?" Ian asked, bending to pick up a book. He looked at the title, then at Julianne, who was still trying to comfort Mrs. Hardesty. "Here's the book on Cajun crafts I was going to borrow. Whoever ransacked this place found it for you."

"Yes," Mrs. Hardesty replied. "The police should be here any minute now."

She walked around, her hands moving nervously as she talked. "They asked us not to move anything until they've had a chance to investigate."

Ian replaced the book on the carpet. "You're absolutely right. We'll have to wait until after the police come before we can start setting this to rights."

"But you don't have to stay. You have a rehearsal this afternoon," Julianne reminded him. "Dad and I will clean this up."

"Of course I'll stay," Ian volunteered. "I can call my musicians."

A few minutes later the police arrived. With methodical thoroughness they swept through the suite of rooms.

The investigation turned up nothing. There were no clues as to who had committed the vandalism, the detective who questioned them concluded.

"According to your statements, nothing seems to be missing," the detective said finally. "Are you sure that no money was stolen?"

"We didn't keep any cash at all in the rooms," Dale explained again. "Julianne and I each had our money with us this morning. The rest is in travelers' checks, and none of them are missing. I've checked each receipt three times."

"Maybe when the burglars realized there was no money, they got mad and began tearing things up," Julianne offered. "Why else would they have resorted to ripping up cushions and even emptying the refrigerator?"

"At least they only damaged one of my figurines," Mrs. Hardesty said, still cradling the tiny dancer in her hands. "They could have broken them all."

Ian's eyes narrowed as he surveyed the ransacked suite. He wasn't so sure the burglars had reacted in anger. What if someone had been after the letters? It was a long shot, but perhaps there was something to the legend about lost treasure, after all.

He opened his mouth to tell Julianne and Dale of his suspicions, then closed it again. There was no need to alarm them unnecessarily.

The police left, promising to look into the matter right away. "If you find anything, or can think of anything that might help our investigation, please let us know," the detective asked.

"We will," Dale promised. "I don't even know where to start in this place," he said, looking around at the mess that surrounded them.

Julianne came out of her bedroom, clad now in blue jeans and an old sweatshirt. She bent to pick up some cushions. "What we need are some paper towels, so we can start cleaning up the spilled milk."

"I can handle that," said Mrs. Hardesty. Another hiccup escaped her. She took a deep breath, trying to regain control, then turned to Dale, who had removed his sports jacket and tie. "If you'll bring those torn cushions downstairs, I'll send you back up with some paper towels."

The straightening moved along briskly. Dale and Julianne worked on the milk and coffee grounds, while Ian, after shedding his own coat and tie, picked up litter. Mrs. Hardesty followed them around with a stiff broom.

"We're beginning to make some progress." Julianne, finally satisfied that all the milk and coffee possible had been removed from the carpet, stretched as she stood up.

"Good heavens! What happened in here?"

Dale's head snapped up at the sound of the low voice. His face turned pink with joy.

"Fiona!" Ignoring the sodden paper towels in his hand, he stood up.

Fiona, her slender figure covered by a hot pink and green running suit, stood in the doorway, hands on hips as she observed the activity. "It looks like you've had some unwelcome visitors."

"We certainly have." Dale quickly explained the attempted burglary of the suite.

"I know something that will work on that milk stain," Fiona said when Dale finished. She pushed up her hot pink sleeves and grabbed a roll of paper towels. "Let's see what we can do."

As the afternoon wore on, Julianne found herself liking Fiona more and more. The older woman had pitched right into the cleanup, offering some excellent suggestions.

Julianne occasionally caught Dale stealing glances at Fiona, and wondered, as she saw the looks the two exchanged, what had happened the night before. Had they had an argument?

It's none of your business, she told herself. Still, it was difficult to control her curiosity.

Finally Mrs. Hardesty set down her broom. "Except for rehanging the curtains, this looks like it did before. I can have those curtains washed and dried by this evening."

Pushing her hair away from her forehead, Julianne sat back on her haunches and looked around. Mrs. Hardesty was right.

"I'm afraid I'll have to get going," Ian said. "I didn't realize it was so late. This is the only chance my group will have to practice before the benefit next week, so I've got to go."

He turned to Julianne. "Why don't you come with me?"

Dismayed, she looked at her grimy shirt and denims. "Look at me. I'm a mess."

"A few minutes more won't make much difference to me now. You look fine to me, especially for a practice session, but if you'd feel more comfortable, that's fine. Why don't you go change? I'll wait," Ian said.

Julianne hesitated. The thought of watching Ian perform, of listening to his voice as it wrapped itself around the haunting Acadian songs, was tempting. She really wanted to go, but would feel guilty about leaving her father to finish the cleanup.

As if she knew what Julianne was thinking, Fiona came over. "Why don't you go? Your father and I can handle anything that's left."

Julianne recalled the glances she'd seen pass between them all afternoon. They probably wanted some time to themselves, she decided.

"Okay. I'll be right back." She hurried into the bedroom to change.

A few minutes later she returned, still brushing her hair as she came out of the bedroom. "I tried to hurry," she said, giving her hair one last swipe with the brush.

Ian's gaze was admiring. "You look wonderful."

She had changed to a soft navy knit skirt and tunic that outlined every curve. A red belt, complete with a gold lion's head buckle, and red shoes in faux alligator added splashes of bright color.

"Thanks." She had taken pains with her outfit, even in the few minutes allotted to her. Ian's praise and the look on his face justified her effort.

She turned to Dale. "Are you sure it's okay if I leave? I hate running out on you."

Dale waved them out with one hand. "Enjoy yourselves. The only things left to do are the ripped cushions, which Mrs. Hardesty says she'll see to first thing tomorrow, and the curtains. Once Mrs. Hardesty cleans them, this place will be almost as good as new."

The door closed behind them, and Fiona sat down on one of the chintz love seats. She plucked at the torn fabric with nervous fingers.

"I came over to apologize for my behavior in the art gallery." Her usually sultry voice shook with emotion. "I've thought it over. In fact—" her voice trembled "—I've thought about little else. I realize now you were only trying to help."

Dale was by her side immediately. He took both of her hands in his. "No, I'm the one who should apologize. I was wrong to make such grandiose schemes and plans without consulting you first."

He squeezed her fingers. "Old habits are hard to break, I suppose."

"Maybe we both were wrong, and both of us were too stubborn to admit it." Her smile was shy. "I would love to start over. I've missed you."

By way of answer he took her into his arms. "I've thought about nothing but you. Poor Julianne. She's been fretting about me since last night. Even in church this morning, all I could think about was you."

Fiona snuggled closer. "Your ideas for the woodworking crafts business are really very good." She thought for a moment. "I think the scale of it all scared me. I'm not ready yet for anything so big, and I may never be."

Gently putting one hand on his chin, she turned his face so that he looked directly into her eyes. "What I really want to do is open a small shop. Let me see how the business progresses before I make any decisions about expanding."

A man could drown in those navy eyes, Dale thought. Fiona truly was beautiful, so much so that he found it difficult to concentrate on what she was saying. With an effort he forced himself to listen.

"I don't care about all those plans," he said, pulling one hand through the silky red hair that lay on his shoulder. "I was so happy to see you walk through that door. That's what I care about."

He pulled her closer. "What I've realized, throughout one very long night and day, is that you're what matters. You're all that matters."

Fiona turned in his arms, her eyes searching his face. She put both hands on his cheeks. "You're all that matters to me, too." Then, with deliberate slowness, she kissed him.

CHAPTER TWELVE

SURE AND STRONG, Ian's voice held the note as he searched the darkness for the one face, the one smile that made the song worthwhile. From his chrome stool in the middle of the stage, it was difficult to see the faces of his audience.

She would be sitting close to the front, he knew, if not in the front row itself. He needed her there, Ian was aware as he shifted on the leather seat, needed her to hear the words he sang for her alone.

Admit it, he told himself. *You need her, period. Pure and simple.* The realization struck hard, almost causing him to lose his balance.

The song, of course, was one he'd known forever, a love song. The French words slipped easily from his tongue, as they always did.

But never before had the words meant so much. Never before had the music struck such a responsive note in his own body. He allowed himself a tiny smile, glad of the darkness that hid all but his face from the audience.

Then he found her. Not that he could see her face that well. There wasn't enough light. But it was Julianne. He could tell by her movements, the shape of her head as she cocked it to catch the almost whispered melody.

He began another song, this one old, an ageless melody of love. His voice deepened, trembling with emotion as the words bridged the short distance to Julianne. He wondered if she knew the song was for her, that all his songs were for her.

Ian's voice filled the small auditorium, which was otherwise completely silent except for the low throbbing of the bass and guitars. Old melodies of Acadia mingled easily with Canadian and American folk songs.

Something magical flowed through the room as he sang, as if the collective yearnings of his listeners had been distilled into melody. Julianne could not take her eyes from his face. Half in shadow, half in light from the single spot, the sharp angles and planes of that face filled her vision, leaving no room for any of the other people around her.

His voice throbbed as he sang a love song, an old ballad with origins in Elizabethan England. Julianne trembled; she saw his eyes reach for her, caressing her as his voice surrounded her, enfolding her in the warmth of the melody.

She'd already heard most of the songs. During the practice session after the burglary the week before, Ian had gone over and over the material, patiently working each one until he was satisfied.

Tonight at the benefit performance, everything seemed different. Now Ian communicated the songs to his audience. Teasing, cajoling, seducing, haunting, he tugged at their emotions, demanding and getting responses from his listeners.

But then, Julianne thought, she was also different, subtly changed from the person she'd been only a week before. Although it hadn't been planned, she'd spent every bit of her spare time since the burglary with Ian. Somewhere during that time she'd changed from simply wanting to be with the man who was singing in the illumination of a single spotlight to needing to be with him.

She leaned farther back in her seat; the memories came back one by one. They'd hiked to Cape Split where they'd

watched the Bay of Fundy tides rush to embrace the land.
She could still hear Ian laughing as he sang an old French
sea chantey to the oncoming waters, could still taste his
kisses in the tangy salt air.

She could still feel his strong arms surrounding her, sheltering her from the wind, holding her close as his mouth
found hers. She could still feel his hands, sure and confi-
dent, exploring, tantalizing. Like his songs, she thought,
forcing her thoughts back to the week's other activities.

They'd visited a fishing village, walking along ancient
wooden piers to view the boats as they came in. Their tired
crews still were friendly enough to wave at the visitors.

One afternoon Ian took her to Windsor, crossing the
modern causeway into the city. They visited the old block-
house, a part of Fort Edward, an early stronghold built for
the defense of western Nova Scotia. Julianne felt an odd
kinship with the uniformed men, dead now for centuries,
who had once guarded the area from the fortress.

The sense of kinship was further heightened by a visit to
the Old Parish Burying Ground. Some of the tombstones
dated to the 1760s, causing Julianne to wonder where Gaston Blanchet was buried.

Probably near a churchyard, she thought as the music
from a lively Scottish reel died away. Maybe during the
weekend she could hunt for it.

Ian's voice changed now, becoming more somber as he
launched into a song about the Acadians. Slowly the sad
story of the Expulsion unfolded, recounting the tragedy of
a dispossessed people.

As Julianne listened, her mind wandered back to the old
Anglican church they'd visited the day before, then to the
Acadian church Ian had taken them to the previous Sun-
day. Something began to nag at her, something about the

Acadian church. She searched her memory, but for a while nothing came to mind.

Then she half remembered something from one of Gaston's letters. Tuning out the music, she concentrated. How did it read?

My heart soars nearly to the very heavens above as, one by one, the stones are placed, building the sanctuary to safeguard my family's heritage.

Had Gaston written about the legacy he'd planned to leave his family? Could those words be the elusive clue to the mystery? Julianne's heart pounded as she thought of the churches she'd visited since her arrival in Nova Scotia. Could the passage refer to one of the churches in the Grand-Pré area? Were any of them standing when Gaston was still alive?

Her thoughts were interrupted when Ian stepped to the edge of the stage. His eyes sought out hers, then he smiled and extended one hand to her.

Mystified, Julianne stood up and walked slowly toward him, drawn by the force of his eyes. He was talking, she thought, even as he took her hand and helped her up the several steps to the stage. Then she realized he was asking her to share a few Cajun folktales with the audience.

Her first impulse was to refuse; a thousand reasons for not joining him onstage went through her mind. Although she loved the ice-pink skirt and sweater she was wearing, the outfit wasn't suitable for a performance. She hadn't rehearsed anything. The audience had come to hear Ian, not a storyteller unknown in Nova Scotia.

Then Ian smiled. His warmth and understanding flowed out to her, ending the stream of questions. Of course she would do it, Julianne decided.

She nodded. Her mind worked frantically to recall some of the stories she knew so well. Then stage fright left her and she recalled one of her favorites, a rollicking tale of an old raccoon hunter and his one-eyed dog.

Slowly, then with mounting confidence, she launched into the story. As she spoke, Ian played softly on his guitar. At the end of the tale, while the audience was still chuckling, he began a charming ditty she remembered from her own studies of Acadian folklore.

The evening went on. They alternated between the spoken tales and songs, delighting their audience with the contrasts. Julianne, listening as Ian mugged his way through a medley of fishing tunes, was surprised how easily they worked together in the impromptu performance.

In turn, as Julianne sketched one last vignette of life in the Louisiana bayous, Ian listened with growing respect for the storyteller. He thought back over the book of Acadian folktales he'd discussed with his agent. It could be an excellent series, he realized, something that would appeal to Acadians and Cajuns alike.

Julianne, with her gift for legends and folktales, would be a wonderful partner. But then, he thought, she would be a wonderful partner in anything.

He was beginning to find it difficult to imagine embarking upon any venture without her. The realization shook him.

She turned to him, her smile mischievous. "It's all yours, maestro."

Ian grinned. "Oh, no. This last one we'll do together."

With no warning, he reached for her hand, gently pulling her to his side as he shifted the guitar into playing position. Then he began the last song, a happy nursery rhyme sung entirely in French.

Julianne couldn't resist the man or the music. She sang along with him, blending her clear soprano with his warm baritone.

Ian looked at her in surprise. She had a beautiful speaking voice. How had he not realized that Julianne was also a natural, talented singer?

They finished and the audience came to its feet, applauding generously. Ian took her hand again and led her to the front of the stage.

"Take a bow," he whispered. "You were wonderful. If you ever need a job as a singer, just let me know."

Julianne glowed. His praise was sincere, she knew; she took another bow.

After the houselights came on, a constant stream of people, most of whom Ian knew, came over to compliment them both on the performance. Julianne felt almost overwhelmed by the enthusiastic response.

"Tonight's performance was wonderful. In fact, we're going to make this benefit for handicapped children an annual event," said a woman whom Ian introduced as director of the university's conference activities.

She turned to Julianne with a gracious smile. "We hope you will be able to come back. We've known for a long time how talented Ian is, but the two of you were something special. I hope this will be a permanent arrangement."

Julianne felt her face flush. *A permanent arrangement?* She managed to mumble something polite as the woman, still beaming, moved away.

With one arm around her shoulders, Ian leaned toward her, his whisper almost drowned by the din around them. "Who knows? After this, record albums, appearances on television talk shows, maybe even Hollywood."

His warm breath tickled her ear, making it hard to concentrate on his words. Julianne turned, to find him grinning at her.

"Talk shows, maybe. But I'll have to check my schedule to see if I can make time for Hollywood," she said with a grin of her own.

"That was outstanding," a familiar male voice said, intruding upon their private conversation. "Simply outstanding from both of you."

Julianne looked up. Professor Godfrey, his face split by a wide smile, stood there, pumping Ian's outstretched hand.

She resisted the urge to smile back. The man wore the same type of rumpled tweeds he wore daily to their seminar. Even his long-outdated tie was askew, as it normally was. The professor turned to her.

"While I was watching you both perform, an idea hit me." He dropped his voice and leaned forward. "Could the two of you work up a presentation on the similarities between Cajuns and Acadians, maybe using some of the music and stories we heard tonight? It would be a real treat, as well as a nice surprise for the other students."

His smile broadened, and his voice returned to normal. "Of course, I would take your efforts into consideration when I add up your grades for the course. Think about it, and let me know what you decide." Still smiling, he moved away into the departing crowd.

"That certainly was a nice offer," Julianne said, when they finally left the auditorium. "Professor Godfrey really seemed impressed."

Ian took her arm in his, and they walked into the clear night. Overhead, the stars seemed unusually brilliant in the summer sky. Buoyed by excitement, Julianne was acutely aware of Ian's nearness.

"He should have been." Ian squeezed her arm. "You added something very special to the performance tonight. I was rather impressed myself."

"Thanks. Coming from you, that means a lot." It did, too, she realized. Without even thinking about it, she slipped one hand into his. The answering pressure on her fingers sent a thrill of pleasure through her whole body.

"I never eat before a performance," he said as they came to the Ferrari. Starlight danced along the midnight depths of the car's shiny exterior.

"So I'm always very hungry afterwards, and tonight is no exception," he continued. "Are you hungry?"

"Starved," Julianne admitted. "I wanted to finish typing the paper that's due tomorrow before the performance tonight, so I skipped dinner. Anyway, Dad was out with Fiona, so there didn't seem to be much point in fixing something just for me."

For a moment she thought about her father and Fiona. Their relationship seemed to be maturing into something very serious indeed. The idea filled her with vague apprehension. What would happen when it was time for the Blanchets to return to South Mississippi?

The thought of Fiona living in her father's house and using Lillian's furniture and other possessions hurt, no matter how much she liked the beautiful wood-carver, no matter how hard she tried to be rational about the situation. Julianne breathed in deeply.

No one had mentioned marriage yet. Maybe she was worrying needlessly.

"It's a little late for a heavy meal," Ian said. "Why don't we stop and pick up something light to eat, then go to the farm?"

Julianne forced herself to put aside worries about her father and Fiona. "That sounds wonderful. How about some of that crusty French bread and maybe some cheese?"

"We can get a bottle of wine from our cellar at the farm. Something deep and rich, like burgundy," Ian suggested.

Sometime later, the Ferrari swung into a long driveway that led to a large home. Although it was night, light from the stars and newly risen moon allowed glimpses of the two-story building, which stood at the top of a small hill. Several huge maples, their branches silvery in the moonlight, dominated the front, while smaller trees shaded two wings that extended on either side.

"Welcome to my home," Ian said, helping Julianne from the car. His voice had a curious note to it, almost one of strain, as if he were nervous about her reaction, she reflected.

"What a lovely house," Julianne said, her sincerity evident in her hushed voice. "It fits right into the setting, as if it's always been here."

"Not always," he said, his tone almost reverent as he surveyed the sprawling structure. "It's about one hundred and fifty years old, according to records we have."

Ian's hand holding hers tightly, they walked up the front pathway to the wide porch. "Did your family build this house? You mentioned it had been in your family for a long time," she said.

"Partially. The man who built it was a farmer, who owned nearly all the land surrounding the hill where the house is situated. He built the two-story portion in the center, then died soon afterward. His wife was from Calgary, so she took her children and went back out west."

Ian produced an ornate key. Moonlight reflected on leaded glass panels in the massive front door as he worked the old-fashioned brass lock.

"My great-great-grandfather, with a few more greats in there somewhere, bought the farm, complete with all the land surrounding it," he said. "Since then, succeeding generations have added to the house. In fact, my parents added this porch we're on now."

Ian opened the door, then waved her in with an exaggerated bow. "After you."

Julianne hesitated, feeling a momentary panic. "But they don't live here, do they?" She remembered him saying his parents lived somewhere else.

"No. My parents turned over the entire operation to me a few years ago. They moved from this house when they retired. They still live on the farm, but in a smaller home my grandfather built. They loved this house, but wanted something smaller and cozier, according to my mother."

He smiled. "It may have been a not so subtle hint from them that it's time for me to start thinking about remarriage and a family."

"Do you ever think about remarrying?" Although Julianne tried to stop herself, she couldn't help asking. Somehow, she knew, his answer was vitally important.

"I didn't for a long time," he replied, his face unreadable in the darkness. "Lately I've thought about it a lot."

Wishing she could see his eyes, Julianne held her breath. Why was he thinking of marriage now? Was she included in his thoughts? What were her own thoughts? she wondered. Her mind spun with possibilities.

Ian pressed a switch, flooding the large foyer with light. "Let's go in. I'm getting hungrier by the second."

Her first impression was of wood, mellowed by age and polished to perfection. Julianne took a few steps forward. It was like stepping back a century.

Oak plank flooring gleamed in the artificial light. A carved oak staircase led upstairs, while more oak framed the doorways that opened onto several different rooms. Carved moldings accented the ten-foot ceilings.

"What lovely oak," she said; her fingers reached out to stroke the shining banister. "Someone must have loved wood an awful lot."

"The man who built the main house was married to a lumber baron's daughter," Ian explained, his pride evident in every word. "Her father personally selected every inch of wood that went into the place. The woodwork is exceptional, as you'll see."

From the foyer they entered a large parlor. "This room is all cherry," he said. "Everything is cherry, from the floor to the ceiling. Even the furniture in here is cherry. Every piece has been in this house since it was built, although the upholstery and drapes were changed from time to time."

Although the room, with its darker wood, could have been gloomy, it wasn't, Julianne decided. Cheerful floral chintz in different patterns upholstered the graceful sofa, love seats and chairs, while pale Oriental carpets covered the floors.

Overhead were skylights that would fill the room with light during the day. Now moonlight shimmered above, casting intriguing shadows throughout the room.

"I forgot to bring in the food from the car," Ian said. "I'll be right back. Go ahead and look around."

As she explored the light-filled rooms, Julianne couldn't shake the sense of going back in time. Each room, filled with antique furniture, had its own personality.

At the end of a wide hall she found a large room that could only be a study. Floor-to-ceiling bookcases lined the walls. A massive mahogany desk faced an entire wall of glass. Although the darkness obscured the view from the windows, Julianne knew it would be spectacular.

Beside the desk were two stands, each holding a covered object. By their shapes she could tell that one was a computer. The other was probably a typewriter.

The room, although filled with books, magazines and papers, was almost obsessively neat. Nothing was out of place.

"This is my study, but I'm sure you've already figured that out."

Julianne turned to see Ian, carrying two large wine-glasses filled with a rich red liquid, enter the room. He handed one glass to her.

Taking a sip of wine, she smiled at him. "I can't believe this is so neat. My office is always cluttered." She shook her head in disbelief. "How can you get anything done with all this neatness?"

Ian laughed. "Annie strikes again, I'm afraid."

She cocked her head. "Annie?"

"My housekeeper. She's about seventy, or at least that's all she'll admit to. Annie's an absolute terror, for all that she's only about five feet tall. She's worked for my family for years, so she listens to nothing I say. I've asked her repeatedly not to touch this study."

His gaze swept the room. "As you can see, she ignores me. I always have to relocate everything after she cleans."

Julianne laughed. She could not imagine anyone bullying the formidable Ian, especially someone only five feet tall.

"You must be awfully fond of her," she said.

"I am. Annie took care of me while I was small. My parents were busy with the farm and Annie loved little boys, so it was a good arrangement."

He walked to the window and looked out at the darkness beyond. "When I worried about ghosts, Annie was always there to soothe me."

"Ghosts? Around here?"

Julianne set her glass on the desk, then joined Ian at the window. She had sensed presences in the house during her exploration a few minutes before, but had decided that her imagination was working overtime.

"Friendly ghosts, I think," he replied. "There aren't any tales of terror or any unhappy ghouls lurking about. My parents felt them, too, usually during times of great happiness. It's as if the former residents come back to share in any joyous occasions."

He glanced at Julianne, then moved away from the window. "You probably think we're imagining things."

"Actually, I don't."

Her expression grew thoughtful as she returned to his desk. Picking up her nearly full wineglass, she swirled its contents gently, watching as the dark liquid picked up stray lamplight.

"Many Cajuns feel very close to their ancestors. Funerals are often a time for reunions, for renewing the ties between family members. Joy and happiness are mixed with our grief for the dead."

"We have much in common, don't we?" His voice was low but intense.

She glanced up, sensing he meant more than Cajuns and Acadians. "Yes, we do," she said quietly, her thoughts concentrated on Ian.

He leaned against a chair, his posture seemingly casual as he studied her. But she felt the coiled tension of his muscles, the hard strength of him, even from where she stood.

The room was absolutely silent as they faced each other. What was he thinking? Julianne wondered. Did he feel the same aching sense of nearness, an attraction as elemental as wind was to rain?

He studied her for a moment, his eyes unreadable. Then, as if he'd won a battle for self-control, Ian turned.

"I believe I promised you dinner."

Julianne tried to relax. For the moment, the super-charged tension between them was gone. But it would return, she knew, and soon. Would she be ready? She tried to suppress a shiver of excitement.

"You certainly did," she answered, hoping her voice didn't betray her inner nervousness.

Moments later they entered the spacious den. Here, unlike the rest of the house, there were no antiques. Instead, overstuffed couches and several wing chairs were scattered about. The effect was one of contemporary comfort.

On one low table Ian placed some small plates, an open bottle of burgundy, several kinds of cheese cut into thick chunks, a few apples, and slices of the crusty bread. Slipping onto the nearest sofa, Julianne took one slice of bread and a chunk of cheese.

"This cheddar smells heavenly," she said, taking a bite. "Tastes heavenly, too."

Leaning against the back of a wing chair, Ian said nothing, simply watching her as she took another sampling of the cheese.

Whether it was the atmosphere of the house, the excitement of the benefit concert, or the intent regard of Ian's fathomless eyes, Julianne suddenly found herself unable to swallow. Carefully setting her plate on the table, she took a tiny sip of wine.

She stood up. Acutely aware of her pounding heart, she faced Ian. "I seem to be unable to eat," she said. "I guess I wasn't hungry, after all."

Unable to move, she simply looked at him. There was nothing left to say.

He moved quickly, closing the distance between them in a single step. Cupping her chin in one hand, he tipped up her head until her eyes met his.

"Perhaps food isn't what you're hungry for."

Her face seemed to burn from his touch. For seconds Julianne could only stare. His eyes were no longer unreadable. Passion burned in their inky depths with an almost frightening intensity. Mixed with the passion was an unasked question.

How could they face the inevitable, the parting at summer's end, with the memories of loving between them? How much harder would it be, how much more agonizing the goodbyes?

But summer's end seemed faraway. This was today. This was now.

If she surrendered to the limitless passion that shone from those eyes, there would be no turning back, she knew. But if she said no, would this time, this moment, ever come again?

Her decision, the answer to his silent question, would be irrevocable. There would be no turning back. But then, she asked herself, was there even any decision to be made?

Without hesitation she touched his cheek. Her fingers trembled as she felt the beard-roughened skin.

"You're right. Food isn't what I'm hungry for."

In answer he leaned forward, touching her lips gently at first, then with increasing pressure. Julianne slipped her arms around him. Even as she did so, his arms came around her. One hand found the small of her back and pulled her close.

He tasted of crimson burgundy, but the rich sweetness was Ian himself. Her heart beat erratically as he teased her mouth open, alternately demanding a response and cajoling her to give one.

She answered eagerly, firmly, and something quivered, then blazed up inside. Her feet threatened to give way, and she leaned heavily against him.

Surprised, he hesitated. Then he reluctantly pulled his mouth away from hers.

"Julianne?" His arms tightened around her, and his hand found her chin again.

How could so much emotion be contained by one word? When had her own name ever sounded so wonderful? she asked herself. Suddenly shy, she gazed at him.

"I...I'm okay." She stopped. Would he understand what she was trying to tell him?

"I've never felt like this before, so intense, like I'm on fire inside. I guess it surprised me."

With one finger he traced a pathway from her forehead to her still-moist lower lip. She felt the pressure on her back increase as his hand pulled her closer.

"Funny," he said, kissing the pathway's starting point. "I always thought," he said, as his mouth came down to the tip of her nose, "you'd be the sort—" he nibbled at her upper lip "—who'd enjoy surprises."

The fire spread to her face, making coherent thinking difficult. "Uh I don't," she managed to say, then his mouth landed on hers again.

His eyebrows came up. "You don't enjoy surprises?"

"Actually—" she stood on tiptoe to reach the tip of his nose with her own mouth "—I love surprises."

His mouth sought hers again, fanning the flames as his fingers pulled through the strands of her hair, then blazed a trail down the downy smoothness of her neck. His lips followed, his breath hot against the bare skin.

Julianne answered back with kisses of her own, opening her mouth to him as he sought out the moist, warm, secret places. She moaned, the sound soft in a room that was silent except for their breathing and the pounding of two hearts.

He was still kissing her, taking what she gave so willingly, when in one fluid motion he scooped her into his arms. Greedy, she kept his mouth on hers, making him walk the entire way to his bedroom with only partial vision.

She felt his muscles tremble around her as he lowered her slowly to the bed and followed her down. His fingers found the tiny pearl buttons at the neck edge of her sweater. He kissed her shoulder as he carefully undid each one.

How warm he was, she thought, as cool air caressed her skin.

How tender, she decided, as he gently removed the sweater and skirt, then the lacy bra and panties.

How handsome, she realized, studying the lean angles of his face. She ran her own fingers through the thick mane of hair, feeling the difference between it and the curly mat on his chest.

Then their bodies came together, soft against hard, smooth against rough, fire into fire. Now she knew that he was essentially male.

"You're lovely," he whispered. With a heart-stopping gentleness his hands found each curve of her body, exploring the feminine secrets she yielded up so willingly. "Such a contrast of dark hair against skin so white."

Touching and teasing, first his fingers, then his mouth feathered the silky surface of each breast. Julianne held her breath, afraid to inhale as the peaks hardened in response. She felt an answering hardness where he lay against her.

Ian played her body with unrestrained passion, a passion tempered by sensitivity as he sang his songs. Now he sang to an audience of only one, she exulted, hugging that thought to herself with what remained of coherent reason.

His lips blazed a new trail, this time down the smoothness of her belly. "And so soft." He found all the sensitive places and then invented some more.

Julianne moaned softly; her body began to ache with longing and need. Wherever he touched she burned with a delicious, slow searing.

Ian burned, too, she thought, running her hands down the surface of his chest and catching her fingers in the curly hairs as she stroked.

Julianne laughed softly, feeling a sweet abandon she'd never known. She nuzzled against him, her nose catching the scents of moss and woodlands intermingled with another, elementally male aroma.

"That hair is like the rest of me," he murmured. "It doesn't want to let you go."

"I'm not going anywhere," she whispered, letting her hands roam his body. "Except here."

Her fingers found the hardness they sought, and he groaned. His breath rasped as she stroked him, her fingers like velvet on the quivering surface of his skin.

In answer, his hands moved to the dark mound that was protected by her legs. With tantalizing slowness he feathered the crisp hair, seeking the softness below. His fingers found the innermost recesses, caressing and stroking until she cried out his name on a moan.

Somewhere deep inside she was still capable of reason. So this was what it felt like to be on fire. Such an exquisite burning, such pleasurable agony. She could hear their mingled breathing now, heavy in the quiet room, and the sound of the mattress moving under their combined weight.

She felt a hand come up beneath her, supporting her. With one arm he shifted her beneath himself. His other arm cradled her, holding her tightly.

"Ian," she whispered. The flames burned now with an urgency, an overwhelming need, while his fingers moved surely along her body.

"I know, darling."

Always beautiful to her ears, his voice deepened, whispering endearments in French and English. His breath warmed her temples as he found the opening he sought.

He entered her, and the last vestige of rational thought fled Julianne's mind. Only sensation remained, sweet and exquisite, searing and scalding.

His name came to her lips again and she moved with him, their bodies matched in an ancient rhythm. Her fingers dug into the muscles of his back, tracing their corded strength as she touched her tongue to his neck.

Salt, her brain recorded somewhere; Ian shuddered. He tasted musky and salty and clean. Her fingers found the beads of perspiration along his forehead. She smoothed them away.

"I've never felt anything like this before," Ian gasped. He hugged her tightly one last time, then gently rolled beside her. He slipped one arm under her shoulders and drew her close.

For a while they were silent, basking in the afterglow. Her body still tingled, Julianne realized, but it was a satisfied tingling. Content, she listened as Ian's rapid breathing finally slowed to its normal rhythm.

"Are you okay?" He kissed her ear, his teeth teasing the tiny lobe.

"I've never been more okay." She fitted against him perfectly, Julianne decided as her thought processes gradually began to function once again. Perhaps they could stay there forever, she thought drowsily, just the two of them in a huge bed in an old ranch house somewhere in Nova Scotia.

"Julianne."

She opened her eyes to find Ian watching her, his hand propped beneath his chin. "I love the way you say my name. It's more of an enfolding."

His finger circled her cheek. "And I love you."

For a heartbeat the world seemed to stop. Ian loved her. The words shimmered between them, almost visible in the darkness.

"I've known for a while now, but onstage tonight I realized every word of love was for you." He stroked her raven curls, pushing the hair away from her face so that he could see her eyes.

"I've been reluctant to say anything," he continued, "because I know how you feel about your home and your commitment to the cultural center."

His lips sought and found her earlobe again. "I can't help but wonder what will come of a long-distance love."

The world revolved on its axis. Julianne felt herself stiffen in his arms. She floundered for words.

"I love you," she said finally.

She saw the joy in onyx eyes as he reached for her, kissing her with unrestrained passion. Finally he released her mouth, but kept both hands on her face.

"Then that's all that matters."

Julianne looked at him, afraid of the radiant happiness she saw in his face. It made what she had to say all the more difficult. She picked her words with care.

"I love you. More than I ever knew I could love anyone." She paused, suddenly aware how true her words were. It made her next statement even harder to make.

"But I don't know if I could handle a long-distance love, as you put it."

She watched the joy fade from his face, but had to continue. There could be no less than absolute truth between them.

"I can't leave South Mississippi." She propped herself on one elbow. Her eyes were riveted to his face as she continued.

"The reasons are so complex. I'm not sure I understand them all myself."

He said nothing.

Julianne inhaled sharply. "There's my father, of course. Losing my mother is still so fresh in his mind. If I move so far away, it will be like losing us both."

His look indicated protest, but she continued. "I know it's not the same, but I still won't be there to do the little things for him. He won't be able to drop in when he's lonely."

She took another deep breath. "And I've worked for years on the Cajun Cultural Center. It's part of my life." She swallowed. "I'm not sure I could leave it, either."

That was what he was asking, she knew. Though his question had been silent, he was asking her to leave her father, her home and everything she'd worked so hard to accomplish.

She touched her fingers to his cheek. His face was rigid; she could feel the taut muscles underneath the skin.

Finally Ian spoke. He knew he was being irrational, but couldn't help himself.

"Joanna couldn't handle leaving her home, either." The words were clipped; he rolled away from her.

Julianne gasped. This wasn't the same. The circumstances were different, completely different. Couldn't he see that?

Before she could say anything, he went on. "I know it's unfair to compare your reasoning to Joanna's, but isn't this desertion, too? Isn't your unwillingness to give up your work in South Mississippi the same?"

"It's not the same at all." She reached for his shoulder, wanting to pull him close, to feel his warmth against her. He didn't move.

She tried again. "It's not just the center. It's my father, too. He needs me."

"Dale seems to be doing fine. If I'm not mistaken, right now all he can think about is one red-haired Fiona Graham."

His words were like a physical blow to Julianne, but he was right. Dale's thoughts were centered entirely on Fiona. Perhaps he didn't need his daughter as much as she thought he did.

She felt a dull throbbing in her head; the words, spoken so harshly in his beautiful baritone, swirled around. With one hand she turned his face toward her.

"I know you feel rejected. It's the last emotion I wanted you to feel. Perhaps we both need time to sort all this out, Ian."

"Perhaps."

His expression softened slightly. "I hadn't thought of rejection. Maybe you're right. Maybe we both need time to think about this."

Julianne sat up, unconscious of the grace with which she moved. Ian held his breath.

"It's late, and we have class tomorrow morning. We probably ought to head back to the inn," she said.

Maybe he would protest, she thought. They could make long, slow, delicious love again and postpone their problems.

But Ian, after searching her face, assented. "You're right. It's late."

The drive back to the inn was silent. Julianne wondered if he would, in his usual fashion, walk her to the door. She was almost surprised when he did.

She turned to go in and he caught her arm. Before she could move, he pulled her close and kissed her, so quickly that she had no time to respond.

"I love you," he said as he released her. "No matter what happens, remember that I love you." He was down the steps before she could reply.

CHAPTER THIRTEEN

"GO AWAY!"

The alarm shrilled again, a rude intrusion upon her restless slumber. Julianne rolled over and touched the reset button with a sleepy movement. A few minutes more, she thought. That was all she needed.

Get up, Julianne, she told herself. This was the third time she'd punched the reset button. It was time to put away her thoughts of the night before. It was time to get ready for a morning at school.

Yet she lingered, reluctant to leave the warmth of her comfortable bed. Her thoughts focused, as they had throughout the restless night, on Ian.

He loved her. She remembered the words in that rich voice, caressing, filling the air around her.

Ian loved her. She loved him. So why, when she should have felt aglow with love, did she feel empty inside?

There were no easy solutions to their dilemma. Ian still bore scars from Joanna's desertion. He'd have to live with those, she knew, but his feelings had to be reckoned with.

He was tied to the land where his family had lived for generations. He was tied by his passionate feelings for his homeland and culture. His roots went deep into the soil of Acadia. She hadn't realized just how deep until the night before.

Yet she had her own strong ties. There was her father, of course. Perhaps Ian was right about Dale's relationship with

Fiona. The signs of a romance between the two were certainly all there.

She had deep feelings, too, especially for what she was trying to accomplish at the Cajun Cultural Center. It was her idea, an idea she'd nurtured through its rough beginnings, through the skepticism of bankers and state officials, through the often rocky fund-raising efforts, and throughout the long search for a competent and dedicated staff.

Her years of hard work were finally paying off. She'd found that competent staff. The center was making great gains. How could she leave it all now?

Sighing, she got out of bed and headed for the shower. The warm water felt good, soothing a body still tired after what should have been a good night's sleep.

How would Ian react when he saw her in class? she wondered. Apprehension nibbled at her as she rubbed off, refusing to leave her alone as she dried her hair, put on her makeup and dressed.

She paused after the last swipe of her hairbrush almost brought order to her unruly curls. Smudges under her eyes revealed her lack of sleep. She sighed again, then left the bedroom.

"Well, hello there, sleepyhead." Dale, just coming out of his own bedroom, greeted her with a kiss.

She nestled against him for a moment, feeling the security of her father's arms. "Good morning, Dad. You're looking awfully chipper today."

He beamed. "Isn't it great? What a grand morning, all sunshine and blue skies. Makes a man want to do wonderful things. Climb mountains, dive into the deepest ocean and all that."

Julianne groaned, then gave him a quick peck on the cheek. "Spare me all this cheerfulness, please. You forget, I haven't eaten breakfast yet."

His eyebrows rose. "I know. I was beginning to wonder if you thought today was Saturday again."

"No," she answered. "I guess I didn't sleep too well last night."

His expression grew thoughtful. "Can I help with anything?"

Tempted by the offer, she hesitated. It would be so easy to tell her father everything, to listen to his usually wise counsel. Dale excelled in problem solving, she knew from experience.

It had been a long time, Julianne thought, since she'd taken her problems to her father. She was used to handling things herself. With a sigh for the bygone days of childhood, she headed for the small refrigerator.

"Thanks, Dad. I guess this is one I'll have to work out for myself." She took out a pitcher of orange juice and poured some into a tall glass.

Then she turned and smiled at her father. "But I love you for asking."

She busied herself getting out a small bowl and plate, then a box of cereal. "So, do you have a busy day planned, or do I even need to ask?"

Still regarding her thoughtfully, Dale sank into an overstuffed chair. "Fiona and I are going to scout some locations for a wood-carving shop she's thinking of opening. I'm supposed to pick her up in a little while."

Hearing the joy in his voice, Julianne looked up from her bowl of raisin-dotted cereal. Now his expression radiated happiness.

For a moment she forgot her problems with Ian. Her father was in love, she realized, absolutely head over heels in love. Why had she not realized it before?

An image formed in her mind, one of Dale, Lillian and herself at a very young age, a picture frozen for all time. She felt a brief, sharp pang for the family they had been. It would all change now, she knew, completely and irrevocably.

But to be fair, Julianne told herself, her father's falling in love with Fiona hadn't begun the change. It was Lillian's death that had altered their little family unit forever.

Now Fiona would fill the terrible void in Dale's life. She pictured Fiona, with her laughing eyes and the hair that seemed to flame with a life all its own.

Fiona, with her innate kindness and generosity of spirit, would be good for Dale. Any doubts Julianne once might have had about the older woman were swept away by the happiness in her father's face. Julianne put down her cereal spoon.

"Dad," she said slowly, "why do I get the distinct impression that I may have a stepmother soon?"

She arched her eyebrows. "Very soon, in fact."

Dale grinned. "Your mother always said you look just like me when you raise your eyebrows."

Avoiding her eyes, he looked at his watch. "I'm going to be late again if I don't hurry."

"I also get the distinct impression that you're avoiding my question."

"If you want a ride to school, you'd better get a move on. It's time to go."

Still avoiding her gaze, Dale stood up, hooking both thumbs into his belt and swaggering toward the door. "This train is about to leave the station."

Julianne laughed. Her father was a master of evasion.

"Okay, Dad," she said. "You win this time. Just let me know in enough time to plan something smashing to wear to the ceremony."

Father and daughter were still chuckling when they went outside. "Don't forget," Julianne said as she got into the car, "we're supposed to visit Thérèse this afternoon. She's looking forward to finally meeting you."

A long black car slid into place beside them. Julianne looked up to see Jean Blanchet waving.

She got out and walked over to Jean. "Hello, Jean."

"I hope I'm not delaying you," the attorney said with a wide smile. "I saw you leaving and thought I'd find out if you were having any success with your treasure hunt."

Julianne shook her head. "Not yet, but we really haven't had much time for exploration."

"Did you hear that our suite in the inn was burglarized last week?" Dale asked.

Shock appeared in Jean's eyes. "A burglary! I can't believe it." He got out of his car.

"A burglary," he repeated, his expression still puzzled. "I can't imagine why anyone would want to rob you. Did the robbers take anything of value?"

"No," Dale said. "Of course, we didn't have much cash, anyway. Whoever tried to rob us did cause a lot of damage to the suite, but Mrs. Hardesty has everything back in order now. There's no sign the place was ever ransacked."

Jean's eyebrows narrowed. "Do you suppose whoever it was could have been after the letters Gaston wrote to Anne? Were any of those taken?"

"Absolutely not," Julianne reassured him. "Thankfully, the letters weren't here at the time. I was having copies made, so we wouldn't have to handle the originals any more than necessary, and I hadn't picked them up yet."

She paused, her eyes thoughtful as they rested on Jean. "Why did you ask about the letters? They're simply correspondence. As far as we can tell, there are no maps or anything like that. The only clues to the treasure, if any exist, are some vague descriptions of land."

"Besides—" her look was questioning now "—I don't think ordinary burglars would have been after the letters. There are only a few people who even know of their existence."

Jean still seemed upset. "That may be, but you still should take care of those letters. Maybe there's more to them than anyone knows yet."

He dropped his voice. "I think I should tell you something else."

Almost reluctantly he continued. "My cousin Marc may be having some financial difficulties at his bank. I don't want to say anything more about that, until I have more to go on."

"I'm sorry," Julianne offered. "Are you sure?" Although she'd had a few misgivings about Marc, she couldn't imagine the banker being stupid enough to embezzle.

"No," Jean said. "Right now I've only got some suspicious circumstances. However, since you visited him, Marc has talked of little else but finding a long-lost fortune."

Julianne couldn't keep the surprise from her voice. "But I told Marc there probably was nothing to those old legends."

Jean shrugged. "Who can say how another person thinks? Marc is sometimes difficult to understand. Anyway, in light of what I've told you, perhaps you would feel better if the letters were put into safekeeping. I have a vault at my office. I'd be happy to store the letters there for you."

"That's kind of you." Pleased by the offer, Julianne smiled at Jean.

"But I'm not convinced that the burglars were after the letters," she continued. "I think I'd rather keep the letters with us. Dad and I can take care of them."

"She's right," Dale added. "Our family's had those letters in our care for many years, and nothing's happened to them yet. I'd feel a lot better having them in our possession."

"Perhaps you're right." Jean smiled. "Please remember I'm here to help you, if you need it."

As the attorney climbed back into his car, Julianne remembered Marc's telephoned warning about his cousin. Strange, she thought, how the cousins mistrusted each other.

She wondered if she should tell Jean about Marc's warning, but something held her back. Anyway, it was too late. The black automobile was already heading down the street.

Perhaps it was just as well, she thought as Dale started their car. There was no need to stir up any more bad blood between the two cousins.

She was still thinking about Marc and Jean when she entered the classroom a few minutes later. Professor Godfrey wasn't there yet, she noted, heading for her desk.

But Ian was, his dark head bent as he read something on his desk. Her heart tripped as she studied his profile, so strong and so loved.

Forcing her feet to take each step, Julianne made her way to the desk and slid into the chair. She felt the seat beneath herself and exhaled slowly.

The soft touch on her arm came as a complete surprise. She looked up to find Ian's eyes on her face, but his expression was unreadable.

"Hi." His whisper was too low for any ears but hers. "I've been waiting to talk to you."

Love swept through her, love tempered by fear of what could happen. She stared at the face she knew so well. Ian, she thought, Ian. His name tumbled over and over in her mind as she leaned forward to listen.

"I love you," he said, enunciating each syllable. "We have problems to work out, but I love you. I need to be with you. All I can think about is you."

"I know," she whispered back. Somewhere in her stomach, the knot of fear dissolved. "I couldn't sleep last night, thinking about you. I love you, too."

For a moment they stared happily at each other. So what if they had problems? she thought, lost in the euphoria of the moment. They were both reasonable, intelligent adults. Surely they could work out solutions that would please them both.

They were still lost in thought when Professor Godfrey entered the classroom. Quickly Julianne found her pen and opened her notebook. It was time to turn her attention to Acadian folklore.

As THE PROFESSOR ended his lecture, Julianne glanced at Ian. As usual, Professor Godfrey had delivered a fascinating talk, but she'd found it difficult to concentrate. For once she was glad that the class was over for the day.

"Dad and I are going to see Thérèse this afternoon," she said over the noise of students gathering papers, books and other paraphernalia. "Why don't you come along?"

"I'd like that," he answered. "Maybe later we'll have a chance to talk."

Julianne had no more time to think about Ian. Dale, grinning with happiness, met them at the doorway to the classroom.

"I'm so glad it's you and not me having to sit through those lectures," Dale said. "I had more than enough college to suit me in my younger days."

Without waiting for a reply, Dale headed for the exit. "The car's right outside. Let's go, before the campus cops decide to ticket me for parking illegally."

A short time later they arrived at Thérèse's elegant home. Julianne rang the doorbell.

Thérèse herself opened the door. "You're exactly on time. I thought punctuality was something revered only by older generations."

Julianne hid her smile. The old lady was going to be in rare form.

After Dale was introduced to Thérèse, they went into the cozy sun porch. "You'll have to help me with tea," Thérèse said with an apologetic look.

"The tray is all ready except for hot water," she continued. "I'm sorry the water isn't ready, but I've had to do it all myself. Miss Roberts went grocery shopping and hasn't come back yet."

"Don't worry about it," Julianne replied. "We'll have it ready in no time at all."

Thérèse and Dale chatted, acquainting themselves while Ian and Julianne found the tea tray in the vast, old-fashioned kitchen. They came back into the sun room to find Dale listening intently to his older relative.

"I didn't understand what the lady at the bank said at all," Thérèse was telling him. "I rang them up earlier to ask about my bank statement. It was for a little savings account I've had there for years."

Ian set the tray on a low table and Thérèse, with increasingly agitated gestures, continued. "So I called the book-keeping department at the bank. Of course, it's the bank where Marc works. My family's dealt there for many years, since the bank first opened its doors, in fact. I used to know everyone there, but all that's changed now."

"Not that they aren't friendly," she said, her tone wistful. "Everyone is always chirping about having a good day or some such nonsense. But I don't know them. The names aren't familiar."

The plaintive statement, coming from a woman of Thérèse's immense dignity, tugged at Julianne's heart. "Did you find someone to help you?" she asked.

"Finally," Thérèse admitted. "But she was wrong."

"She said the statement was correct, but it isn't," she continued with a determined expression. "I know there should be more money in there, a lot more. I haven't made a withdrawal in months."

With surprising agility she stood up and made her way to a corner desk. "Let me show you." She handed several papers to Dale.

Thérèse sank back into her chair and Dale scanned the bank statement. He tried not to show the surprise he felt. Thérèse kept thousands of dollars in what she termed "a little savings account."

The record indicated systematic withdrawals during the three-month period covered by the statement. Dale rapidly calculated the amount withdrawn. About ten thousand, if his addition was correct. He made a mental note to ask Marc which bank officer was responsible for his aunt's accounts.

"There do seem to be a number of withdrawals, Thérèse," he said finally. "If you don't remember making them, maybe you should ask Marc to investigate." Dale handed the statement back to her.

The older woman's expression suddenly closed. "Maybe. I don't know what I'll do. Miss Roberts is supposed to handle this for me. I'll have her look into it when she gets back."

As if on cue, Miss Roberts came into the room. Her normally pale face was flushed, as if she'd been hurrying.

"I'm sorry I'm late," the companion said. "The market was unusually crowded today." She surveyed the room. "May I get more tea for anyone? Or something else to eat? There are some sandwiches in the refrigerator."

"That would be nice." Thérèse handed the bank statement to Miss Roberts.

"When you have a minute, I want you to look this over. There are some discrepancies, I think. Call Marc at the bank and ask him to look into it."

Miss Roberts took the statement. Without looking at the figures, she folded the sheet of paper and put it into her skirt pocket.

"Certainly. I'll do it this afternoon," she said in a soothing voice. "Right now I'll get those sandwiches." She bustled from the room.

"That's better," Thérèse said. Her face relaxed and she turned to Julianne. "Now, my dear, I've thought about something that may interest you."

Thérèse seemed more sure of herself now that Miss Roberts was back, Julianne thought. Perhaps Thérèse had merely forgotten the withdrawals.

She smiled at the older woman. "Have you found a clue to the whereabouts of Gaston's legacy?"

Their hostess chuckled. "Maybe. I've been studying Anne's letters to Gaston again. Oh, I know I've probably read them hundreds of times, but each time I discover something different."

Leaning forward in her chair, she continued, her voice becoming excited as she talked. "After we spoke last time, I became intrigued by the possibility of some sort of family inheritance or treasure. So I reread every single letter, searching for hints."

"Do you think there may be something to the old legends then?" Ian inched forward in his own chair.

"I do," Thérèse replied. "I copied several passages that could be clues." From a pocket she extracted several folded sheets. "I want you to take these and study them."

Her dark eyes glistened with excitement. "Then let me know what you think."

Further conversation about the letters was forestalled by the arrival of the sandwiches. Ian regaled them with funny stories about stage mishaps while they had tea.

Afternoon shadows danced across the sun room; Ian finished yet another story. Thérèse finally held up both hands. "Mercy! My sides are beginning to hurt from laughing."

"You've tired yourself out again." Miss Roberts, looking somewhat like an avenging angel, appeared from nowhere. "It's time for your nap."

Overwhelmed by guilt, Julianne quickly stood up. Thérèse did look tired.

"I'm sorry. We have overstayed our welcome," she said.

"Nonsense," Thérèse snorted. "I haven't had this much fun in a long time. It's not often a woman my age has two such handsome men to keep her company."

"But it's time to go," Ian said. He helped her to her feet, then kissed her on the cheek. "You've been a wonderful audience."

"I know you've got more stories to tell," Thérèse replied. "You'll have to come again soon."

They left the house, then Julianne turned back. Both Thérèse and Miss Roberts stood in the doorway. Miss Roberts glowered at them and closed the door.

"Thérèse didn't want us to leave, did she?" Julianne said to Ian, who'd dropped back to wait for her. "I feel sorry for her."

"I know. Somehow she seemed a little lost this afternoon, like something was bothering her."

"She was awfully worried about that bank statement. I hope Miss Roberts can get it straightened out for her."

"I do, too." Ian took her hand. "I have a show at the Bearded Lion tonight." His eyes found hers. "Can you come?"

She had studying to do, but Julianne didn't hesitate. "I'd love to."

CHAPTER FOURTEEN

"Do you think Thérèse is simply forgetting withdrawals she's made from her account?" Julianne waited for her father to unlock the door that led to their sitting room. At Mrs. Hardesty's insistence, they now locked the door to the suite each time they left.

"I don't know what to think."

Dale opened the door, then took the key from the lock and slipped it into his pocket. "She's very old, over ninety, you said. She might be starting to forget things, although I don't think so. Her mind seems clear enough to me."

Julianne moved about the sitting room, turning on several lights to chase away the early-evening shadows. "I guess it's possible she's being forgetful, but I agree with you. When I'm around her, I get the impression that her mind is still razor-sharp. Mentally she's usually two steps ahead of everyone else."

"I know. That's what bothers me. I wonder what's happened to the money in that account," he said.

Dale's expression reflected his bewilderment. "I suppose Miss Roberts will handle the bank statement," he said. "She seems like a very efficient type."

Julianne laughed. "In a Gothic sort of way, I suppose. You're right, Dad. Miss Roberts will handle it. But I hope Thérèse will let us know if she has any more problems with the bank."

She opened the door to the small refrigerator, then looked back over her shoulder at Dale. "Are you hungry? I think there's some leftover salad in here."

Dale grimaced. "No thanks. I'll get something to eat at the Bearded Lion. Something more substantial than leftover salad."

Taking a small glass bowl from the refrigerator, Julianne found a fork in the silverware drawer, then ambled to the table and sat down. She eyed her father, who was pacing back and forth.

Something was up. It wasn't like Dale to be so agitated. She knew from long experience that the only time he paced was when his mind was in turmoil.

"I'm glad you decided to come tonight," she said. Maybe Ian's performance at the Bearded Lion would distract her father from whatever was bothering him.

Dale reopened the silverware drawer, selected a fork, then came to the table. Disregarding her mock scowl, he stabbed at a chunk of avocado in Julianne's bowl.

"So am I."

He stole another bite of avocado, then stood up. "I think I'll call Fiona. She might like to come along."

His tone was casual on the surface, but Julianne detected the excitement underneath. She said nothing, however, when Dale picked up the receiver and dialed.

She tried not to listen to the conversation, but with the telephone only a few steps away it was difficult not to overhear. His voice trembled with excitement as he talked with Fiona.

Dale was definitely up to something, Julianne decided. She could tell by his pacing, by the way his hands waved as he talked. He seemed almost like a teenager, eager and impatient. But for what?

A grin almost split his face in two; he hung up the telephone. "She's finishing a wood sculpture and can't stop. But she'll meet us at the show."

"That's terrific." Julianne's appetite suddenly faded. She pushed the bowl away, then regarded her father.

"May I ask you a question?"

"What am I up to?"

His grin widened at the look of surprise on her face. "I could see it in those expressive eyes of yours."

Julianne flushed. "I didn't realize I was being so obvious."

"You forget, daughter mine, I've had about twenty-seven years of reading your face." Dale's own expression grew serious, and he returned to the table.

He sank into his chair, unconsciously drumming the table as he talked. "I've come to a decision about something. I've been giving this a great deal of thought."

Trying to ignore the sinking feeling in her stomach, Julianne waited silently. Her father always gave any course of action, major or minor, great thought before pursuing it. She knew his thoroughness had had a lot to do with his success in business.

"I'm going to ask Fiona to marry me."

He looked directly at Julianne, his eyes bright with excitement. "Tonight, after the show."

Julianne tried to keep her face from betraying her inner turmoil. She'd known this was coming, hadn't she?

Of course. So why did she feel as if she'd just been kicked by a mule?

She knew her father was waiting for a reply. His expression was bland, but inside he was probably apprehensive about his only child's reaction.

What is my reaction? Julianne asked herself. Fear—mixed with joy for the happiness her father had found, Julianne decided.

The fear was all too real. Was it too soon after her mother's death? Could Dale, bereft by the loss of his beloved wife, be mistaking loneliness for love?

How would having a stepmother affect her relationship with Dale? The knot in her stomach grew bigger.

There were so many questions, so few answers. Now was not the time for her to work things out, Julianne knew. That would have to come later.

For the moment she could only give him her blessing. She would have to sort out her feelings when her father wasn't sitting there, waiting so expectantly for her reaction.

She reached for his hand. "Dad, I'm so happy for you. I don't know Fiona very well, but I have the feeling I'm going to love her."

Something unreadable crossed Dale's face. Relief, probably.

Now happiness suffused his face; he squeezed her hand. "I know you will. I do."

He stood up. "It's so strange to be falling in love all over again at my age. I almost don't know how to act."

Julianne smiled. "Just keep up whatever it is you've been doing. She can't help but love you back."

"I hope so. I sure hope so."

IAN'S VOICE was unusually rich, full of warmth and promise as it traveled through the crowded room. Looking around in the dim light, Julianne could see the intent faces of the audience.

The women, judging by their expressions, were half in love with the singer. That certainly was understandable, Julianne told herself. He was easy to fall in love with.

It was almost a shock when the houselights came on. Startled, Julianne looked at Dale, who was polishing off the remains of a club sandwich.

"I can't believe the first show is already over. It seems like it just got started," she said.

"I know," Dale agreed. He looked again at his watch, something he'd done constantly since arriving at the Bearded Lion.

"I wonder where Fiona is. Maybe I should go call her. Something may have happened."

"She'll be here soon. Try to relax."

Seeing her father's worried expression, Julianne tried to offer reassurance. "Remember, Dad. Fiona's an artist. She probably got lost in her work."

Ian, shaking hands as he made his way through the audience, appeared at the table. His eyes found Julianne's.

"Hi. Did you enjoy the show?"

Her heart did a tiny flip-flop at the sight of him. His navy turtleneck and slacks accentuated his dark good looks. More than a few female heads turned in his direction.

"It was wonderful," she answered. "I watched the audience. You had everyone spellbound."

Ian studied Julianne's face as she spoke. She was smiling, but the smile didn't quite reach her eyes. What was she worried about?

"Julianne's right," Dale added. "You could have heard a pin drop in here, everyone was so quiet."

"Thanks," Ian replied. "I hope the second show goes as smoothly."

Even Dale seemed distracted this evening, Ian decided. The man's eyes reflected the worry he saw in Julianne's. Looking from father to daughter, he wondered if there was a problem between the two.

But there was no time for further speculation. Glancing across the room, Ian saw Fiona enter. Masses of hair floated around her, creating a flaming aureole of reddish gold. She surveyed the crowd, obviously searching for someone.

Catching sight of them, Fiona waved, then began to make her way to their table. Nearly every male head turned, Ian noted.

The woman was stunning, he acknowledged. Tonight she wore a skirt and sweater of sea-foam silk that rippled around her slender legs as she navigated the room. Her smile, the kind that could melt icebergs, flashed as she neared.

Fiona reached their table and bent her shining head to kiss Dale. The older man's face lighted at her greeting.

As he watched, Ian saw Julianne grow stiff. *So that's it,* he thought. *Dale is in love with Fiona. And Julianne isn't sure how to handle it.*

Ian chatted with them for a few moments more, then gave Julianne a quick kiss on the cheek. "It's all going to work out," he said so quietly that she almost didn't catch his words. "Don't worry."

Startled by his understanding, Julianne touched his arm. Her eyes shone with gratitude. "Thanks."

Then he was gone.

A few songs into the second show, Julianne became aware that the atmosphere in the room had changed. If possible, the audience was even quieter than before as Ian almost whispered into the lone microphone.

Soft words enfolded the audience like velvet warmed by sunlight. As the French words penetrated her consciousness, Julianne realized he was singing a love song, reaching out to her with his incredible voice.

That voice mirrored his character, she thought. The man exuded passion and mystery. Caught by the spell of words and music, she couldn't look away.

Finally the song ended. It was nearly a minute before the audience responded with enthusiastic clapping.

Onstage, Ian winked at Julianne, then grinned. He launched into a varied medley of western songs, music from the American West and the plains of Western Canada. Now the audience was cheering and clapping, even singing along as he took them all on a musical journey.

Then he slowed the pace again. His voice took on a poignant quality as he sang of love in Appalachia, then Acadia. Julianne felt herself relaxing.

Soothed by Ian's voice, her mind began to wander. She glanced at Fiona and Dale, who sat close together, obviously only half listening to Ian. They looked like any happy couple in love, she thought.

Dale used to gaze at her mother that way, Julianne recalled. But Lillian was different from Fiona.

Her mother had been a traditional wife and mother, content to be a homemaker. Fiona, she knew, would never fit into such a traditional category. She wondered if Fiona even knew how to cook.

Julianne grinned to herself. Probably not, and she probably didn't do housework either, but Dale wouldn't care. He would simply hire a housekeeper.

No, Fiona would always be full of surprises. What kind of home would Dale and Fiona have, she asked herself, if they did indeed marry?

She was still imagining their unconventional household when the houselights came on. The show was over, and applause erupted all around her.

Without warning, Fiona reached across the table to touch Julianne's arm, smiling as she did so. The smile seemed to promise understanding.

Startled, Julianne could feel the empathy coming from the older woman, as if Fiona understood the thoughts that were troubling her. Grateful for the gesture, Julianne smiled back.

The room quietened quickly. A few people lingered, still dawdling over late dinners, but most of the audience slowly left.

"Are you sure you won't need the car?" Dale asked his daughter. "Fiona has hers here, so we could take it." He smiled happily at Fiona, who returned it with a dazzling smile of her own.

Shaking her head, Julianne waved them on. "No. Ian is going to bring me home. You two go on. I'll see you later, Dad."

They were anxious to get away, she knew. Especially her father; he was, she observed, nearly dancing with excitement. Fiona had evidently caught his mood. Her navy eyes shone with emotion.

Her thoughts still centered on Dale and Fiona, Julianne waited for Ian and the members of his group to put away their instruments. It was a long time before Ian came over to where she sat.

"Thanks for staying," he said, gently pulling her to her feet with both hands. "Let's go to the farm. I've got a bottle of wine."

Julianne needed no urging, though during the drive she stayed quiet, lost in her own thoughts.

Ian, respecting her need for silence, concentrated on his driving. And after pouring out so much of himself during the night's two performances, he was grateful for the interlude, he told himself.

Once inside the farmhouse, he poured two glasses of wine, then led the way into the den. Julianne sank onto the comfortable sofa. Ian curled up beside her.

He touched the wineglass to his mouth, then set it on the table. With gentle fingers he turned her head so that she faced him.

"Would you like to talk about what's bothering you?"

Julianne wasn't sure. Normally a very private person, she had difficulty in confiding her problems to anyone, although as a youngster she had gone to her parents.

Now her mother was gone and her father was part of the problem.

But this was Ian. She trusted him.

Slowly she told him about Fiona and Dale. Then she related her own ambivalent feelings.

Aware that Julianne needed to talk the situation through, Ian listened without interrupting. From time to time he gave her an encouraging smile.

Finally Julianne sighed. "I guess the hardest part is wanting so much for my father and Fiona to be happy together, and trying to reconcile that desire with the difficulty I'm having accepting Fiona—or anyone really—as a replacement for my mother."

She looked up at him with liquid eyes. "Do you understand what I'm saying?"

Wordlessly he took her in his arms. For a moment he simply held her.

"Didn't you tell me once that one of the reasons you wanted to come to Nova Scotia was to shake Dale out of his rut? He was moping about the house, with little interest in anything anymore?"

"That's right," Julianne agreed. "He didn't want to do anything but brood."

"Well," he said as he stroked her hair, "maybe having Dale fall in love with Fiona, or anyone else for that matter, wasn't what you had in mind. But love," he said, pulling her even closer, "isn't something anyone ever plans. It simply happens."

Julianne listened, letting his words penetrate the fog of hurt feelings. Ian was right, she knew. He was very right. No one ever chose the time or place for real love. It simply happened.

"Love is never the same," he continued. "Somehow it always depends on the people involved. Although it is love, if what you're telling me is correct, Dale's feelings for Fiona have nothing to do with how he felt about your mother."

"I know. I kept telling myself that. Hearing it from you helps a lot."

"Have you talked with Dale or Fiona about your feelings?" he asked. "They may be anxious about you. I'm sure your father can sense your distress."

"No," she admitted. "I probably should talk to Dad. He's usually very understanding. I think I've been too wrapped up in my own feelings to think about theirs."

Ian took another sip of wine. "If Dale and Fiona do end up getting married, where do you think they'll live?"

Julianne sat up, startled by the question. "Where will they live?" she repeated as if the question made no sense at all. "They'll live in Ocean Springs, of course."

"Are you sure about that? What if Fiona wants to stay here?"

His quiet words exploded into the silent room. Julianne stared at Ian.

It had never occurred to her that her father would ever live anywhere but Ocean Springs, Mississippi. It was his home, as it had been home to generations of Blanchets be-

fore him. He loved the little city situated between huge bayous and the Gulf of Mexico. He would never leave.

Or would he? Deep down, a tiny seed of doubt took root.

Julianne had always assumed that Dale would never leave
Ocean Springs. Indeed, she'd never even considered the
possibility of her father moving somewhere else. Now she
realized for the first time that her assumption could be
wrong.

"I've never really thought about it before. It's difficult for
me to imagine Dad leaving South Mississippi, but I suppose he might."

Gently turning Julianne so that her back touched his
chest, Ian's strong hands massaged her rigid shoulders. "I
wonder," he said, so softly that she almost missed the
words, "I wonder if, for love, Dale could give up his home
if Fiona wants to stay in Canada. Or if Fiona could leave her
home here to go with the man she loves?"

Was Ian asking her, or were his questions directed to
himself? With her back to him, Julianne couldn't see his
eyes. She turned to face him.

"You aren't really asking about Dad and Fiona, are
you?"

She caught the surprise in his eyes and probed relent-
lessly. "You're thinking about us," she continued. "How
will we work out our own situation?"

"I guess I am," he admitted. "I've been thinking a lot
about what will happen when this summer is over. I'm not
sure I really want to know."

"I don't know what will happen either," she said slowly.
"I've been thinking about it, too."

Her knuckles whitened as she gripped her wineglass. "I
can't help my own feelings. I don't know what's going to
happen with Dad and Fiona, but I can't move away from
him as long as he needs me nearby."

She swallowed, forcing herself to continue, although she knew her words could signal the end of their relationship. "And there's the cultural center. It's almost part of me. It was my dream, and I made it become reality."

"Not by myself, of course," she added. "I had a great deal of help. But it was my vision, my commitment. The center is part of me. Now that it is finally successful and achieving results, I can't leave it to someone else."

She stopped suddenly, searching his face for the understanding she hoped would be there—but found only the taut angles of his almost perfect profile.

"I guess I could say I don't understand how you feel," he said at last. "But that wouldn't be true. Your feelings are very much like mine."

"Acadia is part of me," he continued. "It's the air I breathe, the music of my soul. Each time I leave, even for a little while, I feel the tug of this land and the people who live here."

His voice vibrated with the intensity of his feelings. Julianne couldn't resist putting her hand on his as he continued. His fingers tightened around hers.

"My family has owned this farm for generations now. I was born in this house," he told her. "My father was born here, and his father before him."

He paused, as if organizing his thoughts. "We've never been absentee farmers. This farm is a legacy I want to pass along to my own children."

Something sharp tore at Julianne; she thought of Ian's children. They'd be beautiful as their father was, she knew. Dark-eyed and dark-haired, they'd probably have wonderful singing voices and minds alive with creativity.

As if he sensed her thoughts, Ian turned the full force of his gaze upon her. Passion leaped in his eyes and he pulled her close.

His kiss caught her by surprise, but she responded immediately. It was gentle at first, as if he wanted to comfort her, but slowly fire ignited between them.

Their lips parted and Julianne caught her breath. She felt the need and desire emanating from the powerful body so close to hers, a need and desire echoed by her own aching being.

Without a word she moved back into Ian's arms, wrapping her own around his neck. His dark head came forward to kiss her again. It was tempting to let her own control go, to give in to the desire that was raging through her like fire through a drought-ravaged woodland.

She loved him and he returned that love. Love should have been all that mattered.

But this wasn't the time. Gently she pulled away from his searching mouth. There were still problems between them, problems that would still be there long after passion's fires had died away.

He held her for a few moments more, reluctant to let her slip away. "I know," he said finally. "We've reached an impasse."

Julianne put her fingers to his lips. "I don't want the summer to end with each of us going our separate ways. There has to be a way to work this out."

He kissed each finger one by one. "There will be. There has to be."

For what seemed like hours they simply looked at each other, wordlessly conveying their fears of what might happen. The magic was gone from the night. With a heavy heart, Julianne forced herself to get up from the couch. She knew it would be a long ride back to the inn.

DALE'S FINGERS CURLED around Fiona's delicate hand. "I love the feel of your fingers," he said. "They're so long and so expressive."

Sounds in the busy restaurant seemed to fade as he looked at her, first at the hand returning his gentle pressure, then at her face. Even in the dim candlelight, her beauty tore at his heart.

"Coffee, sir?"

Startled by the interruption, Dale looked up. The young waiter addressed his question to Dale, but his eyes were riveted on Fiona.

"Fiona?" Dale kept his hold on her hand. "Would you like some coffee?"

"I'd love some." She flashed a wide smile at the waiter. "Black, please."

Dale grinned as the youngster hurried away. "That smile of yours probably made the poor kid's knees buckle. It's a wonder he can still walk."

"Thanks for the compliment." She regarded him thoughtfully. "Didn't you like the food here?"

He looked down at his plate. The remains of his dinner seemed to reproach him.

"It was excellent. This was a great choice of restaurants, actually." He fidgeted in his chair.

"I'm too excited to eat," he said finally. "I feel like that poor young waiter when I look at you."

Her graceful brows came up. "Dale, what is it?"

"I was going to wait until later, when we were alone. But I can't wait one second longer. I love you."

Dale's face lighted up with emotion. "There. I've said it. I love you. Absolutely and totally."

He pushed away the plate and reached for her other hand. "You've brought me happiness and joy I never thought to have again. I want to spend the rest of my life with you, if you'll have me.''

Unable to contain himself, he leaned over and gave her a brief kiss. "Please say yes."

Fiona sat absolutely still for a moment, as if stunned. Then, with Dale watching anxiously for her reaction, she smiled. Her eyes sparkled with happiness.

"I love you," she said finally. Her already low voice dropped to a whisper. "It's been a complete surprise for me, too. I never expected to fall in love again."

Dale beamed. He felt for the ring in his suit coat pocket. In his excitement he'd forgotten all about it. He'd hunted for days to find exactly the right combination of sapphires and diamonds.

Sapphires to match those unmatchable eyes, he'd thought when he finally found the antique ring. It would be a fabulous engagement ring for Fiona.

"I want to live with you, too," Fiona continued. "I was going to suggest it tonight, anyway. Why don't we get your things after dinner? You can move in tonight. I'm sure Julianne won't mind."

The ring box dropped back into his pocket and Dale stared at her. The smile disappeared from his face.

"What did you say?" he stammered. Surely he hadn't heard her correctly.

"I said you can move in tonight," she repeated, still smiling. "Julianne's a very modern young woman, if that's what you're worried about."

With eyes alight with love, she gazed at him. "I'm sure she won't give it a second thought."

"Well, Julianne might not give it a second thought, but her father certainly will." Unaware that his voice was rising, Dale went on. "Move in? Without getting married first?" Dale was shocked to his traditional core. His voice trembled. "I can't believe I heard you even suggest such a thing."

"Shh." Fiona bristled. "Lower your voice. People around us can hear you."

"Then they should mind their own business," he said. His words were loud enough to be heard across the room. He glowered at several eavesdroppers, then turned his attention back to Fiona.

"I have no intention of moving in with you, Fiona Graham, unless there's a marriage ceremony first." The words came out crisp with anger.

"I can't believe I'm hearing this." Fiona, her eyes now roiling pools of navy, threw her napkin onto the table just as the waiter returned with their coffee. Then she stood up.

"I never said anything about marriage. Not one word. If you really loved me," she declared, "you'd move in without a second's hesitation."

Without skipping a beat, she turned to the hapless waiter, who blushed to the tips of his ears. "I won't be needing that coffee after all," she snapped.

The young man gaped at her. Red-gold hair flew around her head as Fiona, her head held impossibly high, stalked from the restaurant.

Speechless with surprise and shock and frozen to his seat, Dale watched her leave.

CHAPTER FIFTEEN

THE COMPUTER PRINTER suddenly went silent. Ian pulled the last pages from the tractor feed, then gathered up the stack of manuscript pages.

Adjusting the miniblinds to block out most of the strong afternoon sun, he sank into his desk chair and began to read. His fingers played with the rim of an old coffee cup as he scanned the pages.

The tales of Acadia seemed to come alive on the crisp sheets. Ian finished the entire stack, then sat back to let the words jell.

Even to his critical eye the work was excellent, some of the best he'd ever done. Without a doubt, the summer school course was good for him.

He took a swallow of coffee, then scowled at the cup. The stuff was too strong and already cold. He half rose from his chair, then slid down again.

The scowl reappeared. He'd had too much coffee already.

Yes, the university course was good for him, except that he saw Julianne every morning. Every morning he had to pretend nothing was wrong, when everything was. Oh, he was good at it, very good, Ian thought grimly. But every day it was getting harder to keep up the pretense.

She was friendly, but in rare, unguarded moments he could see the hurt in her eyes, the bewilderment that wouldn't go away. Most of the time her head stayed bent over her notebook. Her long, black curls always shielded her face, hiding her thoughts from him.

He glanced at the calendar. Friday. It was Friday again. How many days had it been since he'd last held her? How many hours?

"Stop it," he said to no one but himself.

He stood up and ripped the page from the calendar with one swift movement. He wanted no more reminders of the passing days.

Over and over again he told himself that he was doing the right thing by not calling her, by keeping away from the one person he most wanted to see. He knew they couldn't go on seeing each other, tormenting themselves with a love that wasn't meant to be.

Just seeing her every weekday in class was too difficult, thinking of her when he should be listening to Professor Godfrey, aching with need and longing every time she was near. He'd thought several times of dropping the class, but couldn't quite bring himself to do it.

No, dropping the class was the last thing he needed to do. He wanted to continue learning about Acadian folklore. It was good for his writing. The manuscript on his desk bore mute testimony to that.

Admit it, Ian told himself. The real reason, the important reason why he couldn't drop the seminar was Julianne. If he didn't go to class every day, then he wouldn't see her.

Love was so complex, he thought. He loved Julianne and she loved him. Yet they couldn't be together. And that was what he wanted. More than anything he wanted to be with Julianne.

What was it he'd told her during their last evening together? The words that he'd used to reassure her mocked him, tore at him.

"Love is never the same," he'd said. "It always depends on the people involved." Now the words simply echoed in his mind. An image of Joanna slipped unbidden into his mind, Joanna, with her tiger's mane of hair and her brittle laugh. It was still incredible that he'd ever been married to her. They'd had so little in common.

He would never have given up his home in Acadia for Joanna; Ian knew that now. The thought jolted him, filling him with sadness. It was yet another measure of how little he'd loved the woman who once had been his wife.

Julianne was different. He loved her with a love that went to his very core, far deeper than anything he'd ever felt for Joanna.

Would he be willing to give up his home, the family farm, for Julianne? Could he leave the legacy of generations of Rosses for love? The questions hit hard.

These were questions he'd never asked himself before. There were also questions, he knew, for which he had no answers—at least not yet.

The telephone interrupted his reflections. Ian hesitated. He was expecting the call, but was reluctant to give up dreaming of Julianne.

The telephone shrilled again. Ian sighed. He couldn't spend the entire day—or the rest of his life—in indecision. He picked up the receiver.

"Ian?"

Ian recognized his agent's gruff voice. "Hi. Thanks for returning my call."

"I hope this is good news."

The pause at the other end was significant, Ian thought, a true waiting pause. Without Julianne, he found it difficult to classify any news as good, but the manuscript seemed excellent and he was excited about it.

"It is," he said finally, then smiled. Despite the miles between Acadia and New York, he could almost feel Jock rubbing his hands together.

"I HAVE ANOTHER IDEA about those letters Gaston wrote to Anne," Thérèse said. Her voice quavered.

"Can you come over about four o'clock today? I'd like to talk with you about my idea and we could have tea."

"I'd love to." Julianne hung up the phone, then stood up, uncurling her legs from their cramped position. One foot was asleep, she realized. Thérèse had been unusually long-winded during their telephone conversation.

It was nice to have something to look forward to, she thought as she stretched, then walked to the window. There'd certainly been precious little of late.

She checked her watch. It was a few minutes after three. There was still time to finish the day's classroom assignment.

But she lingered at the window, looking at the garden below. What was Ian doing? she wondered. Was he looking out at the same brilliant afternoon sky, thinking about her as she was about him?

Probably not, she admitted; the thought hurt. Ian was a busy man. Writing, singing and farming kept him going all the time. He probably could not spare precious minutes to stare out a window.

She forced her thoughts back to Thérèse. What "idea" did Thérèse have? she asked herself. Perhaps she was thinking that they were wrong about the churches.

From the hints supplied by Gaston in his letters to Anne, both Julianne and Thérèse had thought that Gaston's treasure might have been hidden in one of Acadia's stone churches. To fill the empty days she'd had lately, Julianne had explored the churches in the area.

Her search had turned up nothing. Of course, the church at Grand-Pré wasn't original; it was a replica of the building Gaston had worshiped in. And the few other churches had all been built too late, she finally realized.

One hand smoothed the heavy lace curtain. There probably was no family treasure, anyway. Whatever Gaston had so carefully preserved for Anne had probably been found—or lost—years ago.

She moved away from the window, still lost in thought. Then there was Thérèse. Her strange behavior of late was also discouraging.

The elderly woman really was convinced that someone was stealing her money. She rambled constantly about discrepancies in bank balances, missing stock certificates, misplaced bonds and other mysterious disappearances.

To allay Thérèse's fears as well as to quell her own worries about the alleged disappearances, Julianne had a long and private talk with Miss Roberts. She could still recall their conversation in detail. The companion reassured her with quiet efficiency.

"Nothing is missing," Miss Roberts said with certainty. "I checked with the savings department at her bank. Mrs. Blanchet withdrew that money herself to buy stock certificates. Mrs Blanchet," said her companion with a sad shake of her head, "is having difficulty remembering things. Her behavior is becoming increasingly erratic." Miss Roberts's voice dropped to a whisper. "I don't know how to say this. I wonder if Mrs. Blanchet is ill or even—" her eyes widened in horror "—senile."

Julianne did her best to reassure Miss Roberts. "I haven't noticed any such lapses," she said. "To me, Thérèse seems as mentally alert as ever."

Privately though, Julianne wondered if Miss Roberts's speculations were not, after all, well-founded. The companion was with Thérèse all day long, whereas Julianne saw the elderly woman only infrequently.

Despite Miss Roberts's assurances that all was in order, Julianne still worried about Thérèse's allegations. Were there gaps in the accounts? How could the companion be certain that Thérèse was buying stock certificates with the missing funds? Miss Roberts was a devoted companion, but the woman might not have any head for business.

Julianne understood that Marc Blanchet was responsible for his aunt's accounts at the bank. During her last few conversations with Thérèse, Julianne had found herself plagued by an unwelcome but growing suspicion.

What if Marc was embezzling Thérèse's funds? As a highly placed bank officer, it probably would be very easy for him to fool Miss Roberts.

Something clicked in her mind. Jean had warned her about his cousin, she remembered. Didn't he say Marc was under suspicion at the bank?

Horrified by the direction her thoughts were taking, Julianne came back to her desk. What should she do? She certainly didn't want to worry Miss Roberts. Despite her Gothic appearance, the woman was a faithful companion. She certainly had enough to do, taking care of an increasingly querulous Thérèse without entertaining suspicions of embezzlement by one of the old lady's own nephews.

No, she couldn't bother Miss Roberts. Of course, she couldn't say anything to Marc, either.

She could tell her father, but Dale had his own problems. He said little about his relationship with Fiona, but Julianne had pieced together what had happened from remarks he'd dropped here and there.

Her father was in love with Fiona, passionately so. Fiona was in love with Dale. But they were both too stubborn to work out their problems about marriage. Much too stubborn.

A sigh escaped her. The situation was much like her own, in fact. Neither Dale nor Fiona would compromise—and neither could she and Ian.

Ian's image formed in her mind. The now familiar sense of loss cut through her again.

Ian. She could see him spotlighted onstage. His voice surrounded her, pulling her into its magic.

But there was no voice, no Ian singing on a stage. There was only loss.

She came to her feet. Ian would help with Thérèse. He cared very much for his old childhood friend.

It would also, she had to admit, be a good reason to see him again outside the classroom. Maybe they could talk their own problem out again.

Before she could change her mind, Julianne dialed his number. The line was busy.

She tried again. Only after several more attempts did she give up.

As she replaced the receiver, her hand brushed against one stack of letters that was still sitting on the desk. The copies of the correspondence between Anne and Gaston had been weighing heavily on her mind lately. She picked up the stack, thumbing through it once again.

Several phrases caught her eye as she settled down to read. Maybe if she read the letters one more time, Julianne thought, another clue about the treasure would emerge. Now that she had copies not only of the letters Gaston had written to Anne, but also of those that Anne had written in reply, maybe some previously hidden fact would reveal itself.

But as she read the letters, filled with unselfish love and longing, with the tiny details the lovers knew were important to no one but each other, Julianne became aware that she faced a dilemma similar to the one that had separated Anne and Gaston so many years before. At summer's end, she and Ian would go their separate ways.

I weep for the many months lost, these long days and nights of separation from you, my beloved Gaston. I cannot help my feelings of despair. We are helpless in this cruel world, caught in a perilous situation not of our making. And yet my love for you remains strong. If I close my eyes I can see you still, laughing at the raindrops, which came so suddenly that day near the ocean. Your son sometimes laughs the same way, lifting his face to the sky so the sound travels up. Ah, I miss you so.

Poor Anne and Gaston, Julianne thought. *Poor Julianne and Ian.*

She loved Ian, but they were being forced apart by circumstances, as Gaston and Anne had been. The circumstances were not the same, however. They were not the same at all.

Her ancestors, practically torn from each other's arms by a political situation which neither could control, had no choice but to acquiesce in their separation. She and Ian, on the other hand, were *making* the decision to be apart from each other.

The realization stunned her. She shifted uncomfortably in her chair as questions tumbled through her mind. How could they choose to be apart? If they loved each other, then they could find a way to solve their problems.

The door slammed and she jumped. Her thoughts scattered as Dale entered, his face a study in frustration.

Under one arm he carried his wood-carving tackle box, while a cloth-covered object rested in his free hand. He caught sight of his daughter and smiled briefly.

"Sorry. I didn't mean to close the door that loudly. Both hands were full, so I was trying to do it with my foot. Guess I pushed too hard."

Setting the tackle box on the table, he proceeded to unwrap the object he'd brought. A half-finished owl emerged.

"I like the owl," Julianne said. "What kind is it?"

"A terrible one. I've been working on it for a week now, but the carving is going badly."

He set the bird beside the tackle box, then sighed. The sound seemed too loud in the quiet room.

"I guess I can't take my mind off Fiona." He slumped into a chair.

Julianne knew how he felt. "Have you seen her lately?" She kept her tone neutral, knowing her father wouldn't want her sympathy.

"No." His chin stiffened and he sat up. "No, and that's part of the problem. We won't solve anything if we don't talk about it."

Dale got to his feet and checked his watch.

"Fiona is supposed to be giving a wood-carving demonstration right now at the university. I'm going to go right over and talk with her." He strode toward the door.

"Dad, wait." Julianne remembered her tea date. "I'm supposed to go to Thérèse's house at four."

She looked at her watch. "I've still got thirty minutes before I have to be there."

"That's okay," Dale replied. "I'm not going to take the car. I want to walk, so I'll have time to organize my thoughts before I see Fiona."

Julianne grinned. That was typical of her father. Mr. Organization, she'd called him often enough.

"Poor Fiona," she said. "The woman doesn't stand a chance against all those brains—and Cajun charm, too."

Dale rolled his eyes, then grinned back. "Let's hope you're right."

After Dale left, Julianne picked up the letter she'd been studying. There was still time to read more of the Blanchet correspondence.

She sorted the copies, hunting for the last one Gaston had written to Anne. As she scanned the old-fashioned script, one phrase repeated itself in her mind.

"Rocks soaring to heaven," Gaston had written. Was there a clue in those words? Julianne pressed a hand to her temples.

She stood up suddenly. Because of the references to rock, she'd been thinking all this time of churches. But what if Gaston wasn't referring to churches at all?

Julianne felt excitement rise within her. Like the wood that the Cajuns would use later to build their cabins along the banks of steamy rivers and bayous, rock was a cheap and plentiful building material in Nova Scotia.

The Acadian settlers had constructed most of their buildings from rock, she knew, even their farmhouses.

Farmhouses. Gaston had built a farmhouse, a structure now owned by Thérèse Blanchet. Although the old building had deteriorated, perhaps there was still a clue to be found there.

Julianne tried with little success to control her growing excitement. This probably was yet another blind alley.

Still, she thought as she folded the copy of Gaston's last letter and put it into her pocket, there might be something in her idea. She started for the door, then paused.

Perhaps she should try Ian one more time. Fingers trembling, she dialed his number.

This time the phone rang. Once. Twice. She felt her pulse race as Ian's fluid voice answered the summons.

"Hi. This is Julianne."

She stopped, feeling foolish. Of course he knew who it was. There was an answering pause at the other end.

"Hello," he said finally. "I didn't expect to hear from you."

Ignoring the pain his words caused, Julianne swallowed. "I need your help. I'm very worried about Thérèse. I know how much you care about her, and I thought you would want to know what was happening."

"Thérèse? What's wrong? Is she ill?"

Hearing the concern in Ian's voice, Julianne relaxed. She'd done the right thing in calling him. "No, she's not sick, at least I don't think so."

Quickly she told him about the continuing disappearances of money from Thérèse's accounts, then about her conversation with Miss Roberts. With some hesitation, she also told him about her suspicions of Marc Blanchet.

Ian listened until she finished. "I think you're right. Something is wrong."

He paused. "Something about all this is bothering me, but I can't figure out what it is. Something is eluding me."

He thought for a minute more. "I think we need to take immediate action. Go ahead and keep your tea date with Thérèse this afternoon. In the meantime I'll call Jean and Marc to arrange a meeting, this afternoon if possible."

"Is that wise? Wouldn't you be alerting Marc?" she cautioned. "We don't have any proof that he's actually embezzling."

"No, we don't," Ian agreed. "But Jean evidently knows his cousin pretty well."

He hesitated, then said, "I'll talk to him first. I think Marc would have a tough time withstanding both his cousin and me if we confront him."

For the first time, fear nibbled at the edges of her consciousness. "Please be careful." Julianne was glad he couldn't see her trembling hands.

Hearing the concern in her voice, Ian felt something unwanted melt inside him.

"I'm glad you called," he said slowly. "Once we get to the bottom of this mystery with Thérèse, we have some problems of our own to solve."

Joy poured through her. "I'd like that." Julianne's heart was still pounding as she hung up the telephone.

CHAPTER SIXTEEN

RED-GOLD HAIR tumbled into the wood-carver's face as she worked, oblivious to the small crowd gathered around her table. The wooden owl in her slender hands took shape rapidly as her deft fingers worked their magic with chisel and carver.

The curtain of hair blocked her view from the left, so at first he couldn't see the newcomer, he realized as he gently pushed his way to the front of the assembled onlookers, murmuring apologies as he went.

Still unnoticed by Fiona, he stopped directly in front of the worktable to watch her hands. His pulse raced. Her fingers fairly flew as she carved one outstretched wing.

He loved her, Dale realized once more. He loved her too much to be separated by anything, even by the absence of marriage vows.

The tip of her tongue was caught between her teeth as Fiona turned the bird over. Feeling like a love-struck school-boy, Dale marveled. How could anyone be so incredibly beautiful?

His gaze traveled back to her hands. With a start, he realized that the bird she was working on was an owl.

Thinking of his own unfinished owl on the table back at the inn, he smiled slowly. No matter what their differences were, he told himself, they were tuned into the same wavelength. They belonged together.

Still unaware of his scrutiny, Fiona worked on, pointing out several variations of the carving technique she was using. Chips of walnut fell rapidly.

Dale cleared his throat. It was time.

"Excuse me, ma'am," he said. "I don't think you're doing that wing correctly."

Hair flew around her face as Fiona's head snapped up from the owl. For a moment, joy suffused her face. Then she scowled, though the expression didn't reach her eyes.

Slapping her carving knife onto the table, she stood up and handed him the owl. "If you think you can do better, you're welcome to try."

Dale grinned. "Gladly."

He took the bird from Fiona's outstretched hand, and their fingers touched. She stared at him with wide navy eyes, then gave him an answering smile.

Everything would be perfect again, Dale knew, as perfect as the little owl he held in one hand.

THÉRÈSE OPENED THE HEAVY DOOR herself. "Oh, thank heavens you're here," she said, plucking at Julianne with nervous fingers.

"Miss Roberts is gone," Thérèse said, her voice quivering. "She said she had several errands to run, but she's not back yet. I can't imagine why she's taking so long, when she knew you were coming this afternoon. She knows I have trouble setting up the tea tray."

Alarmed by the quaver in Thérèse's voice, Julianne put one hand on her hostess's shoulder. Through the thin silk she could feel the frail bones.

"I'd love to help you set up the tea tray," she said, following the older woman into the foyer. "Why don't we do that right now?"

Thérèse was still complaining as they made their way into the vast kitchen. "I don't know why she picked this afternoon, anyway. She had all morning to run errands, but she fussed around here like an old mother hen."

Moving briskly, Julianne set the enamelware kettle on the stove to boil. She located the silver tea service, then poured a small amount of milk into the creamer.

"Tell me where the tea is, so I can have it ready." She deliberately spoke in low, soothing tones.

"Well, it's in that cupboard, of course," Thérèse replied, pointing to a site near the stove. "That's where we always keep it. Although lately—" Her voice again dropped to a whisper and she looked around, almost fearfully, before she continued. "Some things haven't been in their correct places. I don't understand why."

Julianne felt faint stirrings of alarm. What did Thérèse mean?

"Are you sure?" she asked.

"Of course I'm sure," Thérèse snapped. The fear left her face. "I've lived in this house all my life. I know perfectly well where things ought to be."

Julianne said nothing for a few moments, letting her thoughts form. What was happening to Thérèse? There had to be some explanations for her distress.

The kettle's loud whistle broke into her reflection. Julianne poured the boiling water into the teapot, then gathered up the tray. She followed Thérèse onto the sun porch.

"I love this room," Julianne said as the old lady lowered herself into her chair. "Even though it's so open, there is always a cozy feeling here."

Thérèse smiled. "This room was my idea. It was the first room to be added on to this house in nearly forty years. I designed it, then my husband oversaw the construction. The room was built twenty-five years ago this week."

She talked for a while about the sun porch, recalling the smallest details of its design and construction a quarter century previously. Julianne marveled at her almost total recall of the event. It only confirmed her conviction that Thérèse's mind was sound.

But there was still the matter of things misplaced. Although she didn't want to upset her hostess, Julianne decided to take the plunge.

"You told me earlier that you've discovered several things weren't in the right places. Can you tell me about them?" She folded both hands across her lap and sat back in the wicker rocker.

Worry puckered Thérèse's still-lovely face. "I've never been a forgetful person. My husband always used to say I was the most organized person he knew."

"It must be a Blanchet family trait," Julianne said with a smile. "My father is the same way."

"Then you understand why it bothers me to find myself misplacing things," the old lady replied. "A jar of face cream wasn't on my dressing table a few days ago. I found it in the bathroom, but I'm so sure I didn't put it there."

Her fingers knotted and she continued. "I had a dental appointment Monday. I was so sure I told Miss Roberts it was for two o'clock, but she said that I told her three. When we got there, the receptionist told me I'd missed my appointment. She rescheduled it."

"There've been other things, too," she continued in a quavery voice. "I couldn't find the snowflakes I've been crocheting for Christmas, and then my small coin purse went missing. We never have found the coin purse. My beauty shop called to find out why I missed an appointment. It was for a Thursday afternoon."

Her dark eyes sparkled with intensity. "I never go on Thursday afternoons. I always go on Friday. But the girl said it was written down in her book."

Julianne looked at her elderly relative with mounting sympathy. "I can understand why you're distressed. You must find this all very frustrating."

"I do," Thérèse said. "I've been wondering if maybe I'm getting forgetful, after all. But it just doesn't seem possible. I don't remember doing any of these things." Her voice rose, then trailed off.

The irony of her statement must have occurred to Thérèse, Julianne thought as the older woman fell silent. Thérèse's face reflected her bewilderment.

Julianne said nothing as she tried to sort out the truth. Such little misfortunes could happen to anyone. A jar of face cream misplaced, even a basket of crocheting missing was plausible, given Thérèse's advanced age. But the woman was so certain that she'd put things in their proper places.

Thérèse began talking again, but Julianne only half listened now. She wondered if Ian had been able to set up the meeting with Marc and Jean. If so, it would be an interesting confrontation.

Was Marc embezzling his aunt's funds? She hated to think that he was capable of such betrayal. Thérèse had griped about not seeing enough of her nephews, a valid complaint in Julianne's opinion, but the woman loved the two men, all the same.

Anything was possible, especially when it came to money, Ian had said. Maybe he was right.

Ian. She could hear him as if he stood next to her. His voice could enfold her, even when he was only talking.

When she'd spoken to him on the telephone earlier, Julianne hadn't wanted to hang up. She'd wanted to keep the telephone line open forever, as if that small act could keep them together.

She caught the names Gaston and Anne and refocused her attention on her hostess. Thérèse was talking with increasing excitement, her hands waving in the air as she spoke.

"I've been rereading the correspondence between those two. Luckily, those copies of the letters haven't been misplaced. In fact, studying the letters has helped take my mind off all these other nagging problems," Thérèse said.

Almost as if she were wondering aloud, Julianne asked, "Was Gaston referring to stone used in churches? I've certainly thought so, but I've been thinking he could have meant the farmhouse he built."

She saw Thérèse's eyes fill with excitement.

"That could be where he hid whatever was so valuable. Right there in the farmhouse, all this time."

Julianne was suddenly certain that there was absolutely nothing wrong with Thérèse's mind. So what about the incidents of forgetting? What about the money and other securities Thérèse had said were missing?

Again Julianne wondered if Ian had been able to set up his meeting with the Blanchet cousins. If so, what was he learning, especially from Marc? There was no way to know until she talked again with Ian.

The other realization, which hit her like the kick of a stubborn mule, was that she and Thérèse were both thinking the same about where Gaston had tucked away his precious cache. She couldn't help smiling.

"I've got news for you, Thérèse. I've been thinking exactly the same thing myself."

Thérèse leaned forward, her face now alive with curiosity. "So, what do we do now?"

Julianne's smile widened. "Anyone listening would think we're a couple of conspirators, plotting to find someone else's treasure."

Thérèse returned the smile. "Well, aren't we? When you think about it, that's exactly what we're doing."

"If there is a treasure." Julianne made up her mind. "Why don't I go explore the farmhouse?"

She glanced through the wide expanse of glass. "There's still lots of daylight left. I could go this afternoon, in fact. Dad probably won't be back until later, so I don't need to think about dinner."

If Ian had been able to set up the meeting with Jean and Marc, she doubted the meeting would be over quickly. She would have plenty of time to do some exploring.

"Just think, my dear. You may discover today what's been hidden for so many years."

Thérèse gave her an appraising look, then continued. "If you find anything at all at the farmhouse, or anywhere else, for that matter, Julianne, I want you to keep it."

Surprised, Julianne shook her head. "Oh, no. Thank you for your generosity, but it's your property. I'm really not interested in the treasure itself, if there indeed is one. It's the mystery itself that fascinates me. I love the idea of finding something Gaston cherished, something he wanted his wife to have."

"I can see that you've overtired yourself again. Talked all afternoon, I supposed."

Startled by the interruption, Julianne looked up to find Miss Roberts standing in the doorway, her back ramrod straight. The woman was scowling, and the full force of her disapproval was clearly directed straight at Julianne. The object of that stare felt almost like a child caught snitching cookies.

When had Miss Roberts come in? The companion's arrival had been so quiet that neither of the other two women had noticed.

"Just look at you," Miss Roberts scolded, her attention now focused on her elderly charge. "I'm sure you forgot entirely about your afternoon nap."

Julianne quickly glanced at Thérèse. A variety of emotions flickered across the older woman's face. Surprise, doubt and something so fleeting that Julianne wasn't sure she'd seen it correctly. *Anger,* she thought with surprise. Thérèse looked angry with her companion.

"I slept for an hour before you left to run those errands," Thérèse said, her words clipped. "You made up the bed afterward."

Miss Roberts stared at Thérèse as if in disbelief. Then she clamped her mouth shut. "If you say so."

Julianne stood up. Privately she thought Thérèse looked fine. The afternoon's talk seemed to have done her some good. She didn't look tired at all.

But Miss Roberts had been with Thérèse for many years. Surely the companion would know what was best for her charge?

"I'll let you know what I find out." Julianne stopped by Thérèse's chair. On an impulse she bent and kissed the dry old cheek. It was like touching faded rose petals, smooth and velvety.

"I'm sorry I tired you," she said.

In answer, Thérèse put a hand upon her arm. "Believe me, my dear. I'm fine," she said in a firm voice.

Julianne straightened. It was time to leave. There was a treasure to find.

CHAPTER SEVENTEEN

CLOUDS, JULIANNE THOUGHT as she turned onto the country road leading to the old Blanchet farmhouse. The cottony shapes from earlier in the afternoon were gone now, replaced by thick masses of gray that moved across the sky in an aimless fashion.

She shivered, trying to figure out when the temperature had dropped. The jungle print shirt and charcoal denim jeans she'd put on early that morning had been fine all day, but now she was getting colder by the minute.

Feeling slightly silly, she turned on the car heater. It was summer. In South Mississippi, air conditioners would be going full blast in both buildings and cars. And here she was, adjusting the heat.

But this wasn't Ocean Springs, she reminded herself. She was in Nova Scotia, far to the north of her Gulf Coast home. It was even beginning to mist.

The mist quickly intensified, changing from sinuous curls of vapor to a gray drizzle. Even the car windows clouded over.

Still shivering, Julianne adjusted the control to Defrost. It was growing harder to see; as land and sky had turned the same leaden gray as the water.

She gripped the steering wheel. Driving in the rain made her nervous, a holdover from the time another car had crashed into her during a blinding rainstorm on Highway 90 in Ocean Springs.

Luckily, neither Julianne nor the driver of the other car had been injured. Her only scar was a lasting dread of driving in the rain.

Julianne peered into the gray gloom. It was about time for her turnoff. As if on cue, the farm driveway came into view. The drizzle and her fears were forgotten, replaced by excitement as she pulled to a stop in front of the old farmhouse.

She sat for a minute, collecting herself and studying the half-ruined structure. Even in the late-afternoon grayness, the house had an expectant air, as if it waited for someone or something.

Now her imagination really *was* running wild, Julianne thought. Ignoring the drizzle, she got out of the car and dashed into the farmhouse. Inside, the lengthening shadows added to the air of mystery.

Something small skittered across the dusty floor. Startled, Julianne took a step back and tripped over something hard. She fell, stifling a scream.

Clouds of dust exploded into the air as she landed with a loud thud on the floor. She sat for a moment to allow her mind to clear and her eyes to adjust to the dimmer light inside.

What had tripped her? Cautiously she looked around.

She spotted a rock behind her. That had to be the culprit, she thought. It had probably fallen from the fireplace.

Stretching, she moved the rock next to the wall and got up.

"Ouch!"

Her backside would be bruised, Julianne realized. She also had a long scratch on one arm. But it could have been worse. She might have broken something, maybe her leg. It would have been hours before anyone came looking for her.

"Okay," she said. "This is ridiculous, Julianne. You're getting psyched by an empty house. You're in full control of this situation."

As if in answer, she heard more shuffling; tiny paws scampered to safety. Outside she could hear the wind moving through the trees. A musty odor, the aroma of years of neglect, irritated her nose.

She laughed at her own fears and heard the sound echo through the silent house.

Where to begin? She knew the answer already. Stone, Gaston had written, stone that soared to heaven. If her ancestor had hidden something away, the most likely spot would be the fireplace.

Ignoring the debris beneath her feet, Julianne moved slowly toward the fireplace. She stood briefly in front of it, absorbing its impact. She hadn't realized before just how high the fireplace was. The stones seemed to reach for the skies.

Kneeling at one edge of the raised hearth, she began a slow exploration of the bottom layer. The rocks, each of a different size and shape, felt cool and damp to the touch. Leaning against the fireplace for support, Julianne could almost smell the smoke from long-ago fires, feel the warmth from the wide hearth, and hear the crackling of flames.

Working methodically, she tested each area of chinked mud for any openings, large or small, where something could be hidden. She hummed as her fingers explored.

What was the melody? she wondered as the song began to penetrate her consciousness. It tantalized, eluding her at the edges of her memory. Finally she recalled the name. It was the love song Ian had once crooned for her ears alone in a crowded club.

So long ago, she thought, as her fingers worked their way along the stone surface. *Ian*. She could see his face, a dear face of hidden depths, one that she loved. What was she going to do about Ian?

Thoughts of him continued to swirl around her like the dust that was still settling. Her fingers stiffened on the stone as the realization hit her. She could not walk away from him at summer's end.

She loved Ian. There was no way she could walk away. It was so simple, she thought, sitting back on her heels. Why hadn't she seen it before?

If it meant giving up her work with the Cajun center, then she would have to do it, no matter how much a part of her the center was. In a few short weeks of summer, Ian had become her heart and soul. Without Ian, nothing else mattered.

Her fingers shook as she leaned forward again. During their phone conversation earlier in the day, Ian said they needed to talk things out.

She would talk with him that very evening, Julianne decided. She would tell him again how much she loved him, then tell him she would stay.

A new thought shot through her. What if Ian no longer wanted her? Maybe that was what he wanted to talk about with her.

He had been terribly hurt by her refusal to remain with him in Nova Scotia. What if he no longer loved her?

Doubt overwhelmed her, causing her hand to stop almost in midair. Then she set her jaw. She would not give in to useless worrying about Ian. Somehow, someway, she knew he must love her still.

IAN FIDGETED inside his car. All afternoon, vague feelings of unease had made the waiting for this meeting nearly intolerable. Then the sun had fled, leaving only a gray gloom. And now this drizzle.

He looked into the wet skies. There were no breaks in the clouds overhead, only the promise of more rain.

He heard a love song on the car radio, a melody that was soft and filled with promise. Ian hummed along.

How was Julianne getting along with Thérèse? he wondered. And was there any truth in the elderly woman's allegations of missing funds?

He checked his watch again. Jean would be arriving any minute now.

The song lingered in his memory after the last notes had died away. It reminded him of Julianne, but then, what didn't remind him of Julianne?

He could remember the texture of her hair, thick and cool as he'd stroked the shining curls. What was she doing now at this very moment? Was she thinking of him?

The long black car slid smoothly into place beside his own. Jean Blanchet, his big frame wrapped in a dark raincoat, got out and Ian followed suit.

"What is this all about?" the attorney asked as they headed for the side door Marc had told Ian about. "Is something wrong with Aunt Thérèse?"

"I'm not sure," Ian replied. "That's one reason I asked for this meeting."

As the two men neared the building, the side door opened. Marc Blanchet, his face a mass of smiles, gestured for them to enter.

"Come on in. It's too wet to stay out there."

He led them to a narrow staircase. "The bank is closing, so we'll take the side way up to my office."

A few minutes later, the men settled into their seats. Ian took a deep breath. The next few minutes probably would be very uncomfortable, he thought, surveying the expectant faces of the cousins.

"Your Aunt Thérèse suspects someone may be tampering with her accounts here at the bank," Ian said without any preliminaries. "She isn't accusing anyone. In fact, she's not definite about the amount of losses. But she is convinced there is money missing."

He glanced quickly at both Marc and Jean. In both faces he read shock and disbelief. They could have been acting, he thought, but their reactions seemed genuine enough.

Marc threw up his hands in protest. "This isn't possible. Aunt Thérèse is mistaken. There's no way someone could be taking money from her accounts."

Jean gave his cousin a level look. "No way, Marc? Come on. Even the most respected of banks can be hit by a smart embezzler. We all know that."

Marc's fleshy face quivered with indignation. "Are you accusing me?"

Jean said nothing for a moment. Tension grew in the silence, while the two cousins eyed each other with suspicion.

Ian, watching them both, sat back in his seat. He curbed his impulse to jump into the conversation. *Let them talk,* he thought.

Clearing his throat, Jean looked his cousin squarely in the face. "You could get access to Aunt Thérèse's accounts. You had authority over them for years."

Marc's face turned a mottled red. "But you're wrong. Thérèse asked the bank to have me removed from authority over her accounts over a year ago."

His hands went up again. "I couldn't believe it. She never said one word to me about it. She just sent a written request to the board of directors."

He leaned forward in his chair. "Since the request was prepared by your office, dear cousin, everything was legal, of course. I immediately turned the accounts over to another officer. Everything was included—savings account, certificates of deposit, trusts—everything. I haven't seen any of them since then."

Ian remained silent, watching the interchange. He sensed the pain Marc felt as the man continued.

"I haven't talked with Aunt Thérèse about her accounts since then. I must admit," Marc said as he folded his hands in front of him, "the entire matter hurt me deeply. You could have come to me first, so we could discuss the matter."

Jean's face was a study in surprise. "But that's absurd. I handle Aunt Thérèse's work personally. My office drew up no such request."

He clamped his lips together in concentration. "In fact, now that I think about it, I think the last work I handled for her was a little over a year ago."

As Jean continued, his eyes studied his cousin's face. "Actually, I knew you were no longer handling Thérèse's accounts, but I didn't know why."

He looked embarrassed. "I thought you were in some kind of trouble in the bank. Maybe even embezzling."

The cousins stared at each other. Realization began to dawn in both minds. Their mutual distrust was based upon a misconception.

"I can't believe what I've been thinking," Marc said. He covered his face with both hands. "I even thought you were trying to get your hands on this supposed treasure, to keep it away from Aunt Thérèse."

"I've been thinking the same about you," Jean replied. "It seems so stupid now."

The silence grew heavier. Ian felt the confusion and bewilderment between the cousins, but said nothing.

"I'm sorry," Jean said finally. "I should have come to you immediately. We could have cleared this up."

Marc's face reflected his inner misery; he looked back at Jean. "I'm equally to blame. I should have known you would have come to me immediately with a request like that from Aunt Thérèse. I'm sorry, too."

Ian remained silent. His gaze traveled from one man to the other. Both men's surprise seemed genuine.

Why, he wondered, would Thérèse have taken such action, without letting her nephews know of her intentions?

They neglected her shamefully, he knew, so she had every reason to be angry with them. But he also knew that Thérèse loved them both. Her anger, although justifiable, would not have caused a woman as shrewd as herself to take such extreme measures unless she were ill or not in her right mind. Somehow he suspected that neither was the case.

As the cousins continued their apologies, Ian's mind sifted through the facts. If Jean's office hadn't prepared a request to have Marc removed from authority over Thérèse's accounts, then where had it come from?

Ian's stomach knotted. He broke into the cousins' apologies. "Marc, would it be possible to look back at the records of Thérèse's accounts? I'd like to know if any large sums of money have been withdrawn or maybe transferred to other accounts within the bank."

Marc looked at the brass clock on the wall. "I'm not sure," he replied. "The bank's been closed for nearly an hour now." He frowned. "On Fridays, everyone is usually anxious to get home."

He stood up. "Aunt Thérèse's accounts were transferred to Henry McGaughey. Sometimes he works late. I'll see if he's still here."

Lifting the telephone receiver, Marc swung into action. He made several quick calls, then hung up, smiling. "We're in luck. McGaughey is still here."

CHAPTER EIGHTEEN

JULIANNE LOOKED at her hands in dismay. Nearly all her fingernails were broken.

She was tired and disheveled. She was also cold. Dampness seemed to chill her to the bone. Thoughts of a hot bath and hot food tantalized her, refusing to go away. With a sigh, Julianne sank onto the hearth.

With one hand she pushed the hair away from her forehead. She was probably leaving a trail of dirt, but it no longer mattered. Even without a mirror, she knew she was covered with dust, grime and debris.

Was it all for nothing? For at least two hours now she'd been exploring, searching every chink and hole in the fireplace, but she'd turned up nothing.

Her muscles screamed at her, especially those in her back and arms. She peered at her watch, then frowned. She'd been working nearly three hours, not two, as she'd originally thought. Small pieces of debris flew from her hair as she shook her head in dismay.

It was time to quit. The light was receding quickly now, fleeing to find sanctuary until morning came. She should be doing the same thing, Julianne thought, looking at the dimming beam of her flashlight.

Like the sunlight, she could return tomorrow. Maybe her father would come with her. Or Ian.

Despite her fatigue and the layers of grime, Julianne chuckled. He probably wouldn't even recognize her in this condition.

She stood up and stretched, trying to relieve the tension. Just a few minutes more, she thought. A few minutes more, then she would go home. Her hands discovered another loose rock. Careful not to scrape her already roughened fingers, she tugged. The rock came out easily.

Julianne inserted several fingers into the opening, then stopped. Her heart pounded; she felt softness against the bruised pads of her fingers.

Slowly she felt it. Then, as carefully as she could, Julianne pulled. In what remained of the twilight, she could make out a small cloth bag. Her chest constricted until she could barely breathe.

She fumbled for her flashlight on the hearth beneath her. Where was it? Then her hand closed around cold metal.

Relief flooded through her. Tucking the flashlight under one arm, she inspected the find.

The fabric was old, she realized; part of it crumbled into her hand. A length of something secured it. Rope, or maybe ribbon, she thought. The tie was so old, it was difficult to tell.

Her fingers trembled as she worked the knot. What was inside? Did this fragile bag contain Gaston's treasure?

She opened the bag and more fabric crumbled. Julianne held her breath and pulled out what looked like folded paper and another, smaller bag. She could feel something inside the inner bag, something heavy.

She exhaled slowly. Despite her best efforts to control them, both hands shook as she unfolded the paper. It was a letter, written in a script she recognized immediately, handwriting she'd read many times before. It was a letter from Gaston to Anne.

In the feeble glow from her flashlight she could barely make out the words, but even across the many years, the faded text tore at her heart. Her eyes filled with tears.

I am dying. Daily my cough worsens. I grow steadily weaker. No longer can I walk outside. I miss the feel of sunlight on my face, the cool breezes. No more will I see the stars overhead, except from my pallet in our home. I will not see your face again, dear one, nor will I see our little son. Not in this world.

The priest brings me food every day. He is a good friend, the only one left, but I have little desire for food. Thoughts of you, and thoughts of our son nourish this body.

A single tear escaped. With one hand, Julianne brushed it away and continued reading.

Someday, my beloved wife, you will return here to our home in Acadia. For you, and someday for our child, I am leaving behind precious treasure, the only left to us, tokens of our steadfast love and devotion.

Overcome, Julianne closed her eyes. Despite Anne and Gaston's insurmountable problems, their love had remained true. Would she ever have that timeless kind of love? Julianne asked herself.

Ian's image formed again in her mind. She could see his face, physically perfect, and what was more important, alive with integrity. He would be steadfast and loyal, she knew. His love would be true, if she gave him the chance.

The smaller bag slipped from her fingers, falling to the hearth with a muffled clink. Julianne picked it up, then loosened the drawstring. Her fingers touched metal.

She drew out two rings, one tiny enough to fit a child or a small woman, the other much larger. Turning them over in her hands, Julianne studied the rings.

They were plain, but perfectly formed. Although the rings had tarnished during their long confinement in the fireplace, she could tell they were gold.

Wedding rings, she thought, recalling the long story told by Thérèse. These had to be the wedding present given to Gaston by his mother.

Of course. The rings, which long ago had shone brightly, were a symbol of the wedding vows pledged by Gaston and Anne. For the two lovers, the plain bands would be the most valuable treasure they possessed.

Their love reached out to her across time. Profoundly touched, Julianne sat still, unable to move. She had found Gaston's treasure.

Something rustled behind her. Julianne's thoughts returned to the present.

The wind was picking up, she decided. It was time to go home. Besides, she couldn't wait to show her discovery to Ian and Thérèse. She slipped the rings back into their pouch.

Her muscles, stiff from sitting so long on the hard stone, protested as she stood. Behind her something fell.

As she turned to investigate the noise, her head seemed to explode. The already darkened room went completely black.

"THIS IS THE LAST ONE." Marc handed the sheets of computer paper to Ian. Then he pointed to several lines of printed figures.

"As you can see, there have been systematic withdrawals for the last thirteen months. Large withdrawals," he added, "just like the others."

Ian looked at the small pile of bank statements and computerized ledgers. The evidence was all there, neatly stacked on Marc's oversize desk.

Someone had been making substantial withdrawals from Thérèse's passbook savings account. At least three certificates of deposit had been cashed.

He looked up at Marc and Jean. "The question now is who? Has Thérèse made these withdrawals, cashed in the certificates, and simply forgotten the transactions?"

The questions seemed to hover in the silent office. Jean and Marc looked at each other. Both faces reflected their bewilderment.

"Aunt Thérèse received a more than adequate income from her investments," Marc said finally. "She owns real estate throughout the city, as well as a nice portfolio of stocks and bonds."

"She lives very simply," Jean added. "Her house is grand, but she only has to worry about upkeep. Her father left the home to her free and clear of any debt."

Marc flipped through the statements, then pulled out several. He handed the sheets to Ian.

"These date back to when I was handling her accounts," he said. "As you can see, she made no withdrawals at all. There was no need."

Ian studied the statements. Marc was correct. There was a long list of deposits into the savings account, but not a single withdrawal.

He looked up at the cousins. "So we're back to my original question. Who?"

A knock interrupted their discussion. Frowning at the intrusion, Marc opened the door.

"Mr. McGaughey thought you might want to see these deposit and withdrawal slips, Mr. Blanchet." The attractive young clerk smiled. "If there's nothing else, sir, may I go ahead and leave?"

"Yes, of course." Marc pulled out several small slips of paper and studied them closely. He handed some to both Ian and Jean.

"Look at the handwriting on these withdrawal slips," he ordered. "It's similar to Aunt Thérèse's but not the same. I've looked at her signature too many years to be fooled by a forgery."

Ian sorted the stack of withdrawal slips until he found several dating back two years. He compared them to the most recent document, which was dated only a week ago.

The handwriting on the newest withdrawal slip was similar to that on the earlier documents, but there were differences. Definite differences, he thought.

Ian set the documents on the desk, then stood up. He faced the two cousins, his expression grim.

"Well, gentlemen. We have proof. Thérèse did not make the withdrawals. So who did?"

He looked from one cousin to the other. Their bewilderment seemed genuine, and their sincerity was obvious. The cousins had nothing to do with this, Ian decided. He would bet money on it.

If not Marc and Jean, the only people who could have had access to her accounts, then who? Ian sat down on one corner of the desk and analyzed the facts.

Marc reached for a small brass lamp on one side of his desk. "I didn't realize it was getting so dark outside," he said, flipping the switch.

Ian looked up in surprise. From his vantage point, he could see only darkness through the broad expanse of window.

It was growing late, he realized. Julianne would probably be wondering why he hadn't called.

Maybe she was still at Thérèse's house, he thought, then looked at his watch. No, Miss Roberts would have shooed her away long before now.

Then it hit him.

"There's only one other person close enough to your aunt to have access to her account records," he said. "I can't believe I didn't think of this sooner."

"But who?" Marc asked.

Jean stared at Ian; understanding dawned visibly. "Of course. She ran all the errands, even the banking. It would have been so easy."

"A trusted companion," Ian stated. "Who would have suspected Miss Roberts?"

"Oh, no!" Marc leaped from his chair. "I can't believe Miss Roberts would do something like this."

"It's the only explanation that makes sense," Ian replied. "I only wish I'd thought of it sooner."

"But why? Aunt Thérèse has been so good to her," the banker continued. "She's paid her an excellent salary, provided a good home and living expenses. Why, Aunt Thérèse has depended on her for years!"

"I don't know," Ian said. "But the sooner we find out, the better. I think it's time to pay Thérèse and Miss Roberts a surprise visit."

CHAPTER NINETEEN

THE SOUND DRIFTED through the darkness. A low sound, Julianne thought, made by someone in pain. Someone was hurt, but it was too dark to tell who it was.

She shivered. It was cold. Why was she so cold? And why was there so little light?

She struggled to sit up, but the pain in the back of her head intensified. The sound again, she thought, listening intently. She moved first one stiff arm, then the other. Each movement brought more pain.

Then she recognized the sound for what it was. It came from her own mouth; she was moaning.

Slowly, like the ebbing of the tide on a Gulf Coast morning, the fog cleared from her head. She tried to remember what had happened, but the memories refused to form.

By squinting she could make out the faint remnants of light that played along a stone surface, puddling in the indentations of the rock. She was in the old Blanchet farmhouse. She'd been exploring for Gaston's treasure, a treasure she'd finally found.

But why was she huddled, stiff and sore, on the cold floor? Had she fallen?

Moving with infinite care, she put both hands onto the floor, then pushed herself to a sitting position. *So far, so good,* she thought. *Now to stand.*

Once again she braced herself with her hands. She felt a large stone beneath one hand. Something sticky came into contact with her palm.

There was enough light to examine her hand, she thought, holding it up to her eyes for a closer look. The dark substance looked like blood. Fresh blood.

She clamped her lips together. With her other hand, she felt the sore area at the back of her head. It too was sticky. Probing gently, she found a small cut.

Thankfully small. She must have fallen and hit her head on the rock.

But Julianne had no memory of tripping over anything. Could the rock have been dislodged by the wind?

There was no point in sitting around in the dark, speculating over what might have happened, Julianne told herself. She was too cold, too sore and too tired to try to puzzle it out. It was time to get up.

She braced herself with both hands and this time, her aching muscles worked better. Then, by grabbing the fireplace, she slowly came to her feet.

She stood for a minute, letting her head clear, trying to chase away the dizziness that threatened to send her right back to the floor. With painful slowness, she moved one foot in front of the other.

"I'm going to be all right," she said to the shadows that darkened each corner of the room. "I really am."

The bag. It wasn't in her hand. She must have dropped it when she fell.

Her foot hit something hard. Ignoring her protesting muscles, she slowly bent and picked up her flashlight. Her heart skipped a beat as she pushed the switch. What if nothing happened?

The light came on, a steady ray in the ever-darkening room. She breathed a sigh of thankfulness.

But even with the aid of the flashlight, Julianne found no sign of the little pouch.

Puzzled, she groped along the hearth, but located nothing. Where could the pouch be? It couldn't have traveled far in her fall. The bag had to be there somewhere. *Unless someone else had found it!*

Julianne's eyes widened in horror. No wonder she couldn't remember what happened. Someone must have entered the farmhouse, struck her in the back of the head with the rock, then left. Whoever it was also took the small pouch and the precious rings inside.

The back of her neck prickled as fear shot through her. Could whoever hit her still be in the farmhouse?

For long minutes she listened. Night sounds were all she heard, the wind as it rustled through the trees and an owl hooting somewhere close by.

Gradually her tense muscles relaxed. Whoever it was, he probably was long gone.

Julianne touched the back of her head again. She was lucky to be alive. She could have died from the blow.

The idea caused another outbreak of trembling. If the rock had been larger or if she'd been hit harder...

She breathed in deeply, forcing herself to calm down. She was okay. Except for a sore head, some aching, stiff muscles and an assortment of bruises, she would be fine.

But why? she wondered. Why did someone hit her, then steal the little pouch? What was more important, who?

Whoever had hit her was someone who knew she was coming to the farmhouse to look for the treasure. But that couldn't be. Only Thérèse had known Julianne was coming to the farmhouse. The idea that Thérèse hit her with a stone, then made off with the rings, was ludicrous. No, she knew it couldn't have been Thérèse.

Back to square one. In her mind, Julianne replayed her visit to Thérèse earlier in the afternoon. The scenes unrolled like a reel of film.

She and Thérèse had been the only people in the house until Miss Roberts came in. Miss Roberts had entered the sun porch so quietly that neither Thérèse nor Julianne had heard her. How long had the woman been listening?

Her hand tightened around the flashlight; now she remembered. They'd been talking about the treasure and about exploring the farmhouse. Miss Roberts had probably heard everything.

Suddenly a lot of unrelated events began to make sense, but now was no time to think things out. Thérèse was probably alone in her house with Miss Roberts. If the woman was vicious enough to hit and possibly kill a strong and healthy young woman for two small gold rings, what might she do to Thérèse, who was frail, elderly and very wealthy?

The thought chilled her more than the cold that surrounded her. She struggled to her feet, ignoring the pains in her head and body. She had to get to Thérèse.

CHAPTER TWENTY

"WELL, this certainly is a surprise. Both nephews coming to visit, and it's not my birthday or even Christmas."

The voice quavered, but there was no mistaking the tartness. Marc and Jean exchanged guilty looks as Thérèse, a frail hand on one hip, swung open the door. Ian moved to help her, but she stopped him with a glance.

"I can manage this door quite well, thank you. I've been doing it for a long time now." She motioned them into the brightly lighted foyer.

"Since all three of you are here, I'm assuming this is not a social call." Thérèse led the way into the immaculate living room, then took her place in a wing chair.

Thérèse was in fine fettle tonight, Ian thought. Ordinarily he would have delighted in her feistiness, but this wasn't the time.

"Where is Miss Roberts?" he asked. He saw no sign of the companion.

"That's a question I've been asking myself," Thérèse replied. "That woman is gone more than she's here lately. I have to answer the door, make my own tea, even answer the telephone," she grumbled.

"As for right now," she continued, "I'm not sure where she is. She spent most of the afternoon out running errands, then came back in time to miss tea with Julianne. After Julianne left, she remembered an errand she'd forgotten. She rushed right out again. Didn't even bother to let me know where she was going or when she'd be back."

Thérèse paused, allowing her glance to travel between all three men. "So, what brings all of you here to see this old woman tonight?"

There was clearly no sense in wasting time with preliminaries. "We've been going over your records at the bank," Ian said. "Someone has been making large withdrawals from each of your accounts for the past year."

Thérèse sat ramrod straight in the chair and studied Ian's face. "So I was right."

From his briefcase, Marc pulled out a stack of withdrawal slips. "We brought these for you to see, Aunt Thérèse. The handwriting doesn't look exactly like yours, but we could be wrong. Did you make these withdrawals?"

Thérèse sorted the small stack. "This handwriting looks somewhat like mine, but it isn't."

"We didn't think so," Ian responded. He took a deep breath, wondering as he did what her reaction would be to his next question.

"Could Miss Roberts have made these withdrawals?" From the corner of one eye he saw both Marc and Jean stiffen. They waited for their aunt to reply.

For a few moments, the room was completely silent, while the old lady studied the documents she held in one hand. Then she raised her head.

Surprised by the shrewdness he saw in her brilliantly dark eyes, Ian exhaled. *She knows,* he thought. She had known something was wrong all along.

Thérèse pushed the deposit slips from her lap, letting them drift to the carpet to land in an untidy heap. Pain replaced the shrewdness in her eyes as she gazed at Ian.

"I've been suspicious for several days now," she said. Her voice trembled.

She took a deep breath, then continued. "I knew I wasn't forgetting where I put things. Those episodes were staged. She wanted to make me think my mind was going, I suppose."

She clenched her tiny hands in her lap and continued. "But Miss Roberts?"

Hearing the agony and bewilderment in the old woman's voice, Ian felt his own hands ball into helpless fists. He wanted to take the pain from her, to spare her the knowledge that her trusted friend had stolen from her. What was worse, Miss Roberts had tried to rob her of her sanity.

But Thérèse would have to deal with the pain herself, he knew. She was tough, made of stern stuff inherited from her Acadian forebears. Could she handle betrayal?

"I didn't want to believe Miss Roberts would do this to me," Thérèse said. The quaver was gone from her voice now, replaced by a growing anger.

"But I know she did." The words hovered for a moment. "The question is, why?"

A sob broke the silence. Four heads turned toward the doorway. There stood Miss Roberts, her face white with shock. Her hands came out, palms up, in a pleading gesture.

"I'm so sorry, Mrs. Blanchet. Sorrier than you will ever know." Her voice broke as she faced her employer.

"But I can't explain it all right now," she continued. Miss Roberts turned to Ian. "I'll tell you everything, I promise I will."

She clutched the doorway, almost staggering. She took a step forward. "But you have to go to the old Blanchet farmhouse."

Ian was at her side immediately. Something was terribly wrong. He could sense it, could see it in the woman's haunted eyes. He grasped both arms to keep her from falling.

"What is it?" He shook her gently. "Tell me what's wrong."

"I may have killed Julianne." The words were followed by another sob.

"What have you done?" His fingers bored into her flesh. "What have you done to Julianne?"

She could only look at him, eyes wide with horror. "No, no, I didn't mean to kill her," she cried.

Julianne? Dead?

Ian refused to accept the message. Miss Roberts stumbled, nearly falling as Ian dropped her arms. He had to get to Julianne.

"Stay with Thérèse," he ordered Marc and Jean.

The cousins, both faces pale with shock, moved quickly to their aunt as if to protect her from Miss Roberts.

Ian ran from the house, his heart pounding with fear. He cleared the porch steps, blinked in the darkness, then someone mercifully switched on the porch light.

Silently thanking the person who had had sense enough to turn on the light, he headed down the footpath. It couldn't be true, not Julianne. She had to be alive. He would have known if something had happened to her.

So intent was he that at first he didn't notice the other car in front of the house, didn't see the slight figure stumbling along the sidewalk.

"Ian?"

The whisper penetrated his fog of pain. It was Julianne.

He scooped her up and clutched her to his chest, searching her face to make sure she was okay. Brown eyes wet with tears stared back at him through several layers of grime.

"Julianne."

For a moment he simply held her, feeling her heart beating against his chest as she snuggled closer into his warmth. Without pushing her away, he lifted her chin, turning her head up so that he could see her eyes. "Are you all right?"

"I think so. My head still hurts where the rock hit me." She felt the strong arms holding her stiffen; she continued. "I don't know how long I was unconscious, but now I'm sore and stiff all over."

A smile trembled at the corners of her mouth. "I must look awful, like I've been rolling in dirt."

He kissed the tip of her grime-streaked nose. "I've never seen anyone so beautiful. Brown and black are good colors for you."

Her laugh was soft. "Thanks for the fashion advice."

"You're welcome."

Despite the warmth from Ian's body, she shivered. "I can't get warm."

"Let's get you inside." Still holding her close, Ian headed back to the house.

Then she remembered. "I think I know who hit me." Now she shook as much from anger as from the cold. "Ian, Thérèse may have been right all along about the money. She could be in terrible danger. Miss Roberts..."

"Shhh." He put a finger to her lips. "We know. Marc, Jean and I pieced it together earlier this evening. Miss Roberts is here now."

Ian carried her straight into the parlor, leaving Julianne barely time to compose herself. It took several moments for the scene in front of her to register.

Miss Roberts, her ashen face a study in misery, gaped at Julianne, while Marc and Jean Blanchet, whose faces registered surprise, seemed to be forming a protective shield around their aunt.

Thérèse simply sat, her eyes studying Julianne.

Then the figures came to life. Still shaken by her ordeal, Julianne flinched. She felt Ian's arms tighten around her.

"Oh, Julianne!" Miss Roberts wrung her hands, and tears began to pour from her eyes. "I thought I'd killed you."

"Julianne." Jean's normally suave countenance reflected genuine concern. "I'm so glad you're here and safe."

Marc left his post at Thérèse's side. "I knew you were all right. I just knew it."

Leaning on Jean's arm, Thérèse struggled to her feet and came to Julianne. She took one shivering hand and held it to her cheek.

"Child, child. I was so worried about you. Are you all right? Should we call my physician? I know he would come right away."

"I'm okay. Really," Julianne said, holding tightly to Thérèse's hand. "I have a bump at the back of my head and a lot of bruises. That's all. I'm feeling better by the minute."

"But your hand is icy." Thérèse pointed to the thick afghan on a nearby love seat. "Ian, put that girl down right there and put that afghan over her."

As Ian moved to comply, Thérèse turned to Marc. "You go put on some tea," she ordered. "Make a lot."

Without a word, Marc scrambled into the kitchen.

"Now, are you sure you're okay?" Thérèse repeated.

Completely surrounded by the soft afghan and Ian's arms, Julianne smiled at Thérèse. "I'm fine."

Some of the anxiety left the old lady's face. She lowered herself into her chair, then turned her attention to Miss Roberts.

"It seems Julianne is all right, no thanks to you," Thérèse said. "I'd like to hear an explanation for this outrageous behavior."

"We want the truth," Ian added. His voice was low, but Julianne caught the steely undercurrent.

Miss Roberts's gaze traveled around the room. Finally, as if she realized there was no way out, she took a deep breath.

She turned to Thérèse. "I've watched over you now for almost twenty years."

Another sob escaped her, then she reestablished control. "I've loved you. I loved you like the sister I always wanted. I thought you cared for me."

Surprise flitted across Thérèse's face, but she said nothing. She motioned to Miss Roberts to continue.

"Last year when I was cleaning out the drawer of your desk, I came across your will," the companion went on. Her face flushed and she stopped.

Then, almost defiantly, she continued. "I knew it was wrong to read it, but I couldn't help it. I couldn't believe what I was reading. Jean and Marc inherit everything!"

Her voice rose with agitation. "Everything! They never come to see you except on birthdays or holidays. Why, you hardly know their wives and children. It isn't fair. What have they done for you?"

Without waiting for an answer, she went on. "I took care of you all these years. Oh, I know I've been paid and paid well. But how can you set a price on love?"

"How indeed?" Thérèse replied in a dry voice.

Marc, who'd come back from the kitchen, exchanged shamed looks with his cousin. "She's right, Aunt Thérèse. We've neglected you."

"Now isn't the time," Thérèse said.

Her voice was stern, but she gave him a gentle look. "Let Miss Roberts continue," she ordered.

Miss Roberts glared at the cousins. "I was so angry, so hurt," she said. "It wasn't fair. I should have been included in the will. Since I wasn't, I thought it was fair to take what was rightfully mine."

Julianne inhaled sharply. So Miss Roberts was admitting her guilt.

Ian's arms tightened. "She's responsible for everything," he whispered.

"I began to put things in the wrong places, so you'd think you were forgetting things." Miss Roberts averted her eyes, unable to face her employer now.

"I wanted everyone to think you were becoming absent-minded. That would make it easier to explain the missing money, if your nephews ever questioned your accounts." She glared again. "Not that they paid any attention!"

"You're wrong, you know." Thérèse's voice was low, but the words were clear. "My nephews may have neglected me, but they've always loved me. As I've loved them," she added.

Jean dropped to one knee beside her chair, then put one arm around his aunt. His eyes glistened. "We've been so wrong, Aunt Thérèse, but we'll make it up to you."

Thérèse patted his hand, then looked at Marc, who stood on the other side. "I've never worried about either of you boys."

Watching the exchange, Miss Roberts's expression changed from defiance to defeat. She sighed. "When I heard about the family treasure, I made up my mind to have it. I deserved some kind of reward for all my devotion through the years. I didn't want the nephews to have it."

She turned her glance to Julianne. "You were a stranger here," she said. "It wasn't right for you or your father to have the treasure, either."

"So you came looking for clues, didn't you?" Clutching the afghan, Julianne sat up straighter. "You're responsible for tearing up our suite at the inn."

Miss Roberts nodded. "Then, this afternoon, when I came in, I heard you and Mrs. Blanchet talking about the location of the treasure. I knew it was time to do something, or that treasure would slip right through my fingers."

"So I waited for a while after you left," she continued, "to make sure Mrs. Blanchet was asleep. Then I slipped out."

Julianne shuddered. Miss Roberts had stalked her, followed her to the farm. She felt Ian's reassuring squeeze on her arm and looked at him with gratitude in her eyes.

"I went to the farm and sneaked in. You were so busy exploring the fireplace, you didn't hear a thing. Then I saw you find the pouch."

Miss Roberts's eyes widened as the memories of her actions returned. "I knew it was the treasure. It was mine! But I had to get it away from you."

"So I picked up a rock," she continued, her voice rising with excitement. "I sneaked up behind you. The wind had picked up and you didn't hear me. I hit you, grabbed the pouch and ran out."

Julianne shuddered again. "You could have killed me. I'm lucky you didn't hit me any harder."

"I know." Miss Roberts's voice broke. "On the way back from the farm, I realized that I might have killed you. I drove around for a while, trying to figure out what to do. I was afraid to go to the police, afraid of what they'd do to me if you were dead."

Loud sobs burst from her. "I never intended to be a murderer. I just wanted what was rightfully mine."

"And you could have had it," Thérèse said. Her voice was colored by indignation now. "Oh, you've been so wrong. So wrong."

Miss Roberts turned back to her employer. "But I read the will."

"The will you found was written more than twenty years ago." Thérèse shook her head. "I intended to destroy it, but never got around to it."

Miss Roberts sank into a chair. Her sobs died away; she watched Thérèse.

"If you'd bothered to read the entire document, you would have seen the date. I made out a new will five years ago, didn't I, Jean?"

He nodded. "Yes. It's in the safe at my office."

"The new will," Thérèse went on, "distributes my estate differently."

She looked directly at Miss Roberts. "Under its terms you were to have a trust fund. Not extravagant, of course, but you would have had enough to be financially independent for the rest of your life."

Miss Roberts stared back at her employer. Her mouth moved, but no sound emerged.

Julianne, watching the exchange, found herself pitying Miss Roberts. Then she caught herself. The woman could have killed her.

Moreover, Miss Roberts's behavior toward Thérèse was cruel. The elderly woman actually had believed that her mind was playing tricks on her.

Ian leaned closer. "Are you warm enough now?"

Snug in the afghan, Julianne nodded. "Finally. I've even stopped shivering."

"Then I need to get up." Reluctantly he pulled his arms away and stood.

"I think it's time to call the police," he said, looking at Thérèse. "Unless you have any objections?"

Thérèse nodded without hesitation. "I have no objections at all. I might have been able to forgive what she did to me, but her attack on Julianne was criminal."

Her words were distinct in the hushed room. "Call the police."

Miss Roberts burst into sobs as he strode toward the telephone. "I'm so sorry," she hiccuped.

Then, as if remembering unfinished business, she came slowly toward Thérèse. She extended one hand.

Jean and Marc, moving in unison, drew closer to their aunt. Jean put one arm around her shoulders.

Miss Roberts leaned toward her employer. In her outstretched palm were two tarnished gold rings.

For a moment the two women stared at each other, each with a new awareness of the other. Then, with trembling fingers, Thérèse took both rings.

CHAPTER TWENTY-ONE

A FAINT AROMA OF LAVENDER clung to the silk dressing gown. A clean smell, Julianne thought as she trailed her fingers over the soft material. It was so nice to be clean again.

It had taken repeated scrubbing to get all the grime from her hair. Now her reflection in the bathroom mirror showed shining-clean curls again. Her face, also scrubbed clean, was still pale.

Julianne pulled a lipstick from her purse and applied it liberally. At least now she wouldn't look so washed-out.

As she came into the living room again, she glanced at Ian. His head was bent, his expression intent as he listened to Thérèse.

It was odd how he had such a calming effect on everyone, she thought. Just being around him made her feel better.

Later, when they were alone, she would tell him of her decision to remain in Nova Scotia. A shiver of anticipation shot through her; she wondered what his reaction would be.

There was no sign of Miss Roberts. Evidently the police had already taken the woman away.

Jean came forward. In one hand he carried a cup of steaming liquid. "Thérèse thought you might like some hot tea after your bath."

Julianne took the cup gratefully, then went over to Thérèse. "Thanks. This is exactly what I needed." She sat down beside the older woman.

"You don't look like you've been through a terrible ordeal, my dear." Thérèse smiled at her. "It's amazing what a hot bath will do for a person."

"You look absolutely beautiful." Ian kissed her forehead, stroking her hair with one hand. "Even with wet hair."

Startled, Julianne felt her hair. It was still damp, especially in back. "I didn't do a very good job of drying it, I guess."

"That's all right," Thérèse said. "You won't be going back out in the cold again tonight, anyway."

"But how will I get home?" Julianne looked at her relative in surprise.

Thérèse's bottom lip quivered. "Of course you're going to stay the night with me, aren't you? Marc and Jean both have families to get home to." Her voice trailed away.

She gave both nephews a fond look. "They both offered, but I said no."

Julianne felt a rush of sympathy. Thérèse was still very upset by the terrible events of the afternoon, especially by her trusted companion's betrayal. Moreover, Thérèse wasn't used to being by herself.

Brushing the dark curls from her face, Julianne looked at Ian. She wanted to be alone with him, but that was out of the question now.

Thérèse needed her. After what the older woman had been through, there was no way Julianne could leave her.

"Of course I'll stay," Julianne said. "You're right about my hair. I don't need to be going out into the cold with a wet head."

She felt Ian's hand on her shoulder. He looked down at her with understanding in his eyes. "Thérèse will feel safer with you here."

Jean set his own cup on a coffee table, then cleared his throat. "Marc and I have been discussing this, Aunt Thérèse. We know someone who might make an excellent companion for you."

Marc smiled at his aunt. "Someone trustworthy, I might add. She's retiring from the bank after thirty years of devoted service. We're all sorry to see her go, but our loss just may well be your gain."

Thérèse beamed. "I'm anxious to meet this person."

"Why don't we come back early tomorrow? We can work out some arrangements then." Jean approached his aunt and kissed her on the cheek.

"I've got to go, now that you're okay. But I'll be back in the morning," he promised.

After making a similar promise, Marc followed his cousin from the room. They were still making plans as they left.

How would Jean and Marc treat their aunt after this? Julianne wondered. She smiled. Much better, if tonight was any indication.

"I have to go, too," Ian said to Julianne. "Will you walk me to the door?"

Nodding, Julianne took the hand he held out to her. With a glance at Thérèse, who gave them both an encouraging smile, she went with him to the front door.

"I understand why you have to stay." He took her into his arms.

Julianne went willingly. Her heart pounded as he pulled her close. Through the thin silk of the dressing gown she could feel the rise and fall of his chest.

"I wanted to talk with you. There are so many things we need to discuss." She looked at him with shining eyes.

"I know. But it will have to wait." He kissed her nose, then her chin. "I have a performance tomorrow night at the Bearded Lion, the last of my summer performances there. Will you come?"

She could see the promise in his eyes. Everything was going to be all right. "Of course I'll come."

NIGHT SHADOWS fell across the skylights; the light from a thin crescent moon filtered into the bedroom. Fiona cuddled closer to Dale. "I love this room. I always know whether the skies are clear or cloudy. When it rains, I can see the drops on the skylights."

Basking in the afterglow of lovemaking, Dale pushed away a thick strand of hair and nuzzled her shoulder. "I haven't noticed anything but you, *chère*."

She ran her long fingers through his hair. "You make me feel like a treasure, precious and protected."

He turned her head so that her navy eyes looked into his. "I love you, Fiona. I've thought about us a lot. If you still want me, I'd like very much to move in with you."

He felt her tense and held his breath.

"I've been wanting a change, anyway," he continued before she could say anything. "Julianne doesn't really need me. She's an adult, living her own life."

He sighed. "My business doesn't really need me either, much as I'd like to think otherwise. So I can easily make the transition. I can always keep in touch with my office by telephone."

The blue eyes were innocent now. She sat up in bed.

"So," she said. "I'm really disappointed."

Bewildered, Dale stared at her. "I don't understand. What did I say?"

"Here I was expecting another proposal of marriage, and the only offer I get is for you to move in with me."

Now Dale sat up. He stared at her with a puzzled expression. "But living together was your idea in the first place. It took me a while to get used to it, of course. I've done a lot of thinking, trying to come to terms with the idea." He threw up his hands. "Now you've changed your mind. I don't understand you at all."

Fiona chuckled, a throaty sound low in her throat. "Don't you see? That's the whole point. You had to talk yourself into the idea of living together."

She traced tiny circles on his nose with one finger. "I've been thinking about this, too. I've realized that you would never be comfortable with living together outside of marriage."

Leaning closer, she kissed the imaginary circles. "But I love you for trying."

"Then you don't want to live together?"

"I've been giving your proposal a lot of thought." She looked up to see hope surging in his eyes.

"Marriage scared me," she admitted. "That's why I reacted so violently, I suppose. When my husband died, I thought I'd never have another relationship like that one."

Dale reached for her. "That scared me, too. My marriage to Lillian was so perfect. I never thought to have anything like that again."

Fiona moved into his arms once more. "I've realized that my love for you is what matters. Our relationship will be different than the ones we had before, but just as loving."

Fiona hesitated, as if she was afraid to go on. Dale's arms tightened around her.

"So I would love to marry you." She looked at him with twinkling eyes. "That is, if you still want to marry me."

In answer, Dale kissed her again and again, leaving her breathless. Finally he paused. "I know where there is a lovely engagement ring, sized just for your finger. Sapphire and diamonds, the blue for those gorgeous eyes of yours, of course.''

Then he smiled. ''But it will have to wait.''

''Until later,'' Fiona replied. Her arms wound around him. ''Much, much later.''

CHAPTER TWENTY-TWO

LIKE SOFT FOG moving in over the Minas Channel, Ian's voice drifted to the farthest corner of the room. Hearing him, Julianne was struck again by the way the man could control an audience with his voice.

Except for Ian's crooning—timeless words of love sung to a simple guitar melody—the Bearded Lion's dining room was silent. No one stirred or coughed, no one shifted in his seat. Even the waiters and waitresses stopped scurrying. Instead they leaned in a line against one wall, as rapt as the rest of the audience.

If he had wanted to, Julianne thought, Ian could have been a world-famous singer, rushing from one engagement to another, making album after album. Paris, London and New York would have welcomed him, she was certain.

But the man preferred Wolfville, opting for the quiet life of a farmer and writer. He sang his songs because of his love for the music and the heritage they represented, not for any financial gain or dream of fame.

How many men could turn their backs on certain wealth and celebrity? Ian was unique, a man of quiet confidence, sure of himself and his talents. He was also the man she loved.

Uncertainty gripped her. Her fingers plucked the cloth covering the small table where she sat by herself. She was glad she'd come although she'd had some second thoughts during the long night at Thérèse's house.

Ian still loved her. She was sure of that.

She'd seen the emotion in his eyes at Thérèse's, especially when he'd carried her inside. Closing her eyes, she could still feel him trembling as he'd swept her into his arms, oblivious to the dirt and grime clinging to every inch of her body.

Yes, he still loved her. But did he still want her?

She opened her eyes, conscious of a sudden silence in the room. On the small stage Ian was smiling at her, holding out his hand.

Without even thinking, she stood up and moved slowly toward him. Gripping her hand in his, he helped her up. His dark eyes tore at her composure.

What was he thinking? she wondered, conscious of the strong pressure of his hand around hers. She felt herself shaking. No, she thought, forcing herself to be calm. There would be time later for them to sort things out.

"Will you tell another story?" he asked, too quietly for anyone else to hear. "I'll accompany you on the guitar." He smiled again.

Julianne nodded, though her composure was almost gone. His smile could start forest fires, she thought, especially the one inside Julianne Blanchet. She took a deep breath, mentally extinguishing the flames. A musician came forward and placed a small stool beside the microphone.

While Ian introduced her to the audience, her mind moved frantically over her repertoire of stories. Which tale should it be?

But there was only one story she wanted to tell, Julianne knew. Her lips curved in a small smile and she stepped up to the microphone.

"Many of you know the story of Evangeline," she said. "Her tale reaches into our hearts, reminding all of us that true love has power beyond simple understanding. Love can touch many more hearts than just those of the two people involved."

Her eyes searched the audience. She felt rather than heard the collective sigh throughout the dimly lighted room.

"Listen to another tale of Acadian lovers, another story of love and devotion that crosses the years, reaching out to touch us even today." She seated herself on the low stool, then lowered the microphone. Her voice began to throb with emotion.

Behind her, Ian waved the other musicians into silence. His fingers touched his guitar, weaving music into her words as he listened. She was telling the story of Gaston and Anne, recounting the tale of timeless love.

Lulled by the throaty pitch of her voice he began to dream. They worked so well together, he knew. If only they could share their words and music for always.

His fingers hit a discordant note, but her voice didn't falter. Julianne simply glanced at him and smiled. The encouraging look on her face reached out to him like the story she was telling. He answered her silently with a smile of his own.

She finished her story and the audience sat quietly for a few seconds. Then applause erupted. From eighteenth-century Acadia Julianne slipped back into the present.

It was a while before she could get away from the many well-wishers who stopped by the stage to congratulate her on her tale. She stole a sidelong glance at Ian, who was saying goodbye to his musicians. Maybe he would come and rescue her.

Finally Ian came up beside her. With a good-natured smile at the people still vying for Julianne's attention, he pulled her away. "Time to go, wouldn't you say?"

Grateful for his timely interruption, she nodded. "I would."

A few minutes later the Ferrari prowled through the quiet streets of Wolfville, heading for Ian's farm. It had been a long evening, Julianne thought; she stared unseeing into the night skies beyond the window, her senses completely attuned to the man sitting next to her.

He was quiet, but she could almost feel his mind working. Leaning against the dark leather seat he seemed relaxed, but she could feel the tenseness, the coiled-spring strength of his body.

Ian remained quiet while he parked the car in front of the farmhouse, and as they walked up the porch steps to the house. Respecting his silence, Julianne said nothing when he ushered her into the den.

Ian disappeared into the kitchen, then reemerged, carrying two crystal wineglasses. Cradled under one arm was a bottle of wine, probably burgundy, she thought, judging by its deep ruby tint.

He uncorked the bottle, then poured shimmering wine into each glass. "How is Thérèse today?"

So he was unwinding at last. Julianne felt something inside herself relax, too. Taking a seat on the sofa, she sipped at the wine. It tasted as rich as its color.

"She did very well all day. She was up before dawn this morning, feisty and full of energy."

Julianne laughed. "Breakfast was ready before I got out of bed. Thérèse made everything herself, then insisted on serving it. It felt strange, being waited on by a woman in her nineties."

Ian grinned, then slid onto the sofa beside her. "I can see her now, fussing over you because of your ordeal yesterday."

His expression changed to one of concern. He explored the back of her head with one hand. His touch was gentle. "You're all right, aren't you?"

She nodded. "I'm fine. A few sore spots and some bruises. The back of my head is still tender, but no dizzy spells or anything like that."

Acutely aware of Ian's leg against her own, she continued. "When I called Dad, he insisted on having a physician come by to check me over. Dr. Gauthier said I was fine, but to take it easy for a few days."

"I think that's good advice." Almost absently he stroked her hair.

"Marc and Jean came back this afternoon," she went on. His touch sent small shock waves through her, making it difficult to think.

"They both brought their wives. Thérèse seemed surprised, but delighted to see all of them."

His fingers paused, then resumed their rhythmic motion. "Maybe now they'll see how wrong they were to neglect her."

Ian's eyes flashed. "When people live busy lives, I know it's tough to remember to include elderly relatives, but that kind of neglect is shameful."

"I agree," she said. "They really need each other. Thérèse has so much to give, a wealth of love and experience to share with both nephews and their families. And she needs the contact with younger people."

"I have the feeling things will change for the better," she continued. "Jean and Marc both asked Thérèse to come live with them."

Ian's eyebrows shot up. "That's unbelievable. I wonder what their wives think."

"Evidently both wives suggested it." Julianne laughed at the expression on Ian's face. "Really. They both think Aunt Thérèse is adorable."

"Adorable? That's not how I'd characterize her, although I'm very fond of her."

He smiled. "She's probably difficult to live with."

"Probably," she agreed. "But there's nothing to worry about. Thérèse refused both offers. She said she needed to be independent."

"But she can't live alone in that rambling old house," he objected.

"Of course not," Julianne said. "Even Thérèse realizes that. When I left, they were all talking about that companion Marc suggested, the lady who's retiring from the bank. Marc talked with the woman earlier today, and she's very interested in the job. I think she was going over there this evening to meet Thérèse."

"Marc and Jean weren't upset, were they?" One arm came around her shoulders.

Julianne considered his question as she leaned into the warmth of his body. "I really don't think so. She isn't going to live with them, but Thérèse did promise to visit their homes frequently. She also wants to take their children on outings."

She paused. "I like the rapport that's been established among all of them. It's fragile, of course, but I think in time they'll all grow to love each other."

His eyes regarded her intently now. Without turning away, he set his half-full wineglass on the table. "And what about our own rapport? What about this fragile emotion, this love between *us*? Will it work out also?"

The words flowed into Julianne as if he were singing, enfolding, caressing, surrounding her with love. Facing him she sat up straight, her own eyes searching his for the emotions deep within. "I love you. I realize now that's all that really matters."

Ian inhaled and held his breath.

"We can't live in two places at once." There was no hesitation in her voice.

"My ties to South Mississippi and the cultural center are important, of course. My father I love with all my heart. But nothing," she said, emphasizing the words, "is as important to me as you. Nothing."

Ian slowly let his breath out, resisting the urge to pull her against him. He wanted to see her face, watch the expression in those luminous eyes. Instead he reached for her hand, playing with her long fingers as he talked.

"Julianne."

To its owner the name sounded like a caress. She watched as he shook his head.

"I've been thinking about this, too. All the time. I haven't been able to think about anything else," he admitted.

He stared at some point past her head. "I stopped loving Joanna so long ago that I can't remember when it happened. Now that I know what love really is, I don't even know that's what I felt for her."

Julianne said nothing. Somewhere inside her she felt an overwhelming joy begin to grow.

"Our broken commitment scarred me too deeply," he continued. "I think because I hadn't faced the issue, hadn't tried to resolve it. But then I had no reason to try. Now there's you. I don't want to sacrifice my future with you for the sake of a past I no longer care about."

"I can go anywhere," Ian said; his fingers tightened around hers. "I can live anywhere, if it means being with you. I love you."

Something elemental flowed from his hand to hers and back again. Julianne had never known that a person could feel love so strongly, simply by holding hands with someone else.

Her words came out slowly. "Since I first read their letters, then heard the story of the love between Anne and Gaston, I've wished that someday I could be part of a love as strong as theirs. My wish seems to have come true. We're both willing to give up parts of ourselves for each other."

For a moment they said nothing; they gazed at each other. Julianne felt the pressure on her hand, but couldn't look away from his eyes.

"Earlier, while you were telling the story of Anne and Gaston at the Bearded Lion, I thought how well we worked together onstage," he said finally. "We were very good."

Julianne nodded. He wasn't bragging, she knew, merely stating the obvious.

"What if we could always perform as a team?" His eyes filled with excitement.

"Why couldn't you start an Acadian cultural center for children right here in Acadia? You could draw on your experience with the original center for its offspring."

Julianne tensed. She felt a matching excitement inside as he continued.

"From what you've told me, your center in South Mississippi is in capable hands. And why not?"

He grinned at her. "You handpicked and then trained every person on the staff. You may have been working yourself out of a job, anyway."

Ian was right, Julianne admitted. Her staff was good, so good that she'd have a tough time picking a new administrator from among them.

"You could build the same thing here," he continued. "If you wanted to, and I'm sure you would, you could link the two centers, which would mean frequent visits to South Mississippi."

Her eyes shone; she considered the possibilities. "I could be a consultant for the Ocean Springs center."

"Exactly." His smile widened. "I could help with the center—with both centers," he corrected himself. "I could bring music to the children. In turn," he went on, "you could be of great help to me."

"How could I help you? Do you mean telling stories on stage?"

"That, and helping me with folktales. I'm planning to write a great deal more than just this first series on Acadian legends."

"What a wonderful idea," she agreed. Then she laughed.

It was Ian's turn to look puzzled. "What's so funny?"

Uncurling her legs, Julianne rose and went to the table where she'd set her purse as they came in. Opening it, she fumbled inside for a moment.

"Here," she said. Then she came back to the sofa and sat down close to Ian.

"Acadians are known for being fey, aren't they?" She laughed again.

"Of course," he agreed, still not sure what it was that she found so amusing.

"It's true. Thérèse Blanchet must have it in great measure." She held out her hand.

Ian caught the glitter of two gold rings. "Anne and Gaston's wedding rings," he said softly. He picked up the larger of the two.

"A gift," Julianne said, her own voice soft. "Thérèse cleaned and polished them herself. She seems to think we'll need them very soon."

Ian reached for her, pulling her into his arms. She went eagerly, her heart pounding with anticipation.

He slipped the ring onto the third finger of his left hand. "It's a perfect fit," he said. His head came down to nuzzle her ear.

"As we'll be," she answered, putting both arms around his neck and holding tight to the tiny ring in her own hand. Her lips found his.

CHAPTER TWENTY-THREE

LIGHT FILTERED through the windows, casting rays of ruby, sapphire, gold and emerald upon the white lace. Julianne fingered the delicate material, watching the play of jeweled light over the intricate pattern.

It wasn't time for her to be in the narthex yet, she knew. By tradition, brides waited with their fathers or other escorts in the tiny brides' room just off this entryway into the historic old church. But she couldn't resist peeking.

From one corner of the narthex she surveyed the guests who were seated in the carved wooden pews.

Julianne thought back over the weddings, baptisms and other ceremonies she'd witnessed here, memories of a lifetime. She'd studied the stained glass patterns during countless Sunday services. In turn, those windows had watched her as she grew from babyhood to maturity.

Julianne sighed. She would miss this church, almost hidden from the highway by centuries-old live oaks festooned with lacy Spanish moss. She would miss the people who had gathered here today, many of them relatives and friends from early childhood. She would miss her home in South Mississippi.

From now on she would attend services in a church in faraway Nova Scotia. Maybe her friends and relatives would visit from time to time. The thought brought a smile to her face.

And she would come back here again and again to visit. This would always be a place of welcome.

A stir behind her caused her to turn. Dale entered, his hands covered by rhododendrons and azaleas. Catching her eye, he grinned, then handed her the bouquet.

Julianne buried her face in the masses of pink, salmon and mauve. "Dad, it's lovely."

"Fiona had to have every blossom exactly perfect. We barely made it on time." He inclined his head. "There she is, slipping in the side entrance."

Julianne turned. There was no mistaking Fiona as she made her way to the pew reserved for the bride's family. Red-gold hair drifted like a cloud around her radiant face, contrasting vividly with the burnished emerald silk of her dress. Julianne could hear an excited humming throughout the church.

She would have a lot of adjustments to make, Julianne reflected. A husband, soon—if Dale and Fiona would ever set a date—a stepmother.

The word didn't fit. Fiona, she knew, would never try to take her mother's place.

Her thoughts went back to her last conversation with the lovely redhead. What she wanted, Fiona had told Julianne with one of her trademark smiles, was a friend.

The organist began to play. Dale reached for her hand. "Time for you to get out of the way, missy. We don't want Ian to see you ahead of time."

With a last look over her shoulder, Julianne followed her father into the brides' room. Only a few minutes more, she knew, but it was hard to control the butterflies that were flitting around in her stomach.

Dale scowled at his reflection in the small mirror. "This thing wasn't made for a human neck."

Glad of something to take her mind off the people seated in the church, Julianne adjusted the offending tie. "There," she said, patting his chest. "I've never seen you look so handsome."

It was true, she thought. Her father looked terrific in his formal attire. She couldn't resist kissing him on the cheek.

Dale glowed with pride. "Stop that now. You'll mess up your lipstick," he fussed, but he held on to her arm for a little longer.

"I have something for you. Did you remember the old tradition?" he asked.

She cocked an eyebrow. "Which tradition?"

"Something old, something new, something borrowed, something blue?" His eyes twinkled.

Julianne frowned. In all the excitement she'd forgotten. Quickly she recalled the words of the rhyme.

"I have the earrings Fiona gave me. Those are new."

She put both hands to her ears, feeling for the brilliant diamond studs. "And so beautiful."

"What about something borrowed?"

"The little Bible from Thérèse." She remembered the old lady putting it into her hands, the tears in her still-bright eyes as she'd hugged Julianne. "I'll carry it down the aisle."

"Something old," he prodded.

She fingered the filigree chain tucked into the high lace collar of her dress. "My jasper pendant."

For a moment the present faded, and she was back on a sandy finger of land overlooking the Bay of Fundy. She could almost feel the sting of the wind against her face, could almost taste the salty air.

"One of Glooscap's jewels," she said, feeling the smooth stone Ian had had made into a pendant for her. "Surely it's very old."

Dale smiled. "And something blue?"

She thought for a moment, then shook her head. "I guess not."

From his pants pocket Dale removed a narrow, velvet-covered box. "Then how about this?" he asked, handing it to her.

Her fingers trembled as she opened the box. On the white satin lay a diamond and sapphire bracelet. Her eyes filled with tears.

"Mom's engagement and wedding rings," she said finally. "And the twenty-fifth-wedding-anniversary necklace! You had them made into a bracelet."

Overwhelmed, she moved into his arms.

"Careful now," he cautioned. "You don't want to mess up your dress."

Dale's voice was gentle, but she felt him trembling. She looked up and caught the glistening of tears in his eyes.

"I know she's with us today." She kissed him again, feeling her love flow out to him.

He fastened the bracelet around her lace-covered wrist. "Your mother would be very pleased," he said.

Before she could admire the effect, he gave her a gentle push. "Come on. They're playing your song."

Slipping her arm through his, Julianne swept from the room in a rustle of lace. Dale walked proudly beside her as she glided down the aisle.

She could hear the murmurs of guests, but her eyes were fixed on the tall figure standing to the right of the altar. *Ian.* An Ian looking impossibly handsome in his formal black, white and gray.

Something mauve nestled against one lapel. More of Fiona's handiwork, Julianne thought.

Then she was beside him. With an encouraging pat on her shoulder, Dale placed her hand in Ian's and moved away, smiling broadly.

Ian's eyes were dark pools as he gazed at her. They faced the altar, then he leaned toward her. "You're as beautiful as a song," he whispered.

She tried to answer, but the words wouldn't come. She could only look at him, knowing that her love was shining in her eyes.

The priest stepped forward and began the timeless rite. Holding tightly to Ian, Julianne followed the beautiful ritual with both mind and heart.

The small ring bearer, with a grin that threatened to split his face, nudged Ian, then offered him the tiny satin pillow. Ian reached for a shining bit of metal, then placed the plain gold ring on Julianne's finger.

Anne's ring, she thought, *and now mine.* She offered a silent prayer that her love would remain as steadfast as that of the ring's first owner.

Then with steady hands she slipped the larger ring onto Ian's finger. Her eyes never left his face. As she drew away, he caught her hand.

"I love you," he murmured in a whisper too low for any ears but hers.

"I love you," she whispered back. The words echoed in her mind like a song she'd always known, Julianne thought. The words were familiar, yet this day, this minute, the words were new, as if meant for them alone.

Happiness surged through her. Her arm tucked firmly in Ian's, they turned to face the world as man and wife. Their song was only beginning, but like every song of love, like the melody shared by Anne and Gaston, the music was ageless.

Dear Readers,

My maternal ancestors came from Acadia. They settled first in South Louisiana, moving later to the Mississippi and Alabama Gulf Coast. Their surnames are inscribed on the brass plaques inside the stone church at Grand Pré. The gleaming tablets commemorate the Acadians expelled from Nova Scotia in 1755.

As a child, I heard the old Acadian stories and myths recalled by my grandmother in her Cajun dialect. Years later when I first went to Nova Scotia from my home in the Arkansas Ozarks, I felt a distant sense of homecoming, a sense of connection to land and people I've never known but have always known, a sense of pride in a unique heritage. *Julianne's Song* came out of those feelings.

KIT BAKKER'S CAJUN RED BEANS AND RICE

Every Cajun cook fixes red beans his or her own way. It's never the same twice. Sometimes I add parsley or omit the ham or sausage, use more bacon, etc. I *always* use genuine Tabasco sauce, made by the McIlhenny Co., New Iberia, Louisiana.

4 slices bacon, chopped
1 onion, chopped
1 large bay leaf
1 lb dried red kidney beans
1 lb hot sausage (kielbasa works well)
1 lb ham, cut in small chunks or a ham bone cut into
    2-inch pieces
2 qts water
6 to 8 cups hot, cooked long-grain rice
1 cut green onion, finely chopped
1 tsb garlic, minced
Tabasco sauce to taste (Careful!)
salt and pepper to taste

Wash kidney beans and rinse well. Soak beans in 2 qts water for at least four hours or overnight in refrigerator. Drain and reserve liquid.

In a 4-quart pot, sauté bacon pieces until transparent. Drain some of the fat. Add sausage to the remaining fat and brown. Add ham. Add both kinds of onion and garlic. Cook five minutes or until onion is translucent.

Stir in beans and reserved liquid. Add pepper and bay leaf. Add ham-bone pieces. Bring mixture to a boil, then simmer over low heat for at least 4 hours, stirring often. If beans seem dry, add water a cup at a time. (I normally end up stirring in an additional 2 cups of water.)

When beans are done, some will split, forming a thick liquid for the rest of the beans. Some people prefer to mash some beans against the side of the pot to thicken the broth.

Remove ham-bone pieces, trim away meat and return it to pot. Discard bones. Add salt, pepper and Tabasco sauce to taste.

Serve over hot rice with a tossed green salad and French bread. Serves 6.

Red Beans takes some time to prepare, but the dish is well worth the trouble. I usually put mine on about 1:00 p.m. to serve about 6:00 p.m. Sometimes I make it the night before, cooking for a hour or so, then refrigerate overnight and finish cooking the next day.

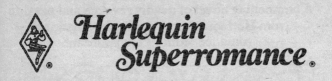

COMING NEXT MONTH

**A compelling novel of deadly revenge and passion
from Harlequin's bestselling international
romance author Penny Jordan**

Eleven years had passed but the
terror of that night was something
Pepper Minesse would never
forget. Fueled by revenge against
the four men who had brutally
shattered her past, she set in
motion a deadly plan to destroy
their futures.

Available in February!

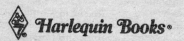

Harlequin Books®

You'll flip . . . your pages won't!
Read paperbacks *hands-free* with

Book Mate • I

The perfect "mate" for all your romance paperbacks
Traveling • Vacationing • At Work • In Bed • Studying
• Cooking • Eating

Perfect size for all standard paperbacks, this wonderful invention makes reading a pure pleasure! Ingenious design holds paperback books OPEN and FLAT so even wind can't ruffle pages — leaves your hands free to do other things. Reinforced, wipe-clean vinyl-covered holder flexes to let you turn pages without undoing the strap . . . supports paperbacks so well, they have the strength of hardcovers!

Pages turn WITHOUT opening the strap

SEE-THROUGH STRAP

Reinforced back stays flat

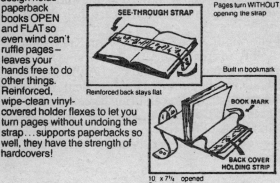

Built in bookmark

BOOK MARK

BACK COVER
HOLDING STRIP

10 x 7¼ opened
Snaps closed for easy carrying, too

HARLEQUIN Temptation

The Pirate
JAYNE ANN KRENTZ

At the heart of every powerful romance story lies a legend. There are many romantic legends and countless modern variations on them, but they all have one thing in common: They are tales of brave, resourceful women who must gentle and tame the powerful, passionate men who are their true mates.

The enormous appeal of Jayne Ann Krentz lies in her ability to create modern-day versions of these classic romantic myths, and her LADIES AND LEGENDS trilogy showcases this talent. Believing that a storyteller who can bring legends to life deserves special attention, Harlequin has chosen the first book of the trilogy—THE PIRATE—to receive our Award of Excellence. Look for it in February.

AE-PIR-1